A BETTER MAN

A BETTER MAN

A Novel

Leah McLaren

HARPER**AVENUE**

HarperCollins Publishers Ltd
2 Bloor Street East, 20th Floor
Toronto, Ontario, Canada
M4W 1A8

www.harpercollins.ca

Library and Archives Canada Cataloguing in Publication
information is available upon request

ISBN 978-1-4434-4156-8

Printed and bound in the United States of America

RRD 9 8 7 6 5 4 3 2 1

For Rob

How can I know who I am until I see what I do?
How can I know what I value until I see where I walk?

—KARL WEICK

CHAPTER 1

Nick

Nick Wakefield is a happily married man. That is the official story.

But even in this moment—a mild, unremarkable mid-week dawn in late September (a "school day," as Maya would call it)— he is clinging to the enviable outward qualities of his life as if to bits of driftwood in a flash flood. It is, by any standard, a good life. A life of privilege and endless opportunities for pleasure. And yet it is also a life that has made him miserable. Slumped over the cool stone kitchen island in a pilled cashmere bathrobe (the perfect Christmas gift for "the dad who has everything"), Nick performs the early morning accounting he's been labouring at each day upon waking for a couple of years now. A keeping up of appearances in his own head. Not a show of gratitude, exactly, but a listing off of the things that, if he could connect himself to the glittering hologram of his own success, he might well be grateful for. These are the things he is sure other people would like to take from him, if they ever got the chance. Topping the slate is this house, the one he's sitting in now—a bombproof Edwardian boulder on a city street that his slick, post-adolescent realtor once described as the "filet of the neighbourhood" (a description Nick secretly relishes but would never have the bad taste to repeat out loud). Then there's the lake house, a cube of glass and steel perched on a slab of pink granite two and a half hours north of the city. The view was chosen for its resemblance to a Group of Seven painting—rocks rising out of choppy waters, a couple of craggy, wind-battered pines emerging miraculously from cracks in the stone. He thinks of the place now and is filled not with pleasure but with the intense desire to buy the uninhabited island opposite. *Always own your view*, his late father—a workaholic, alcoholic dental surgeon—liked to say. It's the single piece of wisdom he retained from the man, and he cleaves to it.

In and around these shelters—these properties that he *owns*, and that no one (not even the bank, since the Duracell job came through) has the power to take away from him—there is all manner of precious things. There are the cars, the boats, the collection of Danish teak mid-century modern furniture, the books and gadgets and photographs, and a few "pieces" by local "sculptors" he long since stopped pretending to understand or care about. There are his bikes, all six of them—two super-lightweight, carbon-framed French road racers in contrasting primary colours; a puffy-wheeled, shock-fitted mountain bike for a month-long race across Mongolia that he had to cancel at the last minute; a half-constructed, custom-built fixed-gear; and two bog-standard commuter bikes from his teens he hangs on to with the idea that he might one day revert to being the sort of modest fellow who cycles to work instead of sliding a luxury sedan into a private parking spot two feet from his office door.

There is more: The collection of copper cooking pots hanging above his head. The specially commissioned, modernist stone birdbath twisting into view like a lost Henry Moore. The empty coffee cup in his hand—white bone china and soothingly logo-free. Although he works in advertising—perhaps because of it—he has imposed a strict "no swag or overtly branded items" rule in the house.

A collection of objects—all of them expensive, solid and, most importantly, *desirable*—parade past his mind's eye. As they do, he feels the old anxiety, that familiar hunted gut clench that wakes him before light most mornings now—eyes springing open, stomach lifting as, *whoosh,* the elevator drops—rising up before it recedes to the background, where it will stay all day like a threat.

Nick pours himself another cup of ethical sludge from the French press and glances at the oven clock: 7:00 a.m. on the dot. Right on cue, the pre-programmed kitchen radio warbles to life, a smug-voiced host analyzing the international misery of the day ("the Voices" is how he thinks of them, having never understood his wife's obsession with public radio, some nerdy hangover of her academic childhood). The Voices are followed almost immediately by the sound of Maya's bare feet moving across the bedroom floor to the master bathroom for her morning ablutions. She will dress in something stretchy and body-contoured— selected from her vast collection of expensive, sweat-wicking exercise togs—before giving the twins their breakfast and supplemental breastfeed (for the "natural antibodies"), dropping them at preschool and hitting the gym.

Nick will go to work and stay there as long as possible, as he has taken to doing for the past several months, ever since Maya settled the twins into a comfortable bedtime routine. It's not that he is avoiding his family, exactly—just that his presence seems to disrupt some precarious balance it's taken his wife sleepless months to perfect. Maya did her best not to let on, but he could sense her bristling at his occasional (now infrequent to non-existent) attempts at New Man domesticity—an awkwardly loaded dishwasher here, a scalding bath there—and now he has given up. There was a time when they had dinner together most nights, gently unwinding the day's events over a bowl of pasta and a glass of wine, but this ritual has long since passed, surrendered to the necessary (no, *enviable*) chaos of buttered macaroni, bath toys and slobbered-on picture books—a chaos he copes with by keeping himself as scarce as possible.

"Daddy?"

A small, sticky hand tugs at his robe, causing it to fall open and exposing his genitals to a gust of cold air.

"Sweetheart, it's rude to yank." He says this with more impatience than he'd intended.

Isla pops a thumb in her rosebud mouth and, with her finger, loops a swirl of red-gold hair around her ear. Her eyes—a clear, glittering blue, unlike his own murky hazel ones—crawl across his face. What are they looking for? Nick reaches down and scoops his daughter onto his lap, but his vague hope that she might zone out quietly while he finishes reading the basketball box scores evaporates as Isla, snuffling with her first cold of the season, squirms around to look at him. It's not that she wants down; it's that she wants his full attention.

"Daddy?"

"Yes, sweetheart."

"Foster sleeps with Garbage Truck and I sleep with Mermaid."

"Is that so?"

"Yup." She nods, mouth twisting. A square crust of snot has formed beneath her upturned nose like a fluorescent yellow Hitler moustache. "Garbage Truck is blue and Mermaid's pink, with green scales for swimming and long hair. Foster's a boy like you, Daddy, and I'm a girl. Like Mermaid. And Mommy."

Nick nods and strokes the whole of his daughter's head, a clumsy palm sweeping over a fragile corn-silk dome. Isla grins, suddenly pleased with herself. Then she sneezes—not once but twice, three times—spraying him with microbial bacteria. Nick winces, and resists pushing her off his lap.

"Girls are nice and boys are yucky. Exthept for Foster, 'cauth he's my twin," she says.

"No, sweetheart—" Nick begins.

But Isla's on a role. "Yeth, Daddy. Boys are yucky."

"Why's that?"

"They like killing games and 'splosions. And they don't know how to love people."

Nick struggles not to react. "Where'd you hear that, baby?"

"Foster tries to make me play with his stupid killing soldiers, but I hate them."

"Not that bit, darling—the second part."

Isla shrugs, pops her thumb back in her mouth, hops off her father's lap and eyes him with something more innocent than suspicion and less affectionate than warmth. Nick wants to press further, but Foster is suddenly upon them, an agent of pure destruction. (Is there no object, Nick can't help wondering, his son doesn't yearn to pick up and hurl to the ground? No system of organization he doesn't long to smash?) Cupboards fly open; pots are banged with wooden spoons; a brand new salad spinner spontaneously combusts, bits of plastic flying in every direction.

"Daddy, Daddy, check it!" Foster's voice rings through the din. He's a tall boy for his age, physically bolder and markedly less chatty than his sister. As the fey, French-braided ladies in his Montessori preschool often gently point out, Foster is "a bit of a handful." He puts a pot on his head like a space helmet, bangs it with a spatula and laughs, delighted by this self-abuse. Noticing his bareheaded sister, he picks up a glass salad bowl and, before Nick can stop him, overturns it on top of her, causing the thing to slip to the floor and shatter, whacking Isla's forehead in the process. The girl is the first to erupt in a squall of hot tears, followed by her brother in a reciprocal howl. (Nick never ceases to be amazed by the way the twins can switch from adversity to unity, hostility to empathy, at a moment's notice.) And of course, it's at precisely this moment, with Nick standing helpless in the shrieking chaos, that Maya chooses to enter the kitchen.

Even now he registers that she's beautiful. Tall, thin-wristed and pale-lashed—she used to joke that without mascara she had no eyes, and she still never emerges from the bathroom without a slick of it. From the beginning, Nick preferred her without— there was a time he felt possessive of her naked eyes, with their translucent, underwater lids. Now he avoids them.

"Foster, apologize to your sister," Maya says, herding the twins out of range of the mess. Without glancing at Nick, who's still standing uselessly by the sidelines, she squats down in her leggings like a rice-paddy worker and scoops the shards of the shattered bowl into the dustpan that has somehow magically appeared in her hand. Isla allows herself to be kissed better, first by her mother, then by her brother. Appeased, she moves toward Nick to complete the circle of comfort. The combination of virus and crying jag has left her face covered in a film of fresh mucus. Nick pulls back on his barstool and grabs a hemp-cloth hanky from a drawer, then attempts to persuade Isla to blow her nose by wrapping the cloth clumsily around her face.

"Blow out, sweetheart," he says hopelessly. The harder he tries, the more she snorts and snuffles, snot plugging all her orifices. Her face is red and scrunched, working itself up to a howl. He can hear the wet congestion in her head as she gulps for breath, and finally—in abject defeat—he allows himself to look to his wife, who has been watching the scene unfold. Maya doesn't look back. She crouches down, takes her daughter's face in her hands, places her mouth over Isla's tiny nose and proceeds to suck out the contents of her daughter's sinuses before spitting it out into the sink.

Nick looks back at the paper. This habit of his wife's—like the extended breastfeeding and the "family bed," which he has long since vacated for the guest room—is part of her firmly held philosophy of child-centred parenting. Since leaving her partner-track position as a divorce lawyer at one of the city's biggest firms, Maya has funnelled all her intellectual and physical energy into moulding and nurturing the twins, making sure they "attached" properly—though to what, exactly, Nick's never been entirely sure. On the few occasions he'd questioned her methods, there'd been an onslaught of disconcerting counter-arguments involving terms like "socio-emotional development" and "hopelessly outdated paternalism." Now Nick's passive resistance is simply assumed.

Maya starts pulling things out of the pantry: dried beans, pumpkin seeds, a bag of leathery kale, apples, some sort of unidentifiable ancient grain product. Supplies that will somehow be turned into edible compost squares, pressed into Tupperware and taken to post-preschool play dates in lieu of "bad snacks" full of trans fats, refined sugar and cancer.

Nick observes this chore with the disinterest of a barfly watching a highlights reel on a barroom TV screen—as if he's seen it all before but is too tired to pay the bill and leave. Finally he blinks himself back into the moment. "How was your sleep?" is all he can think to say.

Maya finishes removing the organic stickers from half a dozen Fuji apples before looking up. "Okay," she says. Then she adds, "Actually, I had a weird dream and couldn't get back to sleep."

He knows he ought to ask what it was about, but for some reason he can't bring himself to do so. Does anyone actually care about someone else's dreams? Aren't they a bit like other people's children? Or minor health ailments?

"Oh, yeah?"

She draws a small but mindful breath. "We were back in university and there was a huge event happening on campus—maybe it was homecoming weekend? I had your varsity jacket, but I couldn't find you anywhere. And then I remembered you were writing a philosophy exam and I was meant to be there too because we'd studied together, so I started running through the halls looking for you. But when I got to the right classroom, the professor stopped me at the door and wouldn't let me in because I wasn't wearing any bottoms—"

"Pants?" Nick asks.

"No, bottoms. Period. I was naked from the waist down."

Maya coughs and keeps talking, and Nick nods and nods, eyes drifting to the box scores until a subtle vibration steals his attention. Even with the phone face down on the counter and turned away from him, his finely tuned antennae home in on that delectable possibility, the promise of all information, his mental lifeline to the outside world: an unknown text-message-in-waiting. Now Maya is in full flow (something about her teeth falling out and a baby lost in the football bleachers), and he's scrolling and scrolling until he becomes conscious of a tonal change. This comes in the form of the sharp, unfamiliar sound of her using his name. "Nick?" she is saying. "Are you even going to pretend to be present?" He thinks this is what she says, but in truth he can't be entirely sure.

"Sorry, babe." He gives her a kiss on the cheek, toward her ear, as far away from her mouth as possible. "Big client meeting today. Gotta run." And he runs upstairs to shower, shave and dress.

In the car, before setting out for the commute downtown, he reads the rest of the text message. *Hey, sailor, when you gonna buy me lunch?* It's from Shelley, the caterer he'd met on set last week, with the ginger bob and the small but promising breasts. His spot for the new music channel had just been nominated for an industry award, so he'd figured he'd reward himself with Shelley's number. Since then they've been exchanging several texts a day, sometimes back and forth at a rapid-fire pace, making up nicknames for each other ("sailor" is new—he isn't sure he approves), sarcastically bantering and generally building up sexual tension like a couple of semi-literate teenagers. She isn't the sharpest tool in the shed, this Shelley, but Nick has decided he likes honing his seduction skills on a pretty girl who is more attractive, yet markedly less clever, than him. He considers it a form of harmless recreation. He is merely exercising the muscle, keeping himself fit in the evolutionary, rather than practical, sense. It's not that he intends to have an affair (he's told himself they'll never actually meet up, and if they do nothing will happen, and if it does it'll be no more than a kiss), more that he likes to keep himself in fighting form. The libido is life force, and Nick intends to keep his stimulated for purposes of professional prowess, rather than tawdry sex. Success is provision. In this sense, when he thinks about it very carefully, he is actually sexting for the sake of his family. He writes, *Aren't you being a bit demanding, little miss? Where are your manners?* There, that would throw her off balance. He smiles, reads the message over once and presses Send.

Backing the car out of the driveway, Nick glances up and sees Maya in the window, half-hidden by the curtains, an apparition of herself. She is watching him from the room that used to be their bedroom. The bedroom she now shares with the twins. When their eyes meet, she shrinks back behind the gauze and is gone.

CHAPTER 2

Maya

Maya is sprawled on the master bed, breastfeeding Foster and reading *The Way: Ten Rules for Seeking Out a Truth Worth Living*. The book, which she drove across town to buy at an independent bookstore, was recommended to her by her personal trainer and life coach, Bradley. Maya knows it's basically crap. She also knows she'll read it right to the end in spite of this. While she normally steers clear of commercial bestsellers, self-help and anything with an embossed cover—she majored in English and can recognize a split infinitive when she sees one—there was something about the manner in which Bradley recommended *The Way* that seduced her. "I think you'd really vibe off it," he'd said, placing a large supportive palm on her forearm for emphasis and really looking at her, almost *into* her, she thought. What was remarkable was not just that she experienced this connection, but that she felt it in spite of his use of "vibe" as a verb. His palm was hot but dry, not moist or slippery in the least. If it had been, she's pretty sure she wouldn't have bought the book, let alone read it. So has she found the promised "ecstatic truth of existence" in its pages? Not yet, but she still has 487 pages to go. She's just finished the introduction, with its breathless blather of string theory and "the law of truth"—an apparently overlooked rule of physics stating that if you speak your heart's honest desire, out loud and often, "the universe will invariably answer." Maya is considering the empirical authenticity of such a law when Foster bites her—a sharp nip with his milk teeth that makes her flip upright, stabbed through by a metal bolt.

"Motherfucker!" She pushes her son's sturdy shoulders away from her chest and watches as his head comes away last, the suction of mouth on nipple breaking with a pop, his head snapping back. On her areola there is black bead of blood; she wipes it off with her thumb and licks it, tasting the sweet, milky mixture of two vital fluids. Foster stares past her, lazy-lashed and drunk on oxytocin, oblivious to her pain. She mops up her breast before tucking it back into the nursing bra. There is no point in scolding him, she knows. *Praise the good, ignore the bad.* It's her own fault for not being able to stop. Every week she promises herself that *next week* she'll wean them for good, but then Monday rolls around and with it the moody morning vicissitudes, the restlessness of bedtime, and she reverts back to the old way. She can feel Nick's silent disapproval mounting with each week the breastfeeding goes on. She knows what he thinks: that she's doing it for her own selfish, needy reasons rather than for the twins' well-being. The truth is, three years after their birth (a botched homebirth turned emergency C-section overseen by a disapproving doula and a team of unflappable thirty-year-old female surgeons), she still finds it hard to pinpoint where she ends and her children begin. She knows people think it's strange—possibly

even disgusting—this business of nursing one's children well past the infant stage. But what about the importance of unconditional love? What about the foundations of security such closeness can bring? What of the natural immunity? Maya wouldn't tell a soul, but a deep-seated part of her believes that she is protecting her children with her breast milk. And that without this magic elixir, intimately administered in the ancient way—skin on skin, nipple to mouth—something awful might happen. Madness, illness, destruction, even death . . . And so she persists.

Now that Foster's finished, Isla, who's been looking at a gender-neutral picture book about dinosaurs, swivels across the bed for her turn. Maya reflects for the zillionth time on how amazing it is that they never refuse it, no matter how much dairy and processed breakfast gluten (she's trying to get them off oatmeal and onto quinoa porridge, to little avail) they clog themselves with first. No matter what, the primordial thirst wins out. Surely they will lose their taste for it eventually, but when will that be? Five? Ten? Fifteen years? Could mammals actually lactate that long without having more offspring? Maya knows such things don't realistically bear thinking about, but she's also secretly pleased with her ability to turn mothering into a kind of endurance sport. Where other mothers detach, she persists—the contours of her existence blurring into her children's development so that all their previous selves, from infancy to kidhood, are imprinted on her skin, a burgeoning palimpsest in bodily fluids.

Isla's on her lap now, head nuzzling under Maya's collarbone, on the spot where she once slept as a baby. (Can she remember this in some subconscious recess of her brain?) She draws her knees up to her chest and wriggles into the fleshy curve of her mother's hips, snuggling down like a baby kangaroo in her pouch. Before Maya even has a chance to unhook, Isla's hand has snuck inside her top. She looks up, face full of trust and wonder, and opens her lips to whisper something. Maya leans in to hear her daughter's secret and decides that this—above all else—is the reason she persists. Yes, it must be.

"Mommy?" says Isla.

"Yes, honey?"

"*Motherfucker.*" And she latches on for her morning drink.

When in doubt, seek professional help. This is one of Maya's core beliefs—one of the few she still seems to share with her husband. For every problem, there is a person whose job is to solve it. She believes this fervently, and yet there is the nagging fear that her mother—a bread-baking retired academic—might be right. That if she keeps on outsourcing more and more efficiently, eventually she will become a tiny bit player in her own life, with all the lead roles taken by talented, competent professionals.

She would be lost without Velma, who comes ten hours a day, five days a week, forty-eight weeks of the year (the remainder a paid holiday). Officially Velma is the twins' nanny, but in reality she's also the family cleaner, cook, gardener, handywoman, finder of lost remotes and socks and keys, putter-together-of-Ikea-furniture, writer of thank-you notes, jump-starter of cars, spiritual counsellor, massage therapist, gadget IT support and, if Maya is honest with herself, the other human adult she talks to most.

Each morning, when the twins are at preschool and Maya has returned from the gym, Velma makes a pot of tea and they convene in the kitchen for girl talk. They would never call it that, of course. Officially, they are employer and employee, mistress and servant, lady-of-the-house and lady-in-waiting. But their chit-chat allows them both to forget this arrangement and act like something less awkward and old-fashioned is going on. For Maya, these bonding sessions assuage her guilt at engaging someone else to hand-wash her delicates despite being unemployed herself. For Velma, a twice-divorced former Brazilian pageant contestant (runner-up, Miss Curitiba 1978) now in her late fifties, it's just a welcome distraction while she gets on with the daily business of sterilizing the counter, reorganizing the fridge and cleaning the corners of the window ledge with a Q-tip. From the cuffs of her tight white jeans to the points of her gel-manicured fingertips, Velma is a superior human being in every way.

Ever since Velma bustled into their lives three years ago, hoisting a bottle sterilizer and case of Diet Coke against her broad and perfumed bosom, Maya's household had ceased to be within her own control. One tearful post-partum call to an upmarket childcare agency was all it took to produce this splendidly tanned and cheaply Botoxed Mary Poppins busting out of an emerald sateen blouse. After casting a spell over the writhing, colicky twins (Velma's method included the ministration of ominous-looking herbal tinctures, some open-handed back-thwacking and swaddling that resembled a straitjacket), she set to work on sorting out the house and, finally, Maya herself. While Velma has succeeded in alphabetizing the spice rack, dry-cleaning the curtains, washing the walls and ridding the pillows of dust mites, her campaign to get Maya to "do something with that hair" and put on a little weight "for the sake of your face" has not been nearly as successful.

Despite this, their domestic companionship has taken on a comfortable rhythm, with Velma running the show while Maya watches gratefully from the sidelines, calling the occasional cue like a well-intentioned but unnecessary stage manager in a long-running Broadway musical. The unflinching competence with which Velma attacks the chaos of a post-breakfast kitchen or soothes a crying toddler is enough to make Maya despair at her own lack of firm domestic instinct. Like all great mistresses of the domestic arts, Velma manages to be bossy and loving by turns. "Watch! Like this!" Velma is always saying, while swabbing gravel from a scraped knee, suctioning water from a toddler's ear or turning over a perfect tarte Tatin. "You see? Easy-peasy." But for Maya, it never feels that way. For Maya, domestic perfection is a daily battle. For Velma, it's a vocation.

In between the cleaning and cooking and childcare, they talk about stuff: Velma's daughters (now twenty-seven and thirty—one a plastic surgeon in Rio and the other a fashion buyer for a major downtown department store), their respective childhoods, places they've lived, holidays they've taken, grooming secrets, cooking tips, celebrity gossip, high-profile murder trials, political sex scandals. But mostly they revert to their favourite subject, which is the twins.

"You should have seen Foster at the playground yesterday," says Velma while polishing the good crystal wine glasses using the espresso machine steamer—something Maya would never have thought of in a million years. "Strutting around like he owned the place. At one point he actually went over to the gate and started choosing which children can come in and which ones he doesn't like the look of. Such a healthy little ego on that boy."

"Let's hope he doesn't have sociopathic tendencies," says Maya. "You haven't noticed him killing any stray cats have you?"

Velma's laugh is a pealing church bell. "Oh, honey, you don't have to worry about that. He's going to be wonderful. He's very proud but also very sensitive and full of heart. Remember the time he knocked Isla off her trike and then tried to take off his Band-Aid to put over her bloody nose? That was so sweet. Come to think of it, he reminds me of my second ex-husband."

"What was he like?" Maya is intrigued. While Velma devotes plenty of airtime to her two daughters, she rarely mentions either of her ex-husbands, both of whom are back in Rio.

"Oh, so handsome. A handsome devil—a salesman who could charm the pants off an Eskimo." Velma is the queen of the mixed metaphor.

"How long were you with him?"

"Only two years. He was a madman—no offence to Foster—but it was worth it because the crazy attraction I felt for him gave me the courage to leave my first marriage. You know *that* one lasted a long time. Over ten years. Much longer than it should have."

"Why?"

Velma shrugs, then gives the crystal glass another blast of hot steam. "I dunno. Why does anything need to end? I suppose I got a bit"—she jiggles her shoulders this way and that, caus- ing her mane of frosted-tips to quiver around her face—"I guess you would call it *restless*. I had to run. To dance. To get a new life! Looking back I've never questioned it. If I hadn't left him,

I wouldn't be standing here today." She spreads her arms, still holding the tea towel with a generous smile.

"But your first husband, you were with him so long. You must have met him very young. He is the father of your children, isn't he?" Maya hears a note of urgency creep into her voice.

Velma looks confused. "Yes? So? People change. Carlos was a good man, but in the end I was so terribly bored. I had to get out or die. And I did, and here I am."

A fizzing wave of anxiety washes over Maya. *This is not about you, silly*, she tells herself. She looks down, blinking and stretching her face at the marble chopping block, but it's no use. The tears have been lurking just below the surface lately, welling up and seeping out whenever she's reminded of the happy past— back when she and Nick could bear to look each other in the eye. Earlier today, after feeding the twins, she spent ten minutes sitting in a chair, attempting to channel the Law of Wanting—a fanciful notion she'd just read about in *The Way*. The idea is to concentrate on the thing you want most, and the universe will hear you and grant your wish. *I want my husband to love me again*, she'd thought over and over, like a mantra. But the wanting only served to remind her of the loss. It wasn't that she wanted love so much as she couldn't figure out where it had gone.

Velma registers the tears and rushes to put her arms around her. "What's the matter? Oh, Lord, what stupid idiot thing did I say? Tell me and I'll chew up my words!" She mimes plucking words from the air and shoving them into her mouth and swallowing.

Maya laughs and wipes her nose with the cuff of her yoga jacket. "It's nothing, really. It's just . . . sometimes I think Nick feels about me the way you feel about Carlos. It's like I'm just there. A fixture he's getting increasingly sick of. Like, like"—she looks around the kitchen, searching for a metaphor—"like an old backsplash."

Velma raises an eyebrow. "A what?"

"You know, a backsplash. The tiles that go on the wall over the counter. People always change them when they renovate. That was the first thing Nick changed when we bought this house. The old terracotta backsplash—unacceptably 1990s, he said. He wanted European subway tiles. The point is, an updated backsplash gives an old kitchen new life." Her voice snags in her throat mid-sob. "I don't know what's wrong with me. I'm sorry."

Velma hands her a hanky, and instead of wiping, Maya pats at her face the way her dermatologist taught her, then snuffles like a congested pug.

"But why do you assume you're the backsplash and not the kitchen?" asks Velma.

"What do you mean?" Maya begins to wonder if this metaphor hasn't run its course.

"Well, you assume *you're* the old backsplash, but maybe you're the old kitchen and all you need is a new backsplash to update your look. Or maybe your marriage is the old kitchen and the two of you can get a new backsplash together and then everything will be fine."

Maya knows she needs to be careful. Apart from the odd eye-rolling joke, she hasn't let Velma in on the hole in the centre of her marriage. In part this is because she doesn't quite know how to articulate what's wrong. She and Nick almost never fight, yet their mutual dissatisfaction is palpable in countless unspoken

19

ways. Maya is suddenly overcome by the unbearable fatigue of long-term denial. She wants to tell someone—anyone, really, but Velma especially—how unhappy she is. But she knows she shouldn't. This house—this family—is also Velma's livelihood. She's as protective of it as Maya is, maybe more so.

"Oh, it's fine, really. Things have just been a bit strained lately. Nick's been working so much and I've been focused on the kids."

Velma uncrosses her arms and places a hand on each hip. "And your sex life?" she says.

Maya cringes. She's always resented the notion that sexual relations could constitute an entire parallel life outside of regular existence. No one asked you about your "eating life" or your "exercise life" or your "sleeping life" or your "job life," so why should sex be any different?

"What about it?"

"Are you doing it? Regularly? Or have you fallen off the horse?"

Maya can't meet Velma's eyes. Her tongue is mossy from too much green tea.

"I think it began to tail off around the time we started co-sleeping."

"You mean after you had the babies?"

"More or less. I mean, yes."

Velma nods, hands on hips. "I know what you need. I read about this in one of those silly magazines, but in this case it's actually a very good idea. It's called the 'date night.' You put on a nice dress, drink a few cocktails, talk about something other than the kids. In my day we did that every weekend. Then again, when my girls were the twins' age I was in my twenties and living with my husband's entire family."

Maya grimaces. "It's true we never go out anymore. I mean, there's his annual awards gala, the whatever-they're-calleds, but I didn't go this year."

"Why not?"

"Isla had a cold. Remember that awful hacking cough she had last winter?"

"And what? You had to watch her while she sniffled in her sleep? I couldn't do that for you?"

"No! She was just being, you know, a bit weepy and clingy, and I felt she needed to know that I was *there*, otherwise her foundation of trust might be eroded or . . . oh, I don't know. Okay, the truth is I just didn't feel like going."

"And *why* didn't you feel like going?" Velma lifts up the elements and scrubs some grease off the stovetop. She stares hard at Maya, indicating she will tolerate nothing less than the truth. Maya feels herself shrink in deference.

"I guess I haven't had much use for parties—or date nights, for that matter—since the twins were born. It all just seems so superficial when there are two small lives I'm now responsible for. Well, *we* are." She smiles sheepishly at Velma.

Velma rolls her eyes with dramatic disapproval. "You're kidding me, honey. Seriously?"

Maya blinks, then blows a wisp of hair from her face. She knows what Velma is going to say without her needing to say it—that the twins are three years old and well taken care of, so why would it be risking their lives to go out and have some fun once in a while? And even more to the point, that it's not in anyone's best interests to sacrifice her relationship with Nick to assuage some deep-seated reptilian fear that if she leaves her children for more than a couple of hours at a time, they will end up corrupted, maimed or buried in an avalanche of refined sugar. She knows all this, and yet she finds it hard to override the anxious primal urges that brought her to this juncture in the first place.

"Have you tried talking to Nick?"

"About what?"

"About this feeling you have—that he doesn't love you the same way anymore?"

Velma says this matter-of-factly, but it still manages to take Maya's breath away.

She shakes her head. "We never talk about our feelings," she says weakly. "But at least we don't really fight. There's got to be some good in that."

Velma looks unconvinced. "See, that's just where you're wrong. A little fighting is *good* for a marriage. Back home everybody says, 'When you fight, you fuck.' Is true, no?"

Maya looks down at her hands. She has heard this theory before.

"Maybe that's what you're missing—the howyoucallit?" Velma plucks an elastic band off the counter and extends it back, letting it snap against her fingers.

"Tension?"

"Yes, the tension! Exactly. This is what holds couples together. Like the sun and the moon."

"You think?" Maya wouldn't begin to know how to pick a fight with her husband, even if she wanted to—or this is what she tells herself, conveniently ignoring the adversarial side of her brain, the side she set adrift when she left the law. The fact is, while she and Nick have almost no conflict to speak of, the resentment between them is constant and palpable—it just doesn't lead anywhere. Not to a fight and not to sex. Their marriage, these days, feels like a state of dull discomfort. A pain so familiar that it wears on her like a chronic injury—too unpleasant to ignore, too boring to mention.

For a moment Maya wonders if it's her fault for not demanding more of her husband. For not calling him at work and ordering him to get home early or bickering over laundry and blown light bulbs. She read a self-help book once about how men prefer bitchy women because their selfish behaviour is a subconscious indicator of self-worth, which men in turn interpret as objective value in a mate. For a while after that, she tried to be difficult just for the sake of being difficult. But her heart wasn't in it. She liked to think of herself as bloody-minded and tough, but in truth, she was in her own life acquiescent and deferential to the point of absurdity. Why else had she failed to wean her babies after three years? Because they kept asking for "mommy milk." Why else had she potty-trained them by eighteen months? Because a book told her that's what good mothers do and she was determined to do things by the book. Another ludicrous case in point: here she was taking marital advice from Velma, a two-time divorcee and avowed singleton (she often said she'd be damned if she ever "washed anyone else's socks again without being paid for it," which Maya thought was eminently sensible).

"You should pick a fight with him and see what happens," Velma concludes, folding and refolding her dishcloth as if to say, *That settles it.*

"If you think so," Maya almost whispers, knowing that she won't.

CHAPTER 3

Nick

SoupCan Productions is located in a former sweatshop in the city's garment district. Nick ascends in the glass elevator and steps out lightly, enjoying the soft spank of leather sole on polished concrete. Even in the flat fall light, the banks of desktops gleam. He does his usual sweep and is glad to note the absence of water bottles and food detritus (both are banned from the office for obvious aesthetic reasons—if employees wish to consume, they may do so in the cafeteria). Hot beverages may be drunk from plain china mugs, cold drinks from heavy-bottomed glass tumblers no more than four inches tall.

Nick has recently decreed that on the first Monday of the month, all employees must shuffle workstations, resulting in a never-ending game of office musical chairs. His official line is that it's for reasons of "sociability and transparency," but actually it's meant to keep people from getting too settled. Nick believes in the power of order and detachment, but also in the importance of changing up the regular. He discourages personalization of the workplace. The office, in his view, should be an escape from the cloying demands of the personal, the messy and the earth-bound. In work there is a controlled kind of freedom—a form of crisp, high-minded play not readily available in any other area of life. It's difficult to be edgy, irreverent and effortlessly on the pulse when constantly reminded that the woman who sits next to you loves her cat.

Nick started SoupCan with his partner and first production accountant, Larry Goldfarb—an unkempt, soft-bellied math whiz and the warm, woolly yin to Nick's cool, angular yang. They met in their early twenties—Nick fresh out of film school, Larry managing a sub shop—and forged a bond while working on Nick's only short film, a state-funded, futuristic art wank inspired by his twin loves, Fellini and Ridley Scott. "There must be a way to make money at this shit," Nick said to Larry one night over cheap draft and soda crackers. When he looked up there was an evil glint in his future partner's eye. Today they are the busiest independent commercial outfit in town, with a stable of producers and directors working with international clients, churning out dozens of slick TV spots a year. As company founder, Nick is now able to cherry-pick which jobs he wants, passing the rest to his preferred directors while retaining a handsome producer fee.

"Mor-ning!" Nick's assistant says brightly.

Ben is trim and scrubbed in a made-to-measure suit. (God knows how he affords his clothes on the pittance he's paid. Nick assumes, as he does with most of his employees, that the kid has family money.) His greeting contains just the right touch of irreverent subservience to make Nick feel simultaneously at ease and important. Ben is immaculate without being anal, animated without being theatrical. It is precisely this level of metrosexuality that Nick specifically looks for when hiring an assistant—a person he secretly thinks of as an extension of his own brand.

"Morning, young Benjamin. How was your weekend?"

"Oh, quiet. Just did a bit of work in the garden, planted some daffodil bulbs for spring." Ben offers a pursed-lip smile that suggests he's actually spent the past forty-eight hours shagging the city while flying on class A drugs. "And you?"

"Oh, you know, the usual. Drunk midget wrestling, appeasing the missus. So what's on again today?"

Ben nods like a naval cadet and lists off a schedule of pitch meetings and casting sessions, followed by the appointment Nick has been waiting for: evening drinks with his old friend Adam Gray.

Nick glides through the rest of the day in a state of pleasant dissociation, skimming along the surface of work in a way that effects maximum output with minimal energy. By the time 6:00 p.m. winds around, he's pulling on his overcoat and feeling predictably numb, considering the meeting that awaits him.

He gets to the Plymouth early to secure a good table. The small hotel bar is widely noted for its stupendously large cocktails and possible connections to the Russian mob. While the weather has cleared up—a bit of late-afternoon sunshine streaks through—Nick chooses a spot in the back, where he and his old friend can conspire like three-hundred-year-old vampires in the murky half light.

Gray is the top-billing family lawyer at the city's biggest firm. Notorious for protecting rich clients by screwing their poorer (and usually markedly better-looking) spouses out of their rightful settlement, Gray is a chronic workaholic who made partner at thirty-three and now charges more per hour than the average taxpayer earns in a week. He is also one of those friends Nick sees as much to measure his own success against as for the pleasure of his company. They meet up a couple of times a year for a drink or six—usually at a dark, leather-scented hotel bar—and reminisce about the old days, back when they were idealistic undergrads chasing hippy girls in ponchos.

Gray is exactly three minutes late, as he is to every meeting—social, professional or otherwise. He is, Nick thinks, the sort of person who commits all errors with purpose. Nick watches his old friend shouldering through the door and blinking around in the dim light, a tall man with the hunched back of a grizzly bear—a shape created from tens of thousands of hours of adversarial paperwork and a diet of ordered-in prime rib and mash.

The two men give each other a rough, back-slapping embrace and a couple of throaty "How're ya's?" then slouch down into the tufted leather booth. It is only after they've sent the waitress for a pair of double Manhattans and a bowl of spiced jumbo cashews that actual eye contact takes place.

"Wakefield, good to see you, man." Gray crunches the words in his throat like a garbage compactor, his voice enhanced by fifteen years of chain-smoking. He reaches into his breast pocket and removes an electronic cigarette—the latest in an endless series of aids in his quest to quit—and takes a deep hit. The tip lights up when he sucks, like a toxic Christmas decoration. Gray holds his breath for a beat, then exhales a strange minty vapour. "Nice suit," he says, looking Nick up and down. "Your stylist pick it out for you?"

Nick fingers his lapel and allows an indulgent smile to spread across his face as he examines his friend's mournful eyes and head of coarse, dark curls. Gray has never been typically hand-some, but he is the sort of man women are naturally drawn to: large, dominant and wounded despite his professional success. The weary, court-battered charm gives him an older man's extra gravitas, but like Nick, he's only just pushing forty.

"You look like shit, as always," Nick counters. "Firm still working you like a diamond miner?"

"I wish. Least then I might dig up something pretty instead of profiting from the proliferation of human misery." Gray says this with a reluctant grunt of pleasure.

"Ah well, there're worse ways to make a living. For instance, you could spend your days casting fitness models to sell body gel."

"Sounds like the lowest circle of hell to me. At least they remunerate us for our suffering."

"Truer words."

Nick gives the waitress a schoolboy smile and removes his cocktail directly from her hand with a dry brush of fingers. She flutters back to the bar. He raises his glass toward his old friend, then tosses back half the drink.

"Thirsty?" Gray is watching him with a quizzical look.

"Mmm, parched." Nick dabs at the corners of his mouth with a cocktail napkin, looks up at the dark mirrored ceiling with its spider veining and waits a few seconds before letting out an old-man sigh.

"How're the custom-built chaos machines otherwise known as my godchildren?"

"Good, good. Busier than me, what with the Kumon, Zumba, Gymboree . . . " Nick tails off when he sees Gray looking at him blankly.

"Was that English you were speaking just now?"

Nick laughs. "Not entirely."

"Maya still keeping up that exercise regimen?"

"Yep, hmmm."

"Is that all you can say, you lucky bastard?" Gray slaps an open palm down on the table, causing the drinks to slosh and the nuts to scatter. "You don't appreciate what you have, my friend. If any of my three ex-fiancées had been within spitting distance of that woman, I'd be a happily married trigamist."

The conversation is not going the way Nick had hoped. Gray's hopeless crush on Maya is a long-standing source of humour between them. Usually Nick thinks nothing of it. Slobbering over his wife is simply Gray's way of winding him up and flattering him at the same time. An intimate form of trash talk. But today Nick finds it getting under his skin, which is of course precisely the point.

"I never should have introduced her to you at the regatta. Should have known she'd chuck me aside for a pretty-boy lightweight like you. Typical fickle sorority girl. Did you know it's one of my biggest regrets in life?"

"So you tell me."

"Should have kept her for myself. Ditched the race and spirited her away to Vegas for a quickie wedding."

"Hard proposition when you're a fat, geeky undergrad."

Gray's face cracks a rare smile. "Fair point."

They clunk tumblers and drink, allowing an amiable silence to descend. Somehow Nick knows it will be his job to break it.

"That's actually what I need to talk to you about."

"I wasn't fat. I was just a bit barrel-chested from rugby—"

"Seriously, dude, I'm being *real*. I need your honest advice."

"Don't tell me we're here to talk about your feelings."

"No, *no*. Well, maybe a little bit." Nick catches the waitress's eye and does the loopy international hand signal for another round. "Actually my feelings are sort of moot. The point is, I've made a decision."

"Which is?"

"I want out."

"Of what?"

"My marriage."

"You're joking."

"I most assuredly am not."

"But you and Maya, you're like Fred and Ginger, Bogey and Bacall, peanut butter and jell—"

Nick cuts him off with an abrupt slice of his hand. Gray is the first person he's voiced this to, after many months of rumination, and he is mentally prepared for a certain amount of resistance.

"Sometimes things are not as they initially appear. Marriages—families—in particular."

Gray takes this in. Employs a swizzle stick to scratch a woolly sideburn. "Okay, I'll grant you that. How should I know what goes on in someone else's marriage? So I take it you're not in love with her anymore?"

Nick winces. Such a harsh way of putting it. "It's not that. And there's no one else, by the way—not in any *real* sense." He looks up at Gray, who gives a skeptical cough. Nick casts his eyes away and continues, "It's more that I don't feel capable of loving her anymore. Or at least not in the way she needs to be loved. I literally can't do it. It's killing me. I feel like I'm drowning or suffocating or—I don't know—trapped in a role. Like I'm understudying the lead character in the movie of my own life. I'm in the wings, watching it all happen. I need to get back on stage. Take control. And the only way I can do that is by making a fresh start."

"Ending a marriage is many things, my friend, but a fresh start it ain't. And lest we forget, your wife is trained in the black arts. Everyone knows you never divorce a divorce lawyer."

"Spare me the homilies, okay? I've thought long and hard about this." Nick can feel the whisky humming over the surface of his skin now, freeing him to say what he likes. What he *means*.

"Oh, I'm not moralizing. I'm just presenting you with the facts. Divorce—if that's what you really want—is not the get-out-of-jail-free card you might imagine. It can be a whole other prison in itself. An emotional Abu Ghraib. And a costly one too—not just financially. On every level. Especially when kids are involved. You should know that going into it."

"You give this speech to all your clients?"

"Only the misguided assholes." Gray leans back in the booth and studies Nick carefully. "And just to be clear, I'm not taking you on as a client. It would be a real conflict. Obviously. And more importantly, you can't afford me. Don't take it personally, bro. Almost nobody can." Nick hoots skeptically, but Gray holds up a hand. "I can offer you my advice—as a friend—but when it comes down to it, you'll have to retain other counsel. I can make recommendations, but I can't act as your lawyer. Is that clear?"

Nick nods and crunches a whisky-laced ice cube. He'd expected this speech and is secretly relieved, since he knows Gray's wrong: he can afford him. But he'd rather not spend a year's earnings on legal fees. He gathers himself, then asks Gray the question he's been waiting to ask: "So how much is it going to cost me?"

Gray doesn't miss a beat. "More than you can afford. On every level."

"I'm talking strictly monetary. Not just the paperwork but the whole settlement. How much?"

"That, my friend, depends entirely on one thing." Gray raises the tumbler to his lips, leans back and drains it. "How much have you got to lose?"

Nick, who has anticipated this moment too, picks up the calf-skin document case that's been sitting at his feet since he arrived and unzips it. He slides a yellow file labelled "Wakefield Family Assets" across the table.

"You tell me," he says.

Gray nods grimly and picks up the file.

CHAPTER 4

Maya

"How long's it been?"

"Just over three minutes."

"Is that all?" Maya's stomach is clenched, her arms trembling. An angry mist of sweat rises off her. "I don't think I—" She is rigid, holding a plank position, hands on the floor mat, feet on a vibrating plate, body a thrum of panic, fatigue and numbness. The idea, apparently, is to trigger the fast-twitch muscle fibres into firing in unison, creating what Bradley calls "a thousand tiny metabolisms" to fuel the larger slow-twitch "central heating system" that is her body's internal furnace. She thinks she might burst—*splat*—like a blood vessel. *People do die from this sort of thing. It's not unheard of.* She sees the headline in her mind's eye: "Housewife Spontaneously Combusts in Exercise-Induced Self-Immolation."

"Hang in there," says Bradley. He is a retired pro soccer player with an undulating West Indian accent and the most magnificent pair of shoulders she's ever seen on or off a sports field. They've been "working together," as he likes to say, for three years now.

He started as her trainer, but six months ago he graduated to life coach after receiving some sort of certification Maya didn't pay much attention to. The only thing that's changed since then, apart from his increased fee, is the specificity of his advice. Where once he used to advise her to drink more water, now it's a glass half an hour before each meal and an additional four glasses throughout the day. Where he once told her to get more sleep, now it's lights out before 10:00 p.m. at least three times a week to optimize the circadian rhythms. Bradley purports to be a firm believer in the mind–matter continuum, but really it's the body he knows how to change, not the brain that instructs it. It's his encouragement she pays for. Those little aphorisms and mantras that enable her to push through to the next level, to force herself toward further heights of self-mastery and optimal humanness.

"This is money in the bank of YOU," Bradley says now. "Dig deep. Give yourself the gift of expending your full effort."

As her trembling becomes a full-out Jello-bowl wobble, he starts counting backwards from ten. Maya makes it to a respectable two before collapsing forehead first on the mat, bile searing her throat, brain crackling with static. For one merciful moment, oblivion descends, and then just as quickly it's gone.

Not cutting it, says the voice in her head (her mother's voice, much as she tries not to acknowledge it) as the familiar wave of self-disgust rises up around her. But before she can be engulfed, Bradley is there, sliding a water bottle into her hand, patting her on the neck with his heavy hand. "Good job, atta girl, looking good." Something deep inside her blooms at the sound of his praise. She wonders if it's possible—or even advisable—to reach a state of psychiatric transference with a fitness professional.

Afterward, she showers and then reconvenes with Bradley for their regular debrief in the club juice bar. After three years of biweekly consultations they have developed a companionable post-workout rapport, one that revolves primarily around discussing Maya's metabolism and Bradley's personal life. Officially speaking, these follow-up sessions are intended as "nutrition seminars" (in addition to being a certified trainer and life coach, Bradley is also a dietary counsellor, whatever that means) to discuss her caloric intake and expenditure, as well as the delicate protein-to-complex-carb ratio, but the topic has been so thoroughly exhausted over the years that now they mostly just chat.

Bradley is twenty-seven and has four children under the age of six with a woman he never mentions. Maya fetches him his regular—a beet-and-kale juice with added protein powder—and gets a green tea for herself. Back at the table, she falls into cooing over the latest baby photos on his phone, a series of snapshots from a backyard birthday party. Little girls in synthetic princess dresses smeared in purple icing.

"Absolutely scrumptious. Look at those cheeks. What a little pudding she is."

"Daddy's little girl. Stubborn as her older sister is sweet. How're the twins?"

"Growing like superbugs." Maya finds herself touching the small pouch of skin above her pubic bone reflexively. The Caesarean scar is the only remaining physical evidence of her first—and last—pregnancy. After the twins were born, Nick had suggested she get her tubes tied—a notion that horrified her, though she couldn't put her finger on why. It wasn't as if she yearned for more children. In any case, the infrequent-sex method of birth control seemed to be working just fine these days. "They've just started nursery school, you know—for socialization reasons—and I'm trying to keep them off sugar and processed food, but it's hard. The other mothers are always bringing stuff in. I've given the teachers strict instructions, but I'm not sure they actually follow them. Last week Isla asked out of the blue if she could have some Smarties. How would she even know Smarties existed? I felt like she'd asked me for a cigarette." Maya takes a sip of bitter tea and tries to focus on the antioxidants.

"I wouldn't worry about it too much," says Bradley. "One little Smartie's not going to kill her, is it?" He slips his phone back in his hoodie and pats his pecs as if to check they're still there.

"Well, no, but it does make me wonder why I bother being so careful when other people are so irresponsible. I don't even allow them wheat products because of the GMO factor. Apparently the strains of wheat we eat now bear no resemblance to the ancient grains, which is why gluten intolerance is so rampant. Anyway, they've had a clean diet, so why shouldn't I try to keep it that way as long as possible? You know studies have linked refined-sugar intake to autism, so it's not like I'm being paranoid here."

"Of course not." Bradley pats her arm, then raises an eyebrow in mock surprise. "Nice tricep, girl."

"Thanks. I have this amazing trainer . . ." Maya feels a smile blooming across her face. Bradley keeps his hand on her a bit longer than usual. When he pulls it away, she feels the skin burning where his fingertips had been. She springs up, suddenly conscious of the time. "I'd better go.

Crazy non-stop day."

Bradley winks goodbye, and Maya hip-swivels her way

through the crowd of stroller-wielding postpartum dieters and single girls clutching yoga mats. Despite her best efforts not to, she imagines Bradley's eyes on her ass the entire time.

Once belted safely into the car, engine purring, Maya tips her throbbing forehead to the cool leather of the steering wheel. She breathes in the correct and conscious way—in through the nose, out through the mouth, letting the air swirl in the back of her throat. She imagines the blood in her veins oxygenating, spreading energy through the outer reaches of her body. Despite this exercise in self-soothing, she gets a flash of herself as a hopeless bourgeois cliché—an overeducated, underemployed housewife on the verge of an affair with her personal trainer—and she is suddenly overwhelmed by the increasingly familiar sensation of waking up after a long, disorienting sleep in a room she's never seen before. *How the hell did I . . . ?*

It wasn't always like this. Back in school, when she first met Nick, Maya was the "together" one. Quietly confident and possessed of a blasé charm, she was the better student of the two, and by far the more socially confident. Nick had to work for a full semester to get her attention. When they first met through Gray, she'd just started dating one of Nick's fraternity brothers, an arrogant rower and engineering major who liked to get drunk and belittle Nick for his fussy taste in clothing. Maya remembers her first feeling toward her future husband as one of pity for the reverse discrimination he endured (she was particular about her clothing too, after all, and why should girls be the only ones to care about their appearance?). Back then, Nick seemed a bit weak to her, a bit too self-consciously fastidious ever to be one of the real men on campus. And yet there was something compelling about him. A sensitivity and patience, a willingness to listen to her yammering about Spinoza as if what she said were a revelation rather than an undergraduate regurgitation. It was a skill the other frat brothers and private school boys, with their fixation on sports and keg party logistics, didn't even pretend to possess.

He reeled her in by listening. Listening to her excitement about some confessional poet or other on the freezing walk from the arts building to her shared student digs. Listening to her story of an argument with her mother as she filled her jumbo Ikea cart with not-yet-assembled bookshelves and plastic kitchen implements. Listening to her pre-exam anxieties as they blew on steaming hot chocolates in the dingy cafeteria under the campus library. And finally, after a drunken night in a smoky fondue joint on the French side of town, listening to her surprise at having ended up sweaty and entwined on her futon on the floor of her bedroom. And that, as they say, was that. Sex bonded them instantly as companions, and from then on it was the Nick and Maya Show, a sold-out run with Sunday matinee in perpetuity. Or so she'd assumed.

It was difficult to put her finger on precisely when the balance shifted. When Nick the slavishly devoted boyfriend and uxorious husband became Nick the eerily remote apparition of his former self. The twins' arrival and Maya's decision to quit the law in the hope of effecting "life balance" seemed to have had something to do with it. In a period of just a few months, Maya had undergone the most dramatic change of her adult life. One day she was a focused, eagle-eyed attorney in a silk suit tackling the business of divorce, and the next she was a harried housewife and budding exercise addict whose biggest daily challenge was determining how to work her private hot yoga session around the twins' nap schedule. It was amazing, she quickly learned, what minutiae could fill your day and—in the absence of court dates, filing deadlines and responsibilities handed down from the fast-retreating World of Work—begin to take on monumentally troubling proportions. Take email, for instance. Where she had once spent the better part of her days and nights connected, practically via implant, to the endless, absorbing cacophony of her smartphone, today she found it a trial to return more than one or two messages in a day. And why should she, when there was never anything interesting enough to demand her full attention? A play-date invitation here, a pre-school newsletter there. A "Hello dear, how are the children?" email from her mother from whatever silent meditation retreat she was on. Reminders and updates from the twins' endless edutainment schedule of intuitive movement, baby yoga, Junior Picasso classes and Suzuki violin. Her inbox—once a place of intrigue, urgency and melodrama—had become a utilitarian emotional dead zone. Apart from the twins, no one *needed* her attention anymore. Not even Nick.

In her first two years of career withdrawal, Maya had made a couple of attempts at "mommy track" sidelines: the hemp-diaper import business that crashed and burned, then a humiliating stint as a self-styled "design concierge" (who knew the rich actually preferred their own dubious taste to that of other people?). But after three years of treading water, Maya has come to the conclusion that it is more dignified simply not to work than to pretend to do so. Nick had supported, even encouraged, her decision to quit the firm (that was around the time SoupCan got the Duracell account, which tipped the balance in favour of his earning power anyway). She could tell that a part of him (probably not the best part) was secretly pleased with the idea of being the sole breadwinner. Perhaps because of his early struggles to fit in, Nick had always had a weakness for status symbols. He took an inordinate interest in material possessions, not for the personal satisfaction they provided but for the outward messages they conveyed. Maya noticed that he liked what an expensive car *meant* far more than he actually seemed to enjoy driving it. And now his wife, in her well-maintained idleness, was one of these possessions. He took a week off work when the twins were born (she thinks she remembers him being there, vaguely—a hand that occasionally appeared holding a blanket or a wipe between the day- and night-nanny shifts), but shortly after that he began to fade from view. Their conversation, once so engrossing and full of secret jokes, suddenly revolved around teething, cracked nipples and sterilization. She sensed his interest waning but was frankly too sleep-deprived to do anything much about it. *He'll be back*, she remembers thinking at the time. Three years later, there was no sign of him.

Maya knows she shouldn't blame Nick for her own restlessness. And yet, like the thief who justifies his crimes through angry entitlement (*Dad smacked me around, ergo I deserve this stranger's flat screen*), she can't help holding him responsible. She knows she shouldn't let her brain get stuck on the repetitive internal monologue of negative thoughts that leads her to believe, in moments like this one, that Nick is somehow conspiring to make her unhappy—that his slow, inexorable fading of feeling is not just passivity but an act of emotional aggression. Try as she might, she can't shake the suspicion that he holds her in contempt. Not just for what she's become, but for everything she's not.

Lately this persistent, unexpressed resentment she has toward her husband brims so close to the surface she can feel it bubbling up in inappropriate moments. The car will stall in traffic and instead of cursing, she'll mutter his name. His face will appear in her mind's eye when she painfully stubs a toe. *Amazing*, she thinks, *the way someone can go from representing everything that's right in your life to everything that's wrong with it.*

Winding her way through the streets around the university, Maya comforts herself with the thought that she was right to extend her therapy with Harriet. If she weren't on her way there now, where else would she be? Probably at the Four Seasons bar, ordering a double vodka for lunch after a round of collagen injections—or worse, upstairs in a suite with Bradley. She lets her mind linger on the notion. As tragic bourgeois clichés go, at least she's picked the least embarrassing option.

Harriet's office is on the second floor of a Victorian building that also houses a small poetry press. Something about the proximity of verse fills Maya with romantic comfort. Harriet's office is a large, airy room with two bay windows that overlook the campus library. As she enters, Maya is relieved to find everything the same. There's an enormous rolltop desk in one corner, two tastefully upholstered wing chairs in the middle of the room and an antique daybed against the far wall. And in the middle of it all is Harriet, a tiny, liquid-eyed woman in an endless succession of black knit dresses and ropes of pearls. She ushers Maya in and, before saying anything, looks at her in a way that manages to be simultaneously empathetic and scrutinizing. Maya falls back on the daybed without even bothering to take off her jacket.

"Tea?" says Harriet, in her customary greeting.

"Only if you're having some," says Maya, as she does every week.

And so they begin. There was a time when Harriet needed to draw her out a bit, but not anymore. These days Maya enters the office already oozing, a bag of milk leaking at the seams.

She starts speaking as Harriet returns with the tea tray. "Remember last week—or was it the week before that?—when I was telling you about how I sometimes have this bizarre feeling that Nick just wishes I'd disappear?"

Harriet glances down at the notepad in her lap and makes a note with a flick of her left hand. "I think you actually said that you felt like *you* were disappearing—that you might cease to exist."

"Yes, but only because he was wishing me out of existence. Me and the twins too. I still feel it, but it's even stronger these days. Actually, it's like he's the one disappearing now. He's there physically, but there's just no sign of the other Nick."

"What do you mean by 'the other Nick'?"

Maya considers the question. "The Nick I married."

"Tell me about *him*." Harriet nestles into her wing chair, slipping off her shoes and pulling a pair of stocking feet up under her like a sparrow settling down in its nest.

"He was . . . beautiful. The most beautiful man I've ever known. Before the twins came we used to lie in bed together for hours on end, talking about everything and nothing—teasing each other, making up a kind of secret language, or at least that's what it felt like. We had more sex then, of course, but it wasn't even like sex in the traditional sense. I felt like we were part of the same space-time continuum, with our outsides just packaging for pleasure."

"You were very much in love," Harriet says.

"That's another way of saying it." Maya smiles, remembering. It's been a long time since she's allowed herself to recall the good times this way. Even in the safe cocoon of her shrink's office, the indulgence seems slightly dangerous. It's as if her tenuously constructed life might fly apart just by admitting to a time when it seemed effortlessly whole.

"We used to go to parties and end up in a corner talking to each other. Not because we were shy but because we were more interested in each other than anyone else. People would come up to us and say, 'Aren't you two sick of each other yet? Haven't you run out of stuff to talk about?' But we weren't, and it felt like we never would be."

"Until now?"

"Yes, I suppose. In a way. Although it's not so much that we've run out of things to say as it is that the things we would say if we could bring ourselves to be honest with each other wouldn't be the sorts of things either of us would want to hear. So we don't say them. But it's like the effort of not saying them—of keeping the unsayable things unsaid—precludes any other kind of real or natural conversation. The kinds of conversations we used to have all day, every day. I think that's what I miss more than anything. Just talking."

Harriet shifts in her cashmere, jots a note. "Let's go back to these unsayable things. Can you tell me what they are?"

Maya frowns, then stops when she feels the crease appearing between her eyes. "For me I guess it would be that there's something heartless about him since he became successful, something hard and dissatisfied, as if he's disappointed all this *stuff* hasn't made him happier."

"And what do you think he might say to you?"

This surprises Maya—the question seems like it's a violation of the cardinal rule of therapy: *The only person you can ever hope to change is yourself—and even then only a little bit.* At first she feels like she can't possibly answer. She is quiet for a long time, picking at her fingernails like a neurotic teenager. Harriet waits, implacable, at ease in the silence between them.

And then suddenly Maya knows the answer. "I think he'd say that he doesn't know how to love me anymore."

Harriet's eyes widen slightly, a rare physical response. "Why do you think Nick doesn't love you?"

Maya shakes her head. "Not *doesn't* love. Can't." What she doesn't add, because it would make Harriet probe more deeply, is that she hardly blames him.

Maya returns home late that afternoon, laden with shopping bags filled with stuff she doesn't need or want or particularly remember buying, and relieves Velma, who has an appointment to get her eyebrows threaded. The afternoon and evening slide by like all the rest, a montage of sippy cups, talking toys, educational books (*L is for llamas, who eat up all the leaves!*), make-believe play and board games (Maya instituted a strict screen ban after reading a study that linked the brain's absorption of LED light to shrinking attention spans), followed by a dinner of spelt-battered chicken fingers and untouched (but dutifully procured) blanched kale. Then it's bath, shea-butter body rub, story, comfort feed and family bed.

It's ten after eight when Maya finally pours herself the first merciful glass of Barolo. The wine untangles the knot in her brain, and for a few minutes she finds she is able to devote herself to the act of reading—something she used to do far more of when she had less time. Tonight it's just an old copy of the *Economist*, a week out of date, but she likes to work her way through in order. She's never been the sort of person who could skim through books, skipping the boring parts and rushing ahead to the relevant bits. Instead, in reading as in life, her talent is diligence and what her mother the architecture professor used to call stick-to-it-iveness. Once set on a course, she will not deviate, pushing through to the bitter end, whatever the cost.

She pours herself a generous second glass and tries to find a comfortable spot on the unforgiving L-shaped sectional she recently had shipped over from Denmark at idiotic expense. (It looked so comfortable online, who knew it would feel like lounging on a church pew?) After half an hour or so, the alcohol that had previously focused her thoughts begins to make her brain murky and restless. A vague sensation of melancholy sets in. She tries to shake it off by fixing herself a dinner of cottage cheese and seaweed crackers and (what the heck?) another glass of wine, making sure to leave a respectable amount in the bottle. She'll use that for cooking, if she ever gets around to cooking grown-up food again—another thing she did more of when she spent less time at home. And when she had a husband who came home before 10:00 p.m.

Nibbling her bachelorette's supper, she wonders what life would have been like if she had ended up just that: a bachelorette. She thinks of her girlfriend Diana from law school, of her immaculate condominium and endless weekend dating dramas. Trawling the Internet for a husband. How depressing to be going through that at this age, when the thought of getting naked in front her own husband—let along a complete stranger—fills her with a dull, throbbing horror.

It's amazing to her that the sex could have stopped when it was once the thing that bound them. A common language and a shared world. In university she and Nick spent what seemed like (and probably amounted to) hundreds of hours in bed, exploring each other, experimenting in physical pleasure, and being swept up in waves of laughter and almost unbearable intensity. The door of her bedroom in the rundown Victorian house she shared with two other roommates (both vegan medievalists) came to seem like a portal to a parallel universe—one that belonged exclusively to her and Nick.

And years later, even after the excitement of marriage and the caffeine-fuelled blur of law school had passed (they'd married in the summer between her third and fourth years, just after Nick set up his company), the physical connection remained. It never took much for them to persuade each other in that direction.

The night is cold and inky, and it feels much later than it is, so Maya wraps herself in a blanket and settles in, abandoning a vague plan to reorganize the mudroom. She turns on the TV and flips around until she settles on a rerun of *Buffy the Vampire Slayer*. An indeterminate amount of time later (could be minutes, could be hours), she's awoken by the bleep of the front-door motion sensor. She struggles to compose herself as Nick's footsteps approach, but the wine has made her bleary, uncoordinated, a person out of focus. He enters the family room, and for a strange, fleeting moment, he looks startled to see her. It is as if he has forgotten who she is, or even that he's married. Then his face recomposes itself into the smooth, familiar mask. His eyes shift to the nearly empty wine bottle on the coffee table, then back to her.

"Need any help getting up to bed?" He hangs his overcoat on a hook, then washes his hands in the kitchen sink before applying lemon-scented lotion.

"I'm fine, thanks." Maya's sitting up now, blinking and smoothing her hair into place. She stands and smacks her thighs to alert her body to the fact that it's time to climb the stairs. "How was your day?"

"Oh, you know, just the usual office shenanigans. How was the, uh, thingy?"

"What *thingy*?"

Nick looks exhausted and on the spot. "I mean whatever it is that you . . ." He searches, then finds what he's looking for. "I was going to say the gym. How was the gym?"

She looks at him and waits for the sting to subside. But the wine, which usually acts as an emotional force field, has somehow lost its buffering power while she slept. A coppery taste fills her mouth and her eyes begin to sting. It feels like an allergic reaction, but then she realizes that for the first time since the birth of the twins, she might actually cry in his presence.

"You should be nicer" is all she can think to say, her voice pathetically smudged with alcohol and emotion. Nick takes this in, rubs his eyes and starts to say something back but decides against it. The set of his shoulders clearly says, *What's the point?* They stand in silence for a minute, until he finally gives a dry little laugh and walks out of the room without bothering to look at her again.

CHAPTER 5

Nick

Nick is relieved to see that Shelley's breasts are every bit as remarkable as he remembered. Small and thrillingly high, they remind him of china teacups or those French ballerinas from the old Impressionist paintings.

He doesn't look at them, of course, but instead shifts his gaze from her eyes—all squinty with laughter at his not-so-great jokes—to the restaurant's front door, just over her left shoulder. He'd suggested the bistro around the corner from the SoupCan offices out of habit and laziness, and is now keenly aware of how this (perfectly innocent!) lunch might look should one of his colleagues happen upon it. Still, he is here and determined to enjoy it.

Shelley is telling him all about her food blog, and how she takes photos of everything she eats and immediately uploads them to her "platforms" so her followers can track her minute-to-minute consumption habits. "It's like an open-kitchen diary philosophy," she is saying, eyes glittering beneath her auburn fringe, "so people can taste what I'm tasting, almost in real time." She is developing an app with a friend to "digitally replicate the experience of smell, texture and taste," which she hopes will "give the experience an added sensory dimension." At present she has over seven thousand followers. Nick pretends to perk up at this, though for all he knows they could be following her just to see her breasts. He certainly would. In fact, he makes a mental note to do so. She keeps talking and talking, and he finds he doesn't mind, since it leaves him free to daydream about exactly how she would look, sitting here in this restaurant, eating bread and butter and drinking a glass of daytime Rioja with her clothes off.

She tells him a long and animated story of how, three winters in a row, she has volunteered as the cook on the canteen bus for a charity bicycle race across Africa. Local villages in impoverished regions across the continent, she explains, send their best cyclist to compete alongside North American riders and raise funds for local schools and hospitals. The trip lasts four months, stretches from Cairo to Cape Town, and is "incredibly inspiring" and has "changed her life."

Nick lets his eye slide down her throat like a finger as she talks. Shelley is sweeter and more earnest than he'd imagined, though not quite as pretty as he remembered. She wanted to meet him, she says, because she has always dreamt of becoming a TV food stylist "for a day job." Presumably she thinks Nick will help her out in this regard. He pushes this from his mind as they continue to talk because he dislikes it when people want something from him.

She is small without qualifying as short—maybe five foot five—and has an overexcited energy that causes her to flutter her hands and open her eyes very wide when trying to make a point, which is most of the time. She wears a pair of smooth black jeans and a tank top that's so worn Nick can sense that if he were to look closely, he'd be rewarded with a glimpse of pale areolae through the nubby cotton ridges (she doesn't seem to be wearing a bra). Her severe red bob is a shade brassier than he remembers, and it reminds him of a Christmas decoration. Not the crafty ones Maya buys but the kind he grew up with in the suburbs. Also, she wears glasses—thick, black 1950s science-nerd specs that look like they might actually cause her head to buckle on her slender neck. He realizes that something about her style is meant to eschew sexuality, to throw up a roadblock to potential suitors or at least send out a signal that this girl means business. Nick isn't bothered by this. A part of him instinctively rises to the challenge.

Shelley holds up her phone and snaps a photo of herself, tongue out, eyes closed, slurping an oyster from its shell. Then she snaps one of Nick.

"What's the problem?" she asks when he shrinks away. Her tone immediately makes him feel ten years older than he is.

He shrugs. "I like to keep my digital footprint to a minimum, that's all."

"Footprint?" Shelley is scrolling through images on her phone now. "Isn't that an environmental thing?"

"I'm not a fan of clutter—physical, virtual or emotional."

Nick takes another look at Shelley, this one openly appraising. He makes a viewfinder with his fingers, Hollywood director-style, and watches with pleasure as her posture corrects.

"You know what?" he tells her. "I think you ought to be one of those people who cooks on TV."

Shelley presses her lips together and rolls her eyes, but he can see she's delighted. She takes a long sip of wine. "You mean like on *MasterChef*?"

"No, no. I mean like one of those shows hosted by women who just kind of float around a kitchen sticking their fingers in everything and licking them."

Shelley laughs, head back, giving him a clear view of the muscles contracting in her milky white throat. "But those women can't cook—not really. And I want to be a *real* chef, not some culinary spokesmodel."

Nick leans back. "Maybe so, but you make people hungry. You should capitalize on that somehow."

Shelley smacks his knee, mock offended.

"Ha! That's almost disgusting!"

Nick's raises his hands like he's been busted by the police and has nothing to hide. "How so? I just have a healthy appetite, that's all."

This is about as dirty as it gets—for now. Less than an hour later, Nick's back at the office sitting in a production meeting to discuss possible locations for his latest spot: a three-part narrative smartphone ad about a hot young couple flirting, fighting and making up—all by phone, text, email and instant messages. He's particularly proud of the log line: *CurvePhones—so you'll never feel alone again.* It's a lie, of course, but a beautiful one. All the best slogans are.

There are five of them around the boardroom table—Nick, Ben, the production manager, the location scout and Larry, who is flipping through a book of location photos while chewing noisily on a peanut protein bar.

"Didn't you see anything more, I dunno, *swank*?" Larry asks the scout, crumbs speckling his chin. Larry has an endearing habit of demanding in the most vulgar possible way that everything be classier. "The actors are kids—but they're rich kids. Don't forget this is a *high-end* smartphone. We can afford to go aspirational on the shag pad here. In fact, I think it's pretty much imperative." He glances at Nick, who gives an almost imperceptible dip of his jaw. It is his habit not to talk in the first half of any meeting, even—indeed especially—if he's in charge of it. That way when he does open his mouth, people actually seem to give a shit.

Larry, meanwhile, continues yakking on in his usual fashion, pushing papers around the table, gesticulating like an angry silverback. On Nick's left, Ben is taking notes, which he will later type up and email to everyone at the table. Nick is comforted by this, because it means he doesn't actually need to listen.

He sifts through the images of antiseptic condo kitchens, fluffy bedroom suites and light-flooded lounging rooms. An industrial loft is perfect except for its floor-to-ceiling bookshelves (too intellectually intimidating for the client); an Edwardian brick house is dismissed as "too grown-up" and a gleaming ultra-modern condo "too clinical."

Just as Nick is beginning to feel almost as agitated as Larry is acting (why can't these people ever find anything new and fresh?), he comes across a printout of an airy, light-drenched space with white walls, an eclectic mix of mid-century furniture and ragtag antiques, a baby grand piano and a distant view of the water. In the corner is a jumble of musical instruments for children, the wooden, painted kind that Nick remembers playing with thirty years earlier—tambourine, xylophone and drum set creep into the frame. Art books are piled on the floor. Worn oriental carpets on barnboards. Oil paintings lean against the wall. Everything about the space suggests a kind of sophisticated domestic peace to Nick. He taps the corner of the photo on the table. "What about this one?"

The production designer—a slim, soft-spoken man with a head of trimmed, prematurely white hair—reaches over, pinches the photo between his fingers and gently, but not without some effort, tugs it out of Nick's hand. "Sorry, Nick. Not sure how that even slipped in there," he says, shoving the photo in the outside breast pocket of his slim black blazer. "It's a place I'm using for another job, starting next week. A family show."

"Give it here," Larry says, plucking the photo from the designer's pocket. "Oooh, I like it. Just the sort of slice of heaven we need. What's the other job? Tell me their budget. I'm sure we can trump them. Have the owners signed anything?"

The designer frowns, his loyalties clearly torn. "I'm afraid it's fully booked. It took us ages to find it. I really can't—"

Larry leans forward, rubbing his hands together and staring straight into the production designer's face. He actually licks his lips. "Our director prefers that location," he says, tapping a thick buffed fingernail on the image. "The question now isn't *if* but *how* you are going to get it for him."

The designer shifts in his seat as though his ass is suddenly itchy, then glances over at Nick, who, despite feeling bad for the guy, betrays nothing. In moments like this, he's learned to let Larry be the heavy. His partner loves a good test of loyalty. The designer rubs his face and thinks, then rubs his face some more. Finally he settles on something he can say.

"Maybe if we did night shoots . . . I could try to arrange it with the owners?" He looks pained.

But Larry is shaking his head. "Nah, fourteen nights in a row with union turnaround time? My girlfriend would kill me. *I'd* kill me. My vampire days are over, man."

For a moment this is the end of the discussion, but then Nick reaches over and plucks the photo out of Larry's hand. He takes one more look at it and knows that's where he's shooting the spot. "I don't mind supervising," he says.

"But you're directing. Who's going to shut *you* down?" Larry says.

"I'm fully capable of producing myself—after midnight, that is."

Larry leans back and considers Nick with a smirk. "Fourteen days of all-nighters just because you like the look of the place? What kind of workaholic perfectionist are you, anyway?"

Nick shrugs. He thinks of last night, finding Maya in a bleary heap on the sofa. The empty bottle of Barolo. The scornful look in her eyes when he woke her. "I just like the look of the place," he says. "I don't mind working nights. Nights are when all the best stuff comes out."

Half an hour later Nick is back in his office, sifting through head-shots of model-slash-actresses (Larry is determined to find a girl with a "classy high school French teacher look"), when Ben knocks on the frosted-glass partition that separates him from the rest of the staff.

"What can I do for you, son?"

Ben arcs his neck around the doorframe at a jaunty angle, causing his linen scarf to fall away from his throat. "There's a very large and scary man here to see you," he hisses. "He seems *awfully* serious."

Gray appears, lugging a wheelie briefcase that's so stuffed full of documents it looks about to burst into a cartoon paper whirlwind. He falls back in a chair without being invited, releases a noisy gust of air, undoes a button and gives his tie a two-finger yank. "This place isn't actually an office—it's some kind of futuristic money-laundering front, right? Those replicants out there pretending to type on their shiny laptops don't even look real."

Nick grins. "Busted. Now to what do I owe the pleasure of an unannounced visit from the city's busiest bloodsucker?"

"I prefer the term 'judicial ambidexter,' thanks." Gray's gaze passes over the smooth, clean lines of Nick's office. For a moment Nick sees it through his friend's eyes. The vast white-lacquer desk, concrete floors and floor-to-ceiling plate glass. A few high-gloss modern art books are stacked horizontally and at odd angles on a shelf "for inspiration."

"Your office is very *American Psycho*. I assume that's the image you're trying to project?" Gray coughs at his joke. "Sorry. It's my walking pneumonia. Chronic, not contagious. Doc says it won't clear up till I've chucked the ciggies for three years straight. Can you believe that?" He reaches into his pocket, pulls out his toy smoke and gives it a long, hard pull, then blows a vapour ring into the air between them. "Twenty-six days clean, not counting my birthday," he says. His face drops into seriousness. "Listen, I was just in the neighbourhood—had a client meeting around the corner—so I thought I'd stop in and share with you, confidentially, some thoughts I've been having on your, uh, *situation*." He reaches into his briefcase, pulls out the calfskin document case and hands it back to Nick. "I thought you'd prefer it if I delivered you the bad news in person."

Nick opens the file and sees that Gray has paper-clipped an extra page of scrawled calculations to the top of it. He casts his eyes down at the columns of numbers. Beside them in Gray's tight, unforgiving handwriting are a series of headings like "family home," "lake house," "daycare and school fees," "nanny salary, taxes and overtime," and more alarmingly, "spousal support," "child support," "equalization of family income," "upfront cash settlement," "legal fees" and "payments in perpetuity." He runs his eyes down to the bottom of the page and settles on a single figure circled heavily and underlined for effect. Its effect on him is, quite literally, staggering. He feels as if someone has wound up and slugged him in the stomach with a kettle bell. His vision goes fuzzy and a strange static invades his head, like a radio on high volume between stations.

All my things, Nick thinks. *All my beautiful things.*

Gray, meanwhile, has adopted his usual sit-back-and-wait-for-the-client-to-absorb-the-bad-news position. He's leaning back in his chair, tie descending in waves over his barrel chest, scrolling through the never-ending flood of messages streaming into his phone. After a minute or so, he looks up at Nick with his unshockable basset-hound eyes. "Figures aren't exact, of course—just a ballpark estimate based on the Divorce Act and my many years of experience."

Nick finds he has to rub his tongue against the roof of his

mouth to generate a film of lubricant before he can get any words out. "So this is . . . normal?"

"Generally speaking, yes."

"But don't people get divorced *all the time*?"

Gray nods with a certain degree of satisfaction. "Sure. People go broke all the time too. If you're looking for numbers, the current national rate's just over a third of marriages—that's down from 50 percent in the mid-1980s, right after no-fault divorce was legalized, though I find that people still cling to that statistic. People who are getting divorced, that is. It's comforting to feel normal."

"But how do they afford it?"

Gray shrugs. "They don't! This is what I've been trying to explain to you, my friend. If you have money, divorce is *expensive*. Why do you think I've got an offer in on a condo in Palm Beach? It's going to cost you dearly. Which is why, if you're interested in keeping the trappings of your precious lifestyle, I suggest you find a way to work out your problems. Try counselling, take a holiday. Join a swingers' club, for fuck's sake. I don't care. Just stay married and save yourself the cash and your kids the therapy." Gray begins buttoning up his overcoat and hoisting himself out of the chair.

Nick motions for his friend to stay put. He is not so easily deterred. Gray must know this, because he sinks back down in his chair, letting his coat flap open. Nick picks up a pen and makes some scratches beside the list of figures. The bridge of his nose burns the way it does when he's thinking too hard.

"Surely there must be a way to bring these numbers down a bit? Take the support payments—why on earth are they so high?

And . . . and this"—he picks up the paper, stretches it tight and flicks it with his index finger so it makes a sound like a snare drum—"this allocation of the value of the house seems completely disproportionate. She hasn't even contributed to the household expenses since the twins were born, so why should she get more of the equity than I do? It makes no sense."

"That, my friend, is precisely where you're wrong." Gray shakes his head at Nick's mental midgetry. "It's precisely *because* she hasn't been bringing home the majority of the bacon—or even the bacon bits—that the court will furnish her so handsomely. I'm assuming you're not planning to seek joint custody of the kids? Given their young age and with Maya being at home, it's highly unlikely you'd get it."

Nick is dumbstruck. With a pang of shame, he realizes he's barely thought about the kids since the idea of separation occurred to him. "I guess ideally I'd aim for a flexible arrangement that works for both of us. Not one of these every-other-weekend deals—I want my kids to know that their father isn't just some guy who buys them a Happy Meal twice a month."

"Well, you should consider the fact that your wife—once she becomes your ex-wife—may not feel inclined to be 'flexible,' as you so diplomatically put it. Once you've left a woman high and dry with two little kids, you can't expect her to be sympathetic to your needs. The same goes for the court, I'm afraid."

All at once Nick sees how high the stakes are—how in seeking to gain one thing he could potentially lose everything else. He sees this and yet he knows one thing with absolute certainty: he has to leave. He has to, because he's already gone.

"I can't stay," he says. "I have to move forward."

Gray makes a palms-up, no-judgment-here gesture. "Then what you're going to be dealing with is an angry, rejected stay-at-home mom with no means to support herself and a whole lot of reasons to hate your guts."

A sick feeling rises in Nick's chest. "That's not true. I've taken care of her and the twins these past few years. Doesn't that count for something?"

"Of course it does—it counts in her financial *favour*! This is what I've been trying to tell you. Maya is now your *dependant*, just as much as the kids are. She may be a qualified lawyer and perfectly capable of supporting herself, but in the eyes of the court she's nothing but a poor, unskilled, unemployed, soon-to-be-single mother—a single mother accustomed to quite a cushy lifestyle. Add to that the fact that she's unlikely to go easy on you considering your recent behaviour—"

"What behaviour?"

"Oh, come on, man! We both know you haven't exactly been Super Dad these past couple of years. Don't forget, I'm your wingman—I've seen the way you look at other women. Don't bullshit a bullshitter."

"No way around it?"

"Nope." Gray is very still.

Something in his posture tells Nick there's more. An addendum to the memo. Gray puts his head in his hands and rubs his eyelids until they turn pink.

"Well, there is one thing. I wouldn't even call it a *thing*. More of a strategy, really. A long-term plan that requires a great deal of self-control, not to mention . . ." he tails off. "Frankly, I don't think you're up to it."

Nick spreads his fingers, places both hands palms down on his desk and stares at his friend. "Try me."

Gray seems bothered—or like he's pretending to be bothered. Nick would find this interesting if it wasn't so strange.

"It's not something I recommend to my clients officially, you understand, but it is something I like to think of as a 'strategic option' in extreme cases like yours."

"And what sort of case is that?"

"The kind where you're about to be taken to the cleaners and hung out to dry." Nick starts to object, but Gray lifts a finger to silence him. "In a way you're lucky, because your situation has what I like to think of as 'room for improvement.'"

Nick straightens in his chair. "Really?"

Gray's heavy shoulders hitch up around his ears. There is an almost imperceptible rip in the silk lining of his coat. Then he begins, "If you want a better divorce settlement, you're going to have to become a better husband first. And by 'better,' I don't mean picking up some tulips and takeout on the way home from the bar on Friday night. I'm talking about a sustained period of commitment and support, resulting in a marked and—this is key—*quantifiable* improvement in conjugal relations."

Nick looks unsure. "But I've already tried to improve things— the point is *I can't*. I've failed. That's why I want to leave and move on."

Gray shrugs. "That's what I figured. Never mind, then. I should get back to the salt mine."

He starts to button his coat, but Nick keeps talking.

"Wait, just . . . first tell me a bit more. What would I have to do?"

Gray takes a deep hit off his e-butt and exhales through his nose like a dragon. "You need to be a better man."

Nick blinks. Laughs uncertainly. "Don't I know it! But what does that have to do with *this*?"

"Everything. Don't you see? You need to transform yourself into a better husband, you selfish cocksucker. Do right by her for a while."

"Look, if I wanted a lecture—"

Gray gives a single exasperated snort. "I'm not giving you one—though you certainly deserve it. You asked me for an alternative strategy and I'm offering one, so if I were you I'd listen carefully."

Nick nods. The back of his neck tingles. "Go on."

Gray begins to speak in a practised monotone that tells Nick he's made this speech many times before. "Tell her you love her. Boost her confidence. Encourage her to go back to the law. Make sure she follows through. Support her pursuit of outside interests—and I don't just mean the gym. Take her away on holiday. Entertain the kids when she's busy. Take a break from your Saturday morning cycling races and actually spend time with your family. Offer to paint her toenails—whatever it takes. Just make sure that when you finally drop the bomb, she can no longer reasonably accuse you of being a bad husband. Not only will this weaken her case financially, but she'll feel subconsciously indebted. The settlement will be tipped in your favour. I've seen it many, many times."

"What sort of a time frame are we talking about here? I want to get on with my life."

"I've never seen it work in less than six months."

Nick leans back, raking his nails through his hair, and exhales. April seems like a lifetime away.

"The main thing is to keep up the act until you see tangible results," Gray explains. "I'm happy to check in every couple of weeks or so to monitor the situation."

Nick rubs his face. "But Maya's a family lawyer. Hasn't she seen this trick before? And even if she does buy it, won't she feel like the rug's been pulled out from under her when I *do* deliver the bad news?"

A look of satisfaction crosses Gray's face. Nick sees that this is the side of his job he loves most: the military strategy of the human heart.

"You see, that's just where you're wrong, my friend. Believe it or not, most people are genetically predisposed to believe good news even when it's patently ludicrous. Even if they are trained—as in the case of your wife—to sniff out a rat when others are being snowed. It's called the optimism bias, and it's what keeps us getting out of bed in the morning in spite of climate change, collapsing economies and the fact that the party's over once the crude oil's gone. Maya may question Nick 2.0 a little at first, but if you're persistent, she'll quickly become accustomed to her new and improved husband. More crucially, when you finally *do* announce that you want out—for reasons of self-actualization, in the most non-acrimonious way possible—her reserves of anger and resentment, which I suspect runneth over at the moment, will be sufficiently depleted to allow a *much* more civilized dissolution of the marriage—that is, one in which she does not end up taking you to the cleaners. You'll still need to do some divvying up, of course, but the final amount will be significantly reduced. Who knows? You might even be able to settle out of court. Especially if you're successful in encouraging her to go back to work."

Nick's closes his eyes and presses a finger to each temple. He thinks of a question. "How much do you figure I can save myself by doing this?"

Gray, who has clearly been anticipating this question, makes a couple of scratches on the calculation sheet and slides it across the smooth desk. Nick barely needs to look down to glimpse the new number.

"I'm in," he says.

Without needing to, the two men shake.

When Gray gets up to leave, Nick hands him back the "Wakefield Family Assets" file.

"I think it's safer for you to keep this—for now."

Gray nods and shoves the file into his overflowing briefcase. And then he is gone.

CHAPTER 6

Maya

Maya's been seeing Antonio at Drama Salon since the late 1990s, when she was a law student posing as a saucer-eyed party girl on the weekends. The salon sits on one of the city's skeeziest corners—she secretly relishes the incongruity of having to weave through a small crowd of crackheads hawking ancient hubcaps to get a headful of premium lowlights and a high-gloss rinse. The salon has no sign and the windows are taped over with tissue paper, giving the place a disused look. Inside, however, the Drams (as it's known among regulars) is a balm for the bourgeois soul—all retro barber chairs, antique gilt mirrors and church pews in the waiting area.

Antonio's three black Cockapoos tear out of the back to greet Maya in a spittle-misted chorus of yelps, ears flying behind them like protest banners. She can never remember their names—a faux pas she tries (and fails) to remedy by sending a magnum of champagne every year on the Saturday before Christmas.

Antonio stands behind her, hands resting firmly on her smock-covered shoulders.

"What can we do for you today, my darling girl?"

He rubs his elegant tapered finger along the base of her skull and lifts up the hair from her neck, making her shiver with delight. Plucking a small tendril away from the nape of her neck, he inspects the ends in a way that makes the roots twirl and sends electric shocks from the crown of her head to the tip of her pinkie toes. She knows he's only checking for damage, but part of her wants to beg him not to stop. Instead she shrugs.

"I dunno . . . the usual? I was toying with the idea of bangs, but I'm still not sure."

Antonio nods solemnly, then closes his eyes and presses his fingers into her scalp as if intuiting the right course of action from her inner hair spirit. After half a minute, he says, "Maybe just a root touch-up and a trim for today. What do we think?"

Maya exhales, relief flooding her body. "Perfect."

Despite Maya's marriage, the birth of her twins and the subsequent derailing of her career, Antonio still tends to her like she's an unspoiled ingenue on the cusp of a great adventure, her whole life waiting to unfold in series of dazzling events, each of which promises to be more glamorous and fascinating than the next, if only—and this is the crucial bit—she can get her hair exactly right. For the past several years, Antonio has been working toward an ashy-yet-lustrous shade for Maya's highlights that he calls gin-and-tonic blonde. Every six weeks, her standing appointment brings them both a little closer to the pinnacle of hair colour nirvana. There is nowhere in the world she is quite so at home.

He beetles off to mix the colour, leaving Maya alone with a two-month-old copy of *Us Weekly*. She is halfway through a story on why Pippa Middleton can't seem to find a husband (apparently she's "too sexy" to be "wife material") when she hears someone air-kissing her way through the salon with loud, smacking "mwahs!" Before Maya can arrange herself more inconspicuously behind her magazine, Rachel Katz is descending upon her with flinging arms and juicy air kisses.

"Oh, my God! THIS IS UNBELIEVEABLE!" she cries.

Maya's not sure if she means their running into each other or the fact that it happened the last time they were here too. She makes a mental note to change her standing appointment.

Rachel is married to Glen, one of Nick's many entertainment lawyers, which has the effect of throwing them together in various social situations throughout the year. Rachel is also one of those people Maya finds she bumps into with random consistency, making them feel more connected than they actually are. In Maya's view, they are not so much friends as co-wives, watching from the sidelines of real life. Nevertheless, in a grand show of intimacy, Rachel tells Maya how gorgeous she looks, and how amaaaazing her perfectly ordinary shoes are. Maya smiles wanly and allows herself to be complimented, then in return tells Rachel how lovely her earrings are (for this, she well knows, is the Girl Code). After they are done making the obligatory fuss over each other, Maya sits there feeling weirdly limbless in her polyester poncho.

"God, it's been a while, hasn't it? I still can't believe you have twins—honestly you'd never know it. So funny how we always end up here at the same time, isn't it?"

Maya smiley-nods and looks down longingly at her unread stack of crappy fashion magazines, but Rachel is having none of it.

She tosses a leather handbag the size of a bowling-ball carrier down on the floor and plunks herself on the next chair over. A shampoo girl hops to it and begins hosing Rachel down in a portable sink, but Rachel doesn't bother to acknowledge her, just continues chatting to Maya with her head thrown back under the suds.

"So what's up with *you*?" Her eyes widen in what Maya recognizes as an unvarnished yearning for scandal and misery. *If I told her Nick was leaving me for a lingerie model, she might actually die of excitement and happiness.*

"Not much. You?"

Thankfully that's all it takes to set Rachel off on a ten-minute monologue about two-year-old Verity's new "boyfriend" at playgroup—a story that is ostensibly about the adorable mating rituals of toddlers but is actually intended to underline the remarkably precocious intelligence, charisma and sex appeal of her genetic issue.

Despite the nature of their non-friendship, Maya's actually known Rachel since her nightclub days, when she was a three-seabreezes-and-a-pack-of-chips-for-dinner kind of girl. Back then, Rachel was a publicist on the hunt for a rich husband, whom she eventually found in the form of Gormless Glen, the most un-entertaining entertainment lawyer in his field. Glen lets Rachel do whatever she wants whenever she wants, and for this she will never forgive him. By the time Antonio returns with his colour cart and begins the fussy work of painting and foiling Maya's roots, Rachel is in full flow.

"I'm telling you, he is *so* bad at gifts that this Christmas I'm actually just taking his credit card, buying my own gifts and putting them under the tree. All the lazy bastard has to do is sign the card, and I'll probably have to nag him for days to do that. Anyway, the upside is I've already got this gorgeous tennis bracelet picked out at the Christie's auction. It's not romantic, but you have to make things easy for men, you know? Like I told Glen, he should consider himself lucky—all he has to do now is press 'spend.'" She cackles at her own unfunny joke.

Maya offers a smile. "But maybe if you gave him a chance . . . ?"

Rachel bats her hands like she's pushing Maya backwards off a cliff. "Bah! No way. I've tried that. If I didn't do it for him, nothing would get done—trust me. It's like everything—marriage, kids, buying a house, renovating, vacations, shopping for friggin' groceries. If I didn't do it, it would never get done. Honestly, sometimes I think if I hadn't showed up in his life and stamped my little foot, he'd still be living in his roachy law school apartment, watching pay-per-view in his tighty-whities. And for this, what do I get? The privilege of buying my own Christmas presents." Rachel shakes her head to convey how utterly convincing she finds herself. "Sometimes I honestly feel like Glen was sent here to help me cultivate patience. Like some kind of test of character from God, do you know what I mean? Surely you must feel the same way about Nick sometimes. How are things going with his company? Is he still crazy busy?"

Maya leans back and one of Antonio's tinfoil flaps falls forward, mercifully concealing her eyes. She knows that in passive-aggressive Rachelspeak, "crazy busy" is code for "workaholic bastard who neglects your every need." Frustrated as she is, Maya has never been able to master the art of venting about her marriage to others. She prefers to keep her unhappiness to herself—not because she's especially private but because co-rumination seems to trivialize things. She likes to think of her marriage as being in a special kind of trouble, rather than the garden-variety type.

"Mmm . . . yeah, most of the time," she mutters. "How's Glen's new practice going?" She knows she should ask about Rachel's work, but she can't recall the exact nature of her pretend job. Something about importing kaftans from Morocco?

"Oh God, you know, the same. *Terribly* important. Takes precedence over everything. Honestly, you'd think negotiating contracts for TV producers was morally equivalent to cancer research. He's so caught up in work most of the time, I feel completely invisible. He never notices if I change my hair or get a new outfit. I feel like I could go on one of those Venezuelan cruises and come back with Eva Longoria's tits and he wouldn't even notice."

"I'm sure that's not true."

"Oh, it is! This summer I was doing that daily fitness boot camp in the park—you know, the one that runs five days a week for six weeks—and every morning I put on the same stretchy yoga pants and top while I was getting my daughter out the door for day camp. Every day for weeks on end, he saw me have breakfast in the same outfit. Then one morning about halfway through the summer, I got up and said, 'Time to put on the uniform.' And he said, 'What uniform?' And I said, 'You seriously haven't noticed that I've been wearing *exactly* the same outfit every day for the past three weeks?' He just gave me that blank look—the one where they've just done something shitty, but if you make a big deal about it, they're going to call you crazy. God, I hate that look. It's so invalidating. Anyway, I completely dropped it. A test of patience. But that doesn't mean I've forgotten."

There's a flustered silence as the girl wraps a towel around Rachel's head, causing her to close her mouth. Maya searches for something to say.

"Have you tried counselling?"

Rachel looks astonished. "No, why would we?"

Maya shrugs, not wanting to answer the question. "Well, it's just that you seem sort of . . . I don't know."

Rachel laughs and shakes her head. "Unhappy? Are you kidding? I'm the happiest person I know—I've got everything I want. My life is perfect. I've just been married for a long time, that's all. You've got to *vent* once in a while. That's what *girlfriends* are for." She gives Maya a meaningful look, reaches over and squeezes her knee. "We should go for margaritas one of these days."

"Yeah, we totally should." Maya wonders how much time to let pass before she moves her knee away.

Mercifully, Antonio breaks the silence. "Ready for a blow-dry, darling girl?"

Maya nods eagerly and lets him lead her over to the shampoo station, already relishing the silence.

When Maya returns home, the house is silent. Since the twins were born, she's rarely come home to an empty house. She walks through room after room, calling out her children's names. When she gets to the kitchen, she picks up the baby monitor and stares at it as if hoping for a message from the beyond. It's nearly quitting time, so Velma won't be at the park. Besides, they'll be hungry for dinner soon. She has a moment of blind panic, in which she imagines a car crash, an electrocution involving a misplaced fork, and the double onset of childhood meningitis all at once. Then she sees the note.

The handwriting is more deliberate than usual but still unmistakably Nick's. "Hi babe," it reads. "Got off work early, so sent Velma home and decided to take the kids to the Jungle House for noodles. Back before bedtime. Enjoy your evening off—relax! Nick."

Beside the note is a jar of lavender bath salts from Maya's favourite French toiletry shop. She picks it up and studies the mauve-and-white label as if looking for clues. As one set of neurotic fantasies evaporates from her mind, another begins to present itself. *Why is he being nice to me?* she finds herself thinking. *What can he possibly want?* She racks her brains for reasons why Nick might be feeling contrite or emotionally indebted. Has he forgotten some major birthday or anniversary? (No.) Is he having an affair? (Maybe.) Is he just feeling guilty for months of stonewalling and emotional avoidance? (Unlikely.) She goes to the fridge and uncorks a half-empty bottle of Pinot Grigio. Pouring herself a generous glass, she thinks about Rachel's monologue on marital depreciation—how it had made her feel sorry for Gormless Glen, a decent, hard-working guy who could never do a single thing right. A man condemned to a lifetime of criticism and failure in the eyes of his spouse.

Maya swallows a bit of wine, letting the acid sweetness roll down her throat to some deeper, fast-warming place. Low in her belly, a coil unfurls.

Whatever Nick's game is, Maya resolves to play along and

avoid giving him the satisfaction of resistance. She knows how guilt works; she isn't going to relieve him of it by being the cold fish to his ingratiating suitor. Whatever he's feeling guilty about, she'll make him feel guiltier still by accepting his every kindness with gratitude and compliance. If he wants her to relax, she'll relax. She'll be the most relaxed and understanding wife on the block—a paragon of well-adjusted reasonability. As if to prove the point, she picks up the lavender salts and marches upstairs to draw herself a bath. *There*, she figures. *That'll show him.*

CHAPTER 7

Nick

There are no two words in the English language that instill more trepidation in Nick Wakefield than those he is being forced to contemplate: date night.

It isn't the event itself that horrifies him—like anyone else, he is capable of enjoying dinner and a movie with his spouse, or has been in better times—but the notion of a life so circumscribed by duty that even a weekly window for romance must be put in dull service to the cause. "Date nights" were for people who read advice columns, joined professional networking groups, signed up for "club cards" at every retailer they frequented, went on package vacations and had their savings swindled away in pyramid schemes. Unimaginative, credulous people, in other words— *normal* people who'd gone without passion in their lives for so long they'd forgotten what real passion felt like (if indeed they ever really knew at all). Dates nights were the death of spontaneity, the gateway into a life defined by middle-class banality. A code word for mandatory sex. And while Nick liked to think of himself as a man with a healthy libido, nothing left him colder than the idea of erotic duty.

Hadn't it, after all, been the performance requirements of baby-making sex that had signalled the beginning of the end of what his own commercials might call the "spark" between Maya and him? Nick hadn't been averse to children—he knew it was part of the deal, and since they'd been married several years, it was getting to be *time*—but he hadn't banked on Maya's goal-oriented approach to the project, a full-on regimen of folic acid (for her), zinc tablets (for him), ear thermometers, ovulation charts and mandatory twice-daily rumpy-pumpy during "the window," followed by weeks-long dry spells in which he was instructed to "save it up" for the next opportunity. All of this was compounded by Maya's mounting anxiety when things didn't go immediately as planned—an anxiety that could be assuaged only by appointments with a private fertility specialist, culminating in hormone injections (for her), hospital-supervised spunk extraction (for him) and, finally, nature's greatest-known obstacle to a healthy married sex life: twins.

Nick had tried to make the best of the news at the time, pointing out gamely that it was "two for the price of one," and that now they could simply get it over with in one shot—the usual gloss people put on the terrifying reality of multiple births. But the truth was, he secretly blamed Maya for the logistical difficulties presented by two babies where one would have sufficed. Because of her hyper-vigilance—her habit of panicking before there was any cause for alarm—they had spent the past three years saddled with double trouble. Considering where appointment sex had gotten him so far, was it any wonder he'd developed a natural aversion to date nights?

And yet he knew what he had to do.

After the success of the bath salts on Tuesday (he'd come

home to find Maya damp and pink-cheeked in her robe, curled up under the winter duvet), he felt emboldened by the plan laid out by Gray. If he was to pull off a convincing impersonation of a good husband, it was going to take time and effort. If he wanted the ultimate prize—the financial and sexual freedom of unencumbered singledom—he was going to have to do many things that didn't come naturally to him. The trick would be in keeping his eye on the ball—remembering that his actions, while purporting to seek one result, were in fact striving toward the opposite effect. In essence, for the next few months, he'd have to commit to a state of supreme ironic detachment—one that would require every ounce of emotional control he could muster. If he was chilled out before, now he would be reptilian.

With this resolve, Nick makes a reservation at Ethel's Kitchen, a newly opened restaurant specializing in high-end Sloppy Joes and single-malt Scotch, for the following night: Saturday night. Date night. He emails his wife to inform her of the plan and is surprised to get an almost immediate response: "Love to. Can't wait. xo M."

The "xo" surprises him. It's been ages since they used terms of endearment in email correspondence. Email, now, is for family logistics rather than adolescent declarations of love. Seems silly and disingenuous to "x" and "o" someone you've given up kissing and hugging in real life. Still, something about Maya's sign-off gives him a moment of pause. He feels a small twist in his lower intestine: the worm of guilt. Is it possible she actually still loves him? After all that he's done (or more to the point, not done)? He pushes the thought from his head. *It's a date, then*, he thinks. *So far, so good.*

The next morning Nick, reasoning that Rome wasn't built in a day, breaks his resolution to spend time with the kids on the weekends. Instead he follows his usual Saturday routine: a fifty-kilometre ride through the ravine system with his cycling buddies, followed by a long day at the office. Pre-production is ramping up on the CurvePhone job, and the thought of hanging around the house fills him with roiling anxiety. He spends the day drifting around the office, looking over preliminary budgets and ducking in and out of pre-production meetings, flirting with the stream of potential wardrobe girls (all named Aynsley or Ashley and wearing jeans and towering heels) who've come in to interview for the job. By the time six o'clock rolls around, he's feeling pumped. He is going to take this date night and *kill it*.

When he gets home that evening he finds Velma in the kitchen, batch-baking sweet potatoes for the following week. He is whistling a Rihanna tune about umbrellas as he tosses his coat over the back of the chair and drops his keys on the table.

"Well, someone's in a good mood," Velma says, eyeing him with mock suspicion.

He takes a bottle of beer from the fridge—some organic microbrewed craft thing—and drinks it half-standing at the kitchen counter, pausing only for a gulp of air and to wipe his mouth with the back of his hand. "Is there something I should be grumpy about?" he says, emitting a silent purr of a belch.

Velma raises an eyebrow. "Careful you don't get drunk. Your wife has been getting ready for hours. I swear she spent half the day just picking out what dress to wear."

So Maya's told Velma about date night. Nick watches her gingerly peeling the skin off the steaming yams and wonders how much else Velma knows. Doubtless she will have noticed a certain amount of discord in the house. Her tone is certainly a knowing one. Will he have to bring her onside too? He takes another slug of beer and considers this. Decides it's too soon to tell.

"Where is that gorgeous woman I'm married to?" He tosses the empty bottle in the recycling.

"Reading stories. You know how she likes to do bedtime herself."

Nick nods. He does know. Maya's bedtime routines are sacrosanct, the indelible framework within which everything else in the household functions. He takes the stairs two at time and pauses outside the master bedroom—the room he used to consider his own but now doesn't enter without knocking. Through the crack in the door, he can hear the well-worn murmur of her voice reciting *Where the Wild Things Are*. He wants to see the twins but remembers that Maya doesn't like him to "overstimulate" them at bedtime—so he decides to take a shower instead. He heads to the spare bathroom, sheds his clothes and is soon leaning into the hot water, blood rising to the surface of his skin in a thousand tiny, delicious pricks.

Warm and scrubbed, he stands in front of the guest room closet, body throbbing, towel on hips, contemplating his clothing options for the evening ahead. While dressing, Nick secretly imagines himself a benign dictator of an oil-rich Third World nation holding a parade in his honour. He sits down on the suede upholstered bench and stares at the open racks of colour-coded dress shirts, the stacks of cashmere sweaters separated by tissue paper, the made-to-measure suits spun from the finest Italian wool and stitched together by his private tailor in Hong Kong. When did he acquire all these beautiful things? he wonders vaguely. Does he even deserve them? The thought paralyzes him for a moment. Then the right outfit comes to him: the lavender V-neck with the grey wool trousers. An ensemble fit for a date night.

He smells Maya before he sees her. Citrus mixed with something darker: liquorice root and burnt cedar. The perfume he bought her while he was shooting in Morocco five years ago. Possibly the last gift he gave her that wasn't chosen by his assistant.

She is actually smiling, a rare surprise. She stands awkwardly, stockinged feet in a simple black shift dress, a pair of high heels in each hand—one gold, one blue.

"Definitely the gold," he says.

Maya puts a finger to her lips to indicate that the twins have settled and must not be disturbed. Then she glances down at the pair of four-inch metallic ankle straps dangling from her fingers. "You mean these?" she says.

"Isn't that what you came in here to ask me?"

"Actually I was looking for the mink oil for my shoes. What time is dinner?"

"Not 'til eight, but I'm sure we can have a drink at the bar first."

He cinches his towel a bit tighter around his waist and looks down at the lavender sweater unfolded on the bench in front of him. Maybe it's not quite right with the grey flannel trousers? He looks to Maya for approval, but she's already left the room. When she returns five minutes later, he's buttoning his cufflinks, having abandoned the sweater for a checked shirt and blazer. She wears the same shift dress, though her shoulders are now swaddled in a delicate mohair wrap. Then he notices her shoes: blue.

"Your car or mine?" she asks.

Finally, a question to which Nick *knows* he has the right answer. "I'll drive," he says.

As soon as they enter the restaurant, Nick can feel her stiffen. He does all the right things—opens the door, takes her coat, places a gentle hand on her lower back as the head waiter leads them to their table—but none of it matters. Maya is on her guard. He can see it in the way her eyes move restlessly around the room, with its mirrored walls and vintage vinyl diner booths, never pausing on any person or thing for more than a second at a time. She opens her menu, then closes it again. At Nick's behest, the waiter brings over two vintage single malts and two glasses of spring water, which disappear quietly and without comment. He exhales with a whisper.

"Where's the wine list?" she says.

He hands it to her with some reluctance. It's thick and heavy as an atlas and he was looking forward to using it as pre-dinner reading material.

"Shouldn't we choose what we're eating first?"

Maya shrugs. "There's not much choice."

Nick glances around the room and registers an alarming number of people in designer pajamas with asymmetrical haircuts eating wet ground beef on Wonder buns.

He bridles slightly—the restaurant was his choice, and one he'd hoped would amuse her—but then he checks himself and forces an indulgent smile to the surface of his face. At first he feels his skin might rip from the effort, but then something loosens behind the surface, like an elastic waistband giving way. "I hope you're in the mood for some seriously high-end slop," he says.

Maya, who's been studying the wine list like it might contain the lost secrets of the ancients, lifts her head and gazes at him evenly, back flat against her chair. "Okay, then," she says. "Let's have the Montepulciano." She hands him the book and taps a buffed fingernail on her selection to make sure he understands.

Second one down, Nick notes with an inward grimace. Everyone knows you *never* order the second least expensive wine on the list, especially not at a restaurant like this—that is, the sort of place where trendy people gather to stare at each other and spend stupid amounts of money. The reason for this rule, as any halfway sophisticated lover of the vine knows, is that the second least expensive wine is invariably the most commonly ordered bottle and consequently the most marked-up. Thus, in choosing what *seems* like the best deal—an inexpensive wine that saves you the embarrassment of looking like a cheapskate—you actually end up getting swindled.

He is compelled to explain this to Maya (again), both to make her realize her mistake in ordering the Montepulciano, and also to point out he's not being cheap by objecting—quite the opposite, in fact. After all, he would happily spring for a pricier bottle, safe in the knowledge it's *actually the better deal*. He hasn't yet opened his mouth to contradict her choice when her objections begin streaming through his mind. *Why do you have to be so stubborn and controlling? Why can't I just make one simple little choice without everything turning into a fight?*

In the middle of this internal bickering, the waiter comes over and asks, with an obsequious little bow, if "the gentleman" has "come to a decision on the wine." Nick doesn't pause to think about it—he just draws a breath and does the thing he knows he must do in service of his New Self: he smiles tightly and orders the Montepulciano. The waiter nods, then reaches out to take away the list. It's only after the second tug that Nick realizes he hasn't—that his hands somehow won't allow him to—let go of it.

"So sorry," he says relinquishing the list and watching the waiter retreat with a quizzical look.

When Nick turns his attention back to the table, he notices Maya staring at him rather intently, eyes wide and blinking double time.

"What's wrong?" he says, suddenly stricken by the idea that she might be about to cry, which she almost never does. For the second time since they entered the restaurant, Nick braces. But then her eyebrows lift and he sees that in fact she's amused. Soon she's sputtering, eyes glistening, cheeks mottled, hand pressed to a trembling mouth, trying and failing to suppress a burst of laughter.

"What is it?" he asks, feeling suspiciously mocked.

She hides her face, waves with her free hand and breathes until her little fit has passed. "Nothing," she says finally. "Nothing at all."

Normally Nick would press her, but tonight he decides to let it go. Because of this, they end up staring silently at their menus—a litany of hand-chopped meats with accompanying "secret" sauces—until the waiter arrives with the wine and makes a merciful fuss about opening it. Before Maya can speak, Nick orders the five-course tasting menu, beginning with the pork-belly mince with Hollandaise sauce and homemade ketchup on brioche for two. She looks at him, startled.

"Are you sure that's a good idea?" she says after the waiter has left.

"Don't tell me you've gone vegetarian again."

She gives him a dead stare. She hasn't been vegetarian since third-year law school, and even then it was only for six months. Nick knows this but still can't resist.

"It's just I was thinking about, you know, Velma at home and everything. Timing."

"What about it?" He slides his hand across the table, thinking this is the moment to fondle her fingers or make some equivalent gesture, but it's dark and the breadbasket and truffle butter get in the way. "We have a babysitter, so let's let her babysit."

"We *are* letting her babysit. It's just a question of for how long. She's not normally there at night. What if Foster wakes up?"

"Then he'll find Velma, his nanny, who he sees every day and is his second-favourite person in the entire world."

"You think?"

"Yes, and she's also certified in first aid and speaks Portuguese, Spanish and English. Says so on her CV. Don't you guys talk?"

"Yes, but reading a CV is different from talking. And anyway, we talk about different things."

"Like what?"

Maya looks at him suspiciously. "None of your beeswax."

"Oh, so it's like that, is it? The sacred pact between nanny and mommy?"

Maya shrugs. "Let's just say we talk about *stuff*. Mostly man troubles."

Nick is taken aback. "You mean you tell her about . . . us?"

"God, no. *Her* man troubles," Maya says. "She's got enough for both of us, believe me."

The waiter arrives with an amuse-bouche of barbeque-flavoured corn nuts, and Maya frowns. Nick remembers why he gave up trying to please her years ago.

"Maya, we haven't been out for dinner in months. Can you just relax for a couple of hours? I know it's hard to be away from the kids, but if we're going to make things better, we're going to have to remember how to spend time alone together. To enjoy each other's company again. Just the two of us. Can you please try to do that for me?"

She cracks a corn nut between her teeth and looks at him with curiosity. "You're really trying, aren't you?"

Nick feels suddenly called out. Blood pounds in his ears. *No, no,* he tells himself. *This is good. Talk about your so-called feelings.* "Yes, I am," he says.

Maya nods and he nods back. Then she smiles and he finds himself smiling too, like he's in one of those strange mirroring games hippie parents play with their babies.

"So we're *trying*, then, are we?" she says. She looks amused by the idea. As though he's just suggested they buy a blueberry farm in New Zealand and she has, on consideration, found herself strangely delighted by the prospect.

"Of course," Nick says, then he smiles again, attempting to put a gloss on the moment. "I mean, really, when were we *not* trying?"

Maya starts on the wine. By now the ground meat and sauce has arrived, and they both begin spooning savoury glup onto their brioche rolls until the bread is swimming in sop. Nick sees he has miscalculated her mood.

"Like, um, maybe for the past three or four years? Definitely the last two," she says. "If we're being honest, I think we should admit that. We haven't been trying. At least not to make things better. I think if anything"—she drifts off for a moment, eyes roaming the room again, before finding her thread and continuing—"if anything, we've been trying to make things worse. I don't mean actively trashing our marriage, but neglecting it to the point of nonfeasance."

Nick swallows hard at the legal jargon (is she on to him?), then decides it's just a flash of the old Maya. At the same time, he's not sure how the conversation came to be so earnest when earnest conversation was the furthest thing from his mind in bringing her here. What exactly *had* he imagined would come of this date night? The first and only such night he'd suggested to his wife, outside the odd obligatory work function, in the three years since the twins were born? He had a vague notion of liberal wine consumption overlayed with lots of tinkling laughter and maybe an accidental brush of thighs beneath the table. (Was it too much to hope she might wear a garter belt? Probably. No, definitely.) Anyway, of all the scenarios he'd imagined, a relationship talk had not been one of them. He is happy to have sex with his wife again in the service of ending their marriage, but he has no intention of talking about his feelings. His real feelings, that is. His fake feelings are another matter.

Maya, on the other hand, seems perfectly comfortable with the way the conversation is going. Nick reminds himself to keep his eye on the ball. *Happy wife, happy life.* He tries to get inside the head of the kind of man who believes this. He reaches across the table again, pushing aside all obstacles, and this time finds what he's looking for. Her fingers shrink away at first, then settle under his like a small animal panicking and submitting. Her other hand clutches at her napkin.

"You're absolutely right," he offers. "We've been bad, haven't we? Especially me. I know I haven't always been the easiest person to live with, particularly since the kids. But I want you to know that I'm here now and things are about to change. I'm going to be a better man—for you, for the twins and most of all for myself. I really do want things to change, and I'm willing to go to the mat to make it happen. Do you believe me?"

As he speaks, Maya drops her eyes to her plate, then looks up. She nods silently and does that undulating neck extension women do when they're trying not to cry. He experiences a small and not entirely unpleasant twinge in the pit of his stomach. Empathy? *No, no,* he decides. *Pity. Pity with a side of guilt.*

At this moment, Adam Gray appears beside their table like a harbinger of doom in a rumpled silk suit. "Well, well, if it isn't the harvest king and his homecoming queen," he thunders. "Out on a well-deserved date night, I see. Very good." He smiles greedily and then kisses Maya's hand in the unselfconscious manner of a Hungarian count. Nick cringes while his wife giggles with delight.

"My God, how are you? It's been forever, hasn't it? How's the law?" Maya looks wistful, as she always does when asking after her former profession.

"Good, good," says Gray, patting his chest. "Actually, horrible. Look at me—I'm a wreck. Be glad you got out when you did,

Maya. You should write a book of health and beauty tips. Call it *Escape from the Salt Mine.*"

Everyone chuckles but no one louder than Nick, who is laughing to mask his annoyance. What was Gray doing by validating Maya's choice to stay home when just last week he'd said Nick's only hope was to encourage her to get a job? He watches them catching up on professional gossip and then it hits him: Gray is using reverse psychology. The more he publically validates Maya for staying home, the more she'll privately long to be back in the thick of it.

As Maya chatters on about the kids and the "utter hilarity" of toddler yoga, Nick lets his mind drift slightly, toward the night's conclusion and what awaits him there. He has sex on the brain. Now what to do about it? He knows they need to end their epic dry spell since the birth of the twins, but how best to go about quenching the Sahara Desert? He watches her talking to Gray, the way her eyes widen with recognition, then crinkle up at the corners when she gets the joke, which thankfully she always does. Nothing about her—skin, hair, the upper-lip divot where latte foam gathers—looks any different to him than the day they'd met. She is the same and yet utterly changed. As she teases Gray about some social transgression or other (hair thrown back, glossy lips parted to reveal the tiny gap between her two front teeth, laughter free-flowing and effervescent), Nick acknowledges how rarely he sees this version of his wife—the one whom he used to know, but who now seems off-limits to him. The wife reserved for friends and strangers at cocktail parties.

"I'd better get back," Gray says finally, giving his bull head a swing toward the corner of the room, where a young woman with a glossy brown side braid cranes her swan neck at the menu. Nick pegs her at no older than twenty-five. "Working dinner with my articling student. Poor kid's been putting in eighty-hour weeks since June. Thought she deserved some overpriced beefaroni, or whatever it is the kids are eating these days."

"How generous of you," says Nick. Maya nudges him under the table.

Gray doesn't bother to protest, just gives a shrug of mild defeat and, before sloping back to his table, says with a look Nick finds altogether too knowing, "We can't all be happily married, can we?"

They wait until Gray is at least eight paces away before discussing him.

"I know we're supposed to feel sorry for him, but I'm not sure I do anymore," she says, twirling a piece of hair between her fingers.

"Don't you think he's lonely and, I dunno, filled with a tragic sense of emptiness?"

"Why?" Maya laughs. "Because he's rich, successful and totally unencumbered? That sounds to me exactly what most men aspire to."

Nick shifts in his chair. "Not men as lucky as me," he manages to say after an awkward pause.

Maya, who's been watching Gray, snaps her head back and stares at him. "Wow, you're really laying it on thick tonight, aren't you?" She says this a little more combatively than she seems to have intended. And for a terrible moment, Nick thinks, *She knows*. But then her expression blooms into a smile and she reaches languidly for her glass. He finds himself admiring, for the thousandth time, the way her arm furls out from the elbow like a ballerina's. She nods her head toward Gray, who appears to be edutaining his date by deconstructing the wine list, bottle by bottle. "Looks like I'm not the only one getting the full charm offensive tonight."

Nick is keen to shift the focus. "Do you think it's actually an Internet date? Do grown-ups really go on those?"

Maya shakes her head. "Nah, guys like that can't date outside their job description, let alone their firm. Trust me, I know the type."

Nick leans back, watching his wife watching Gray. "*Do* you now?" he says with mock surprise, his tone concealing a flutter of something at once prickly and pleasurable. He is thinking of the old her, the one who glided out the door to the office every day in a series of smooth wool skirt suits. A woman who watches—and is watched by—countless men he doesn't know and will never meet.

They're only halfway through their platter of high-end cat sick, and Maya is toying with her glass, the edges of her expression softly blurred with wine. He suddenly knows neither of them will eat another bite. She looks up at him through her hair, which has gone sweetly mussy, and suppresses a giggle. Nick thinks, *If this is the fake me, is that the real her?* He flags down the waiter and asks for the bill.

CHAPTER 8

Maya

Maya wakes up the next morning with a pain in her face and a buzz in her head. A half-dried puddle of spit has gathered in the crease of her pillow, gluing her hair to her cheek and leaving her lips dry and sore, like the sandy edges of a bayou sinkhole. It's not the hangover that hits her first but the dread. The sense that whatever damage was done the night before may well be irreparable now. She has a strong suspicion that her life is ruined. And as a consolation, she wishes someone would bring her a large bag of salt-and-vinegar chips.

With this comes the realization that she is alone in the master bedroom. The twins, she remembers, were put down in their own beds and actually stayed there for once. She has a bleary memory of Nick moving them. He slept here with her, she's sure of that, but he isn't here now. For a moment she worries that maybe he prefers the guest bed after all this time. But then she decides that he must have gone into the office, which would not be unusual on a Sunday.

As disorienting as it is to be alone in her bed, it's nice not to be woken up by sweaty, restless toddlers. She sniffs the air and detects the faintly equine smell of a middle-aged man. The leathery smell of body hair and fresh sweat. She tries to decide whether she has missed his smell and concludes that, in fact, she has.

She remembers it's Velma's day off—a realization that would normally elicit a dim flicker of anxiety overridden by a desire to accomplish things (a day for educational board games, flash cards, rearranging winter closets, making ambitious to-do lists), but not today. The cinderblock of gloom pressing down on her chest is too heavy for that.

But what is she so gloomy about? Surely not the fact that her husband insisted on taking her out for dinner. A real live date night! Imagine that. The two of them going out together just like a normal, functional couple trying to raise a family and fit in some "grown-up time." Finally, Maya had thought, they could actually *be* the people everybody thought they were—even if only for one night. But then she'd ruined it, although she couldn't quite remember how. Things had seemed okay at the restaurant. A little awkward—inedible hipster food—but generally all right. Then the drive home, during which she'd teased Nick for being tipsy and he'd laughed but neither of them had done anything about it. (Drunk driving was bad, she scolded herself. They were *parents* with *responsibilities*, for Christ's sake!) And then paying Velma in crumpled bills from the bottom of her handbag (why not just add it to her monthly take-home pay?) while Nick called a taxi, revealing that he was too lazy (and hammered) to drive her home. She recalls trying to persuade Velma to have a glass of wine—a sign she and Nick were definitely over the limit, since

Velma never drank on the job or even in the house as a rule. For Maya, there was always a moment in every drunken evening when, on reflection, she should have (a) shut up, (b) left the party, or (c) gone to bed. And most often it was (d) all of the above. Velma's exit, Maya now saw, had been that moment last night.

But she hadn't.

Instead, Nick suggested a TUD (their university acronym for "totally unnecessary drink," otherwise known as a nightcap) of cognac in the kitchen, and Maya rejoined with some (even more unnecessary) sloppy dancing to a Motown tune that happened to be on the late-night radio. And then, just when she figured it was time to drop the giggly pantomime and go back to behaving like the responsibly dissatisfied grown-ups they were, Nick had leaned in and kissed her. Not one of the dry, joyless pecks he occasionally dispensed while searching for his BlackBerry before leaving for work, but a real kiss. A multi-levelled communiqué that started soft and gathered momentum, like an absorbing conversation with an attractive stranger. A kiss with a view.

All this was fine, of course. It was during the foreplay that things began to go off course. First Nick lifted her onto the counter, like in the movies, but the angle wasn't right and her tights had to be removed—a process that involved a lot of kicking and squirming and yanking at control-top spandex. That done, they attempted to move to the sofa, but first the curtains had to be pulled shut and the lights dimmed, and by the time Nick had settled down beside her on the merciless sectional, she was feeling chilly and trying to wrap her bare legs in the mohair reading throw he was always complaining was too itchy. Then, in the vain hope of rescuing the moment, she'd attempted to give him a blow job—a skill she'd always prided herself on, aided in large part, she knew, by Nick's legendary responsiveness. There was a time—not so long ago, in fact—when Maya had considered them exceedingly well matched on the blow-job front. It wasn't a complicated equation: she liked administering, and Nick was an avid recipient. But it was the first time she'd gone there, so to speak, in months, if not years. While she felt a bit rusty and thick-tongued with booze at first, her old technique quickly returned, or at least she thought it did. Nick's body seemed to disagree. He wasn't just unresponsive; he (well, *it*, to be precise) actually seemed to recoil from her attentions, like a slug being poked with a stick. Something in Nick's flinch spurred her on, encouraged her in her task, until long after it was clear that nothing would come of the exercise. They'd failed at sex in the past, but this was different. This was the first sex act between them in many months, and her self-esteem was riding on it. Nick, however, responded as though she were attempting to finalize his corporate tax return. There was no communiqué down here, and if there were, the message was cold and clear: Bye-bye now. Don't call us, we'll call you. Please shut the door on your way out.

Finally, Nick heaved a sigh and apologized, murmuring some self-blaming platitude in what seemed to Maya an obviously disingenuous tone. (He was drunk and tired; it was the end of a long week; and so on.) This had been her cue to throw in the towel, wipe the slobber off her chin and gamely laugh it off on her way upstairs to check on the twins. Yes, she should have smoothed her skirt and made some crack about Nick losing his mojo. And that's what she would have done, if it hadn't been for all the wine and the dancing and the disorienting regard (she wasn't used to him paying her so much attention, not in a real way). But no, instead of seizing her opportunity for coolness and bringing the night to a dignified close, she found herself giving in to a competing urge, one that was unfamiliar yet strangely irresistible—and that was the impulse to fall apart. Slumped on the floor beneath him, with her forehead resting on his left knee, she began to sob. Soon the tears were sliding into the crevice of her nose, where they joined a string of egg-whitey snot that descended in a humiliating string from her nostrils onto Nick's trousers, then puddled on the floor beneath his unmoving feet. He let her cry like that for a while—whether out of mercy or disgust, she couldn't be sure, and at the time she didn't care. By the time he hoisted her to her feet, Maya was inwardly despairing (could she actually have moaned aloud?) that her husband didn't want her anymore. After all, what could be *less* attractive than a drunk, insecure, sobbing, unemployed, middle-aged mother of two? The sniffling, convulsing blubfest continued unabated as he helped her up the stairs, unzipped her dress and encouraged her to collapse, face first, on top of the sheets. She remembers nothing Nick may have said while all this was going on, only his silence, accompanied by a grim sense of purpose. His hands firm and determined, like those of a disgruntled but competent nurse.

And now, the morning after the night before, Maya knows there is only one thing to be done. And that is to pretend it never happened.

She lies there, still and disconsolate, watching the sun creep around the edges of the blackout blinds. Yesterday she promised the twins they'd go to the park and jump in the giant piles of fall leaves left there by the city, but now she wonders if they'll hold her to it. They're just starting to remember promises made the day before, which means she'll soon have to adjust her primary parenting strategy of forever-delayed gratification. The park will be cold, the leaves wet. There could be broken glass and used syringes hidden in the piles. Not that the children will see any of that, being children. Guarding against such dangers is what it means to Maya to be a mother.

She needs to get up to pee, but the thought of the bathroom with its multiple reflective surfaces makes her dive back under the duvet. How puffy she must look, how many hormones and antibiotics she must have ingested in all that processed meat the night before. As her thoughts slip into the familiar, and not entirely unpleasant, cycle of self-criticism and plans for purification, she also becomes aware of the inevitability of the day spread out before her—a nannyless Sunday with hours of as-yet-un-planned kid-friendly activities to get through. A day in which a new precedent must be set. A day she cannot afford to waste. She shifts her head to look at the clock: 7:24 a.m. She will allow herself exactly six more minutes to wallow. Six more minutes of sulking under the covers. The seconds slip by, each one more deliciously self-pitying than the next, until the clock flashes 7:30 and she hears the sound of her mother's voice, a tea-warmed hiss: *Pull yourself together*.

Half an hour later Maya is downstairs, second batch of free-range, wheat-free French toast under way as the twins shout their favourite morning stadium chant of "Joos! Joos! Joos!" She is trying to teach them to eat at the table, to cut and chew each bite with the restrained civility of French children (though in truth she's never actually met one).

"Isla, put that down. The maple syrup is for pouring, not drinking."

As if to show her up, Foster grabs the syrup bottle from his sister's hands and upends it into his milk cup, splashing the table with sticky white slime.

"No, no, sweetheart!" Maya feels the familiar flash of exasperation in her chest, the crackling fuse about to blow.

"Yes, yes, YES! Pooey bum head, Mommy!" Foster says triumphantly, smearing the mess as far as he can reach with both hands.

Maya stares at her son, his face flushed with the thrill of outright defiance, and thinks, *You are an asshole.*

She banishes the thought, but it lingers in her consciousness like skywriting dissipating behind a plane. What she ought to do now is muster a tone of empathetic firmness and install Foster on the "naughty chair" in the mudroom so he can "think about what he's done" before offering the obligatory sing-song apology ("Soo-wee, Mommee!") and carrying on with his day unrepentant and unchanged. Maya knows she should do all this, but instead she does nothing. Foster stares back at her, waiting expectantly—almost hopefully—for his punishment. Lashes flutter over the bright whites of his eyes. How are children so poreless, so veinless? So devoid of cracks and crinkles and split ends? She can see that all the parenting experts are right—he craves boundaries, feels protected by them even when he pretends to want to smash them down—but she just can't bring herself to follow through. Not this morning. She takes a cloth and wipes up the mess, then has a go at Foster's filthy hands and face, an act that elicits yowls of protest. Isla is already off her chair and consumed in the project of picking sequins off the Princess Barbie salsa costume that Maya purchased for her in a moment of weakness. Foster just sits there, snuffling in a way that slowly begins to unnerve her, his little hands balled into fists. After a little while he says, "Are you sad today, Mommy?"

"What?" Maya stops. She can't remember another time that he's asked about her. "No, baby. Why would I be?"

Foster shrugs. A tiny adult shrug that is funny and strange. "Maybe because Daddy's not here."

"But Daddy is here; he's just gone out for a bit."

"Not here like you, Mama. Even when Daddy's home, it's like he's away."

"What do you mean by that, darling?"

"Nothing."

Maya looks over at Isla, who is now plucking sequins off her tongue and pushing them up her nose.

"That's not true, honey. Daddy's here lots. He loves you very much. Just like I do."

Foster rolls his eyes, an insolent, stagey gesture he must have learned from one of the older kids at playgroup. "I was just *joking*," he says in a voice she doesn't recognize. "Ha-ha!"

Maya tries to think back to the last family outing they had together, but all she can come up with is a chaotic Saturday trip to Ikea last spring, the highlight of which was Isla barfing up all her Swedish meatballs on the car ride home.

"Mommy and Daddy have been busy, but that doesn't mean we don't love you," she says.

Foster ignores this and demands a marshmallow for "breakfast dessert." When she refuses, he pushes his milk cup off the side of the table and runs from the room. Maya lets her head drop into her hands.

After a minute, Isla sidles over. "Foster's bad sometimes," she says, half as an apology for her twin and half in comparative self-regard.

Maya tries to stop them, but her tears come anyway. Just one or two big ploppy ones at first, and then a steady trickle that has her wiping her eyes with Foster's torn-off terry cloth bib. She's less self-conscious about crying in front of her daughter, mostly because Isla is so understanding about it.

"Mommy, do you want to wear my princess crown?" she says, stroking Maya's knee gingerly.

Maya blows her nose in the bib and ruffles Isla's curls with a watery grin. "No, sweetie. It's okay. I'm fine. Mommy's just tired today, okay? Why don't you go upstairs and put on one of your very prettiest play outfits. Can you do that for me?"

Isla marches out with purpose, clearly pleased to be of service and, Maya suspects, out of her mother's strange, emotionally volatile orbit. Maya sits for a moment, casting an eye over the newspaper, sections spread out before her like a misery buffet. There is a bloody uprising in the Middle East. Another austerity budget on the horizon. Europe is in economic turmoil. Asia's carbon emissions are up. America's struggling and Africa's screwed. She turns the page and half-reads an advice column devoted to relationship dilemmas. A woman has written in to say she's found herself caught between two men. One is a dull but kindly ex who hopes to reconcile, the other a married man with children with whom she's hopelessly in love. What should she do? The expert, of course, cautiously advises the woman to find a way to extract herself from both relationships, which she deems "emotionally unsatisfactory and imaginary" each in its own way, and free herself up for something more "real and right." Maya thinks of the philosophy of Radical Honesty and the promises in *The Way*. She realizes she hasn't spoken her deepest desire out loud because, until now, she didn't know what it was. "I want our love back," she hears herself say. She is surprised because she knows it's true.

She has pulled herself together by the time Nick bursts into the room like a daddy orangutan, one child hanging off his front, the other off his back, two pairs of legs braided around his middle like a sort of writhing snake belt.

"Mwahahaha! I am a kidnapper from Mars!" he declares in his evil-supervillain voice. The children shriek with mock-terrified delight. "I have been transported through several millennia by the speed of light to find you!"

Maya sees from his outfit—a high-tech ensemble of skin-tight, high-visibility microfibres complete with built-in GPS and magical quick-dry properties—that he's been out cycling again. That makes two days in a row, almost like the old days. Foster claws at his polarized, shatterproof sunglasses as Isla begins pressing the buttons on his digital heart monitor.

Maya watches this show while sipping the dregs of her coffee. The twins are keen for more horseplay, but Nick soon shakes them off, shooing them toward their piles of Lego and fixing himself some toast. He asks if he can bring her anything and Maya demurs. For a few quiet moments, they sit side by side reading the paper. Nick hums a grunge rock anthem she vaguely recognizes from their university days and drums his fingers on the countertop. Suddenly his head snaps up.

"I think we should do something fun today." He says this as if "fun" is an exciting new lifestyle trend he's just stumbled across in the paper.

"Okay," she says with caution.

He looks at her, eyes flashing, chin bobbing exuberantly. "What do you think?" he says.

"Of what?"

"Of the day. The whole day we have in front of us. I mean, I obviously need a shower, but after that."

Maya realizes he has no idea what to suggest. For Nick, "something fun" is—and almost always has been—a long day at the office followed by unaccounted-for hours she no longer bothers to ask about. His fun, for as long as she can remember, does not include her or the kids.

She senses this is foreign territory, so she decides to help him a bit. "We could go to the early learning centre and get some new puzzles."

Nick makes a face, so she tries again.

"There's a toddler yoga and meditation class at the gym?"

Nick is already staring at his phone, consulting the Internet. "I said FUN! How about a fall fair? According to the Interweb, there's one just east of the city off the main highway."

"Yaay! Falling fair! Falling fair!" the twins shout.

"Not falling fair. *Fall* fair. Have you never been to one?" Maya asks them, though she knows the answer perfectly well.

They look at each other, then back at her, stumped. Isla pops her thumb in her mouth and shrugs.

Nick starts doing a silly hip-waggling dance around the kitchen. His eyes widen and his voice gets loud and loopy. The children react like he's the Pied Piper, following him around the island. "It's a place filled with nothing but games and treats and rides and music and toys. It's an old-fashioned kid place, like the kind of places Mommy and I used to go to when we were kids."

Isla and Foster are dancing around his legs, howling with delight. "Can we go? Can we? Please, please, *pleeeeze*?"

Nick stops dancing and bends down so his face is level with theirs. His manner is suddenly serious. "It's up to Mommy," he says.

The twins turn to her. "Can we go to the fair, Mommy?" Isla asks, grabbing her fingers for emphasis. Foster just tugs on her arm and lets his sister do the talking. "Can we can we can we, *pleeeeze*? We promise we'll be good!"

Maya shakes them off. "Of course," she laughs. "What did you expect me to say?"

CHAPTER 9

Nick

The Port Mary Fall Fair is a ragtag affair even by theme-park standards—a village of crooked games stalls and rickety rides burping polka music, all framed by a collapsing snow fence in the middle of muddy farmland. At first Nick wonders if they ought to drive back to the city and see the latest high-def computer-animated kid flick instead, but then he remembers Maya's screen ban. If the twins register the fair's crappiness, though, they don't show it. When the car crests the hill and the wobbly old roller coaster soars into view, they squeal like a couple of tickled piglets, straining forward in their car seats and tipping their noses out the window to inhale the carnival smell of burnt sugar and axle grease.

Nick gears down as the Range Rover trundles along the rutted mud path through the fair's arch, a shabby chipboard facade covered in wind-tattered streamers. "ARE YOU READY FOR FUNWORLD?" a goggle-eyed clown's face ominously demands—as if this weren't a carnival but a test of character. And in a way, for Nick, it is.

He considers last night's unsuccessful sex. At first he'd worried that his performance—or lack thereof—was going to give the game away. But Maya's drunken tears provided the perfect distraction. Where once it would have irritated him to see her break down in self-pity over something so inconsequential, he now finds himself oddly sympathetic. *I'd feel bad for myself too if I were you*, he'd found himself thinking as she wept on the floor between his knees.

How does he justify his deception? By telling himself that some forces, once initiated, simply can't be stopped. Attraction is one. Leaving is another. It's pure physics, Newton's first law: an object in motion stays in motion. What he's doing now is simply setting the stage for a graceful exit. The less acrimony the better for the kids, not to mention his bank balance. The irony is that the charade of goodness is getting easier the longer the performance continues. In certain moments, Nick feels almost at one with the Good Husband, the way he imagines a well-rehearsed actor feels about a character who is entirely unlike him. The more he goes through the motions, the more effortless the motions become. They begin to seem almost a part of him, something he was always meant to do. A yogi might call it a "flow," an athlete "the zone," but he thinks of it simply as "the new Nick." What had once been foreign is beginning to feel almost natural. Weirder still, a few times when he wasn't paying attention, he'd accidentally enjoyed himself.

"I go on that one!" Foster's hands are starfished on the car window, eyes trained on the rusted metal Drop of Death ride, which rises up beyond the coaster.

Nick watches as a cramped metal cage full of teenagers is

cranked up to the top, held there for a terrible moment, then allowed to plummet screaming to the earth. He feels his stomach heave and pitch against his lower intestine. He glances over at Maya, whose normally pale skin has taken on a hung-over bluish tint around the nose and lips.

"I'm afraid you're too little for that one. Maybe next year," she tells Foster, who responds with a whine of protest.

"Isla's older—can she go?" Foster hasn't yet grasped the notion that six and a half minutes is not much of an age gap.

"Nope," says Nick.

Foster flings himself back in his seat and emits a pitiful moan.

For a moment Nick wonders if perhaps this wasn't such a hot idea after all. It has been so long since he's taken the initiative in planning a family activity that he's losing confidence. He glances at Maya again, but she's staring out the window at a muddied parking lot.

"I go on the big-boy ride!" Foster's tone has all the raw ingredients for a major meltdown: high-key excitement combined with an unwillingness to let even the smallest defeat go unprotested. Soon Isla is chiming in her support and the atmosphere of the car becomes unbearable.

Nick scouts the parking lot for a spot as close to the entrance as possible, while Maya rifles through her bag and mutters something about not having brought anything for lunch.

Nick shrugs. "We'll just get something in there."

"Really?" She looks at him skeptically. "Do you think they'll have, you know, things they can actually eat?"

"I guess we're about to find out. I'm sure we can find them a corn dog."

Maya takes a breath and stretches her neck. After a beat, she speaks. "I'm not saying they're going to get pancreatic cancer, but is it really necessary?"

Nick stares straight ahead and wills himself not to react. This is one of their ongoing battles: her obsession with nitrates, toxins and evil ingredients, and his happy obliviousness to them.

"No," he says as evenly as possible. "I suppose we can look for healthier options."

They are both out of the car now and unbuckling the twins from their safety seats. Nick struggles with Isla's belt, prompting Maya to reach over and release it with a one-handed flick of the wrist.

"I'm a little rusty at this," he says.

She looks at him with weary affection. "It's okay."

The kids are on the ground and tearing across the wet open field toward the gate. Even above the bleated polka theme, Nick can hear them singing a song from playgroup—something about a quacking duck.

"Okay that I'm rusty, or okay that I'm trying?" Nick is determined to keep the mood light.

Maya narrows her eyes and rolls them at the same time—an expression she's perfected in the past couple of years. "Look, when it comes to food, I'm just saying that everything's a choice. You have to look at the numbers and the potential risks, then weigh them against the perceived benefits—fun, pleasure, etc. And with some things—hot dogs might be one of them—the benefits may not outweigh the risks. I mean, how good does a hot dog actually taste? How much pleasure do you get from it? You wouldn't put heroin in your body, even though I'm sure it feels amazing, because you know how dangerous it is. And you certainly wouldn't give it to your kids, would you?"

They are trudging across the field now.

"I was actually talking about corn dogs," says Nick.

"Ah, well, that changes everything."

He puts his arm around her shoulders and squeezes. She stumbles in the mud, then rights herself with a good-humoured hop.

"What was that for?"

"What?" he says. "I'm not allowed to manhandle my own wife? Tell me, what's the cost–benefit scenario with physical affection? What are the chances of you developing pancreatic cancer if I do *this*." He jabs his fingers under her rib cage and tickles her where he suspects her pancreas might be. Maya laughs, pinkens and pushes him away, though he can see she's pleased. She shouts at the twins to slow down to mask how much he's flustered her.

Once through the gates, Nick hands a man in a fluorescent vest a wad of cash in exchange for a long red serpent's tail of paper tickets, which he folds up and slips into his pocket. Now he is the Dispenser of Fun. Foster and Isla look around at the flashing lights, candy vendors and hanging gardens of plush toys, then press their faces into Maya's legs like Eastern bloc foundlings encountering capitalism for the first time.

"Are you ready for FUNWORLD?" Nick booms in the supervillain voice. The children look unsure, so he casts around for an opening. Beyond the weight-guessing contest and the sledgehammer strength test, he sees a game he's *sure* to win. "Who wants a PET?" he says.

The twins cheer as Maya's expression clouds, but it's too late—Nick is halfway across the grounds, twins trailing after him like groupies. There it is, his favourite fall fair game: the fish-bowl toss. The twins pause for a moment, hand in tiny hand, and stare at an enormous table laid out in a precarious pyramid of teapot-sized fishbowls. Inside each clear glass bowl swims a single exotic-looking fish. They are beautiful and serene—fancy, feathery fins in gleaming jewel tones. There must be at least a hundred of them, each in its own lonely orb. It looks to Nick like a dubious conceptual art exhibit. In a gallery it would make his heart sink, but here at the county fair it fills him with joy.

By the time Maya catches up, Nick's spent eight red tickets on four Ping-Pong balls—one for each of them. The twins clutch their balls to their chests. Isla presses hers to her lips and closes her eyes in silent prayer.

A mustachioed man in a dotted bow tie explains the rules of the game in an auctioneer's holler: "Buy a ball, take a toss, win a fish! One ball, one throw! Get one in the drink, take home your very own pet! Goldfish at the bottom, fancies at the top! Buy a ball, take a toss, win a fish!"

Maya goes first. Her ball bounces off the side of the table, not even touching a fishbowl. She steps back with a self-mocking cringe and encourages Foster to step up. Nick is glad to see that he aims high—for the fish on the upper level—but is less pleased when the ball bounces off the first bowl and then falls to the lower level, spinning around the rim of a goldfish's home before skittering off to the side. Nick slaps his son's shoulder, muttering at the injustice of life, as Foster's face crumples into a sob.

Isla goes next, releasing a gentle underhand toss that to

everyone's delight sails through the air, falls cleanly in the drink with an almost imperceptible plunk and floats above the head of a tiny, shimmering creature. The mustachioed carny, who'd been scratching at a crossword until now, perks up and, with a flourish of his stained white glove, plucks the Ping-Pong ball off the surface of the water and hands the winning bowl to Isla. Her eyes go wide with joy, and she jumps up and down, sloshing water all over her shoes and causing the fish to leap up and almost out of the bowl.

"Would you like a bag?" asks the carny, and before anyone can respond he's pouring the fish and its water into a clear plastic sandwich bag, which he secures with a twist-tie. Isla beams and Foster begins to moan. Maya gives Nick a look that says, *Thanks for the awesome idea.* Nick attempts to distract his son by sliding the last ball through his line of vision with two fingers like a magician.

"Don't worry, Fozza. Daddy's going to win one for you now! Are you ready? On the count of three. One, two . . ." Nick takes his toss, and they all watch the ball arc up and fall. It plinks off the side of the bowl he was aiming for and drops into one he wasn't.

Suddenly the mustache is upon them. "We have a DOUBLE WINNER! Congratulations, sir. You are now the proud owner of two very rare and exotic VIETNAMESE FIGHTING FISH!" He pours the second fish into a bag and hands it to Nick, who marvels at the blue-and-green scales glimmering in the afternoon light.

Foster stares at it open-mouthed. "Is it really mine, Daddy? Really?"

"Only if you promise to take good care of it."

The man in the bow tie bends down and taps Foster on the nose. "Mind you don't put those two in with the rest of your aquarium," he says. "Vietnamese fighters like to be on their own. They have a tendency to get a bit vicious with company. Territorial little buggers."

Foster nods solemnly and clutches the bag to his chest, dangling it in front of himself from time to time to peer at the pet inside.

They walk around the fair like this for a while, the children unsteadily clutching their sloshing fish bags, staring at the games kiosks and the noisy merry-go-round with its wild-eyed horses humping up chipped plastic poles. Nick is surprised when Maya suggests taking the twins onto the haunted house ride, a big black box covered in cotton cobwebs and fake blood. A toy train filled with uncomfortable-looking teenagers moves down a track into the howling mouth of a dodgy Edvard Munch *Scream* replica. A dark, dusky pop song plays over the ghostly sound effects. It takes Nick a moment to place it: "Another One Bites the Dust" by Queen.

"Won't they be scared?" he asks.

"Sure," she says. "But it's fun to be scared sometimes. Isn't that the whole point?"

He looks down at his children and gently lifts away each bagged fish. It isn't hard. They don't have much of a grip. "Go with Mommy," he says, handing Maya the stack of tickets from his breast pocket.

There isn't much of a line, and soon enough they are being tucked roughly into their seats by a fat guy in a Metallica T-shirt who slams a foam-covered safety bar down over their laps and

orders them to keep their hands and feet in the cart. As the ride
jerks forward, Maya, who is sitting between the twins, trying
to hold their hands under the restraints, looks back at him and
smiles a tight little smile. He can suddenly see she is doing this
to please him and the effect is like a tourniquet on his throat. He
feels a sudden compulsion to throw himself on the tracks and
order the metalhead to remove his family from the ride at once.
But instead he just stands there. The music starts up—Michael
Jackson's "Thriller"—and Vincent Price's famous laugh is all can
Nick can hear as the train slips into the howling mouth of the
painted ghost.

He waits there, a fish hanging from each hand like a surreal-
ist weighing scale, waiting for his wife and children to reappear.
When they do finally materialize, several minutes later, cart her-
ky-jerking out of a papier mâché cave strewn with bouncing rubber bats, he finds himself waving like an idiot, fish bags sloshing
and leaking over his coat. But they don't see him. Their heads—
pale hair, delicate faces, so familiar to Nick in both individual
isolation and mutual resemblance—are all fixed forward, eyes
wide, bracing for the next scare. As the cart slips, twists and rattles around the corner, then plunges them back into darkness, he
feels a sharp kick to his mid-zone. He wants to go with them. To
follow his family into the void so he can protect them from its
depths, from the shrieking witches and rattling skeletons, from
the horror of the merciless disembodied laughter. He wants all
these things, and yet of course he does none of them.

When the ride is over, the twins bound off the cart and over
the brown grass toward him, fleece-padded arms stretched out
to reclaim their fish.

"Daddy! Daddy! At first I was scared of the ghost, but I touched it and it wasn't real!" Isla tells him.

Foster is more subdued. He doesn't look Nick in the eye, rubbing his face in a manner that indicates there may have been recent tears. He takes back his fish solemnly and peers into the bag to make sure all's well.

Maya brings up the rear, shoving kid detritus into her handbag—a sippy cup, a toy car, a stray pink mitten. She is three feet away, almost touching distance, when she stops, looks up at Nick and smiles. It's the smile of someone coming home after an extended ordeal, the smile of returning to safety. Nick finds himself taking her hand as they walk, something he hasn't done in years. The light has a honey-coloured tinge to it, though it's just past two. The days are getting shorter, nighttime creeping into day. There is a smell of fried fat in the air, and soon the twins start jostling and asking for food. Nick is worried that if he doesn't find them something, there will blood-sugar meltdowns. He looks around for something—anything—that might meet Maya's exacting standards (a falafel? pretzels?) and sees only cotton candy, swirling ice cream and cages being plunged into bubbling fryers.

"Let's hit the road, kids," Maya says. "There's lots of food at home."

The children look devastated. "Do we *have* to go? We love it here!"

Nick shrugs and reaches deep into the pockets of his oilskin coat. "We could go home or . . . we could have *THIS*."

He pulls out two enormous shrink-wrapped banana–nut bars he pilfered from the pantry before leaving. The twins, who have never seen their father produce anything from his pockets apart from cash and keys, cheer at his newfound powers. They fall upon the bars like starving puppies, mouths and fingers streaked with carob.

When Nick looks at Maya, she's staring across the field at the corn dog stand. "You saved the day," she says—a little flatly, he thinks.

"I hope you don't mind."

"Of course not," she replies. "Someone had to."

CHAPTER 10

Maya

Maya is pre-packing for a holiday. A proper grown-up week away, with beaches and cocktails and sunsets and a huge hotel bed with creamy sheets and fluffy towels and all the rest of the clichéd holiday stuff you'd find in a deliciously cheesy karaoke video. Their flight isn't for more than a week, but Maya can barely suppress a grin as she folds her stringiest of string bikinis (unworn for half a decade) into quarters and presses it tightly in her suitcase alongside the Kenyan sarong, three prize-winning novels and a large spritzer of Swiss-made SPF 50. It will be the first time she and Nick have been away on their own since the disastrous pre-booked heli-skiing vacation they took to Switzerland when she was seven months pregnant (not a memory she wants to relive). It's not just a holiday—it's a *surprise* holiday. A trip to a secret location, planned specially and exclusively by Nick for her birthday. She knows they're going somewhere hot for seven nights, but that's it. "I'll take care of everything," he'd said over dinner at home three nights ago, and she'd had to fake yawn and look at the ceiling to avoid tearing up—not because of the surprise (which was actually a bit unnerving) but because he was being so nice and she really wasn't used to it.

Over the past couple of weeks, ever since the date night and the visit to the fall fair, Maya has seen a strange transformation in her relationship with Nick. It isn't just that he's changed—it's as if some old dysfunctional part of him has been extracted and replaced. A transplant of sorts. The new old Nick is familiar but unnaturally so. At times it feels to Maya as if the past five years never happened. The company, the twins, his success, the end of her career and their slow, glacial drift into parenthood have vanished and they are their younger, unencumbered selves again. The man before her now is wiped clean, almost eerily so. She can sense his urgency to make things right and is sympathetic to it (how could she not be?), but she can also feel how little he wants to talk about where it all went wrong. Every time she tries (albeit clumsily) to bring up their problems—the years of silent resentment—he heads her off with appreciative comments or upbeat talk of the kids. She can't make him a cup of tea for the compliments it inspires. ("Baby, have I told you you're a prize?") Before she can get back on the topic of What Happened to Our Marriage, he's off—making all the right noises, doing all the right moves—until she abandons the impulse to pick apart whatever problems they once had. And perhaps he is right to do so. Nick seems so enthralled by their quick recovery that to retroactively diagnose the illness feels a bit . . . petty. What's the point of dwelling in the miserable past when the future is suddenly so bright?

In her most hopeful moments, Maya thinks it's a return to the natural order. Without discussion, they've resumed many of their rituals from happier times. He brings her coffee in bed every morning. And he gets home earlier too. She waits until he arrives so they can have a glass of wine together—just one each—and then she makes dinner for the two of them. The twins, after a bit of initial caterwauling, are now sleeping in their own beds on the third floor (Velma helped ease the transition by staying over a couple of nights), which frees up space for Nick in the marital bed. Maya still nurses them before they go to sleep, but without them in bed, the night feeds have stopped altogether. At first she was almost disappointed that they didn't cry out for her, but soon she came to realize the benefit: a full night's sleep, something she hasn't experienced in years. And what a difference it makes! She no longer wakes up each morning with an anvil of dread pressing down on her chest. This, she realizes, is what it feels like to be rested. But most importantly, Maya just feels different around her husband. Not just warmer but more *herself.* She is interested in him and—more surprising—feels interesting *to* him, for the first time in a long while.

It's amazing, she thinks, how difficult it is for us to believe things may change. When we're in the bad place, it always seems we'll be there forever. But it's in fact possible that bad places that once were good can be restored, making the bad times seem like no more than a blip. It's amazing how easy it is for her to revert to seeing herself as happily married. She feels a bit like a naturally thin person who, having gained a lot of weight over several years, has gone on a successful crash diet and emerged suddenly skinny again. The relief of returning to her *real marriage* at last.

There is, however, one missing component, and that is the sex. Now that they're sharing a bed again, they are being more physically affectionate (Nick actually scooted across the mattress and gave her a kiss on the shoulder one morning last week), but this proximity hasn't translated into actual conjugal relations. It's not that she doesn't want to have sex with him—it's more that she feels she's forgotten how. After the horror of the botched blow job, Maya opted for a more organic approach. She was hoping that all this loving behaviour would naturally result in . . . well, the ultimate of loving behaviours—that is, the sweaty, stinky, dirty-talking kind. Yet so far, nothing. This, in part, is why she is so keenly looking forward to their holiday. Just the two of them. No twins. A change of scene—ideally one involving an ocean breeze and a strong rum punch—might be just the thing to coax the skies to open up and end the dry spell.

With this in mind, Maya presses a number of flimsy, filmy things into her suitcase—complicated garments with florets and ribbons and hooks and eyes—things she hasn't thought of, let alone removed from their tissue paper, for years. Lifting her robe, she touches the small pouch of skin just above her pubic bone, where the surgeons cut her open to pull out the twins. It's still numb more than three years later, and she can feel where her muscles pulled apart and had to knit back together. The scar is nearly invisible now—the surgeon on duty told her that since the low-rise denim trend, they take care to make such incisions as discreet as possible—but the fact of it being there, and the great change it marks, has altered Maya's perception of her body more than she likes to admit. No amount of exercise and dieting will change that. It's as if her body spent the first thirty-three years of its life existing primarily for her own pleasure, and then one day it grew up and put away childish things. It made a baby. *Two* babies. And then it served as their exclusive food source for months, rose at one and three and five in the morning at the sound of their cries, held them and bounced them two at a time, and generally ran itself ragged in constant effort to keep them alive. Now that they'd survived, it was time to get back to the pleasure principle. People had been telling her this for years. Every lifestyle magazine seemed to feature a story declaring it. Bradley, the trainer turned life coach, never tired of repeating it. Apparently it was *time to have some me time*. She'd heard it all before, but she was only now starting to believe there might be a time when her body's primary function wasn't serving the needs of the twins.

Maya lets her robe slip to the floor with a swish. She stares at herself in the full-length mirror. It's difficult, but she tries to be as forgiving as possible while also being empirically self-aware. This is what she sees:

1. Pale blonde hair streaked silver, shoulder-length, unbrushed.
2. Reasonably decent skin. Some crinkles around the eyes and a vague hint of peach-pit cleavage, but nothing a bit of deep moisturizer and concealer can't fix.
3. Not officially tall at five foot eight, but tallish. (And six feet in the gold heels.)
4. Narrow shoulders and small, almost anxious-looking breasts. Could pass for girlish but for the dark, distended nipples.
5. Square, jutting hip bones. Hips made for carrying a sack of potatoes. Or a toddler. Or both. But usually the latter.
6. Pokey knees separating slender thighs from thickly muscled calves.

7. Long, narrow feet with knobby former child-ballerina toes.

8. A face she finds hard to assess, it's so familiar. Long of chin and wide of eye. A face that wears both makeup and the lack of it well. One that keeps something crucial back instead of giving itself away at first meet.

She curls the corners of her mouth and feels the superficial mood enhancement that comes with even the most forced of grins. She will admit what everyone from her mother to countless construction workers has told her is true: she is prettier when she smiles.

Maya traces her fingertips along her throat, over her breasts, across her rib cage and down her hips, and she feels a familiar shiver of delight. The pleasure-seeker is returning to herself. *I am a happily married woman going on a holiday with my husband,* she thinks. *This is a perfectly normal thing to do. My children will survive a week without me.* And it feels right and true. Like an actress in one of those ads for creamy desserts, she looks at her reflection and mouths the words "You're worth it." Then she lets out an involuntary half-mad hoot.

She is suddenly conscious of the time—her meeting with Gray is in less than an hour—and so she does something she hasn't done in years: skips her usual breakfast of steel-cut oats with flax and pumpkin seeds, which takes twenty-five minutes to prepare, and has a piece of toast instead. She smears it with sugarless fruit compote and takes it out to the car, where she eats it while humming along to Velma's Portuguese pop radio.

When she'd called Gray to suggest they meet, he'd been

oddly apprehensive. He'd tried to hide it with his gruff, good-natured bluster, stammering over which day, which restaurant, what time. She didn't tell him why she wanted to see him, but it was pretty obvious. And no wonder he was wary. The economy was still limping along, law schools were pumping out qualified young attorneys like super-charged automatons, and clients had less cash to splash out on pricey litigation than ever before. Not to mention, any firm that took her on would be obligated to pay her bar fees retroactively. Plus she had two kids now—an unspoken career liability in a profession that demanded sixty-hour weeks at a bare minimum. Maya sternly reminds herself of all this to avoid getting her hopes up. She is just feeling Gray out about the possibility of returning to the law. Just dipping her toe in the water to test the temperature. In fact, she is so uncertain about the whole thing—so convinced it will never work and no one will ever want her in a professional capacity again—that she hasn't even bothered mentioning it to Nick.

Funnily enough, even though she knows he prefers to have her at home, Nick was the one who'd put the idea in her head in the first place. A few nights back she'd used the word "recalcitrant" in passing, and he'd smiled and said, "Ah, my little legal eagle," and ruffled her hair. A gesture that she would have found *infuriatingly* patronizing just a few weeks ago now made her nostalgic for the old days. Now that she had her husband back, Maya could suddenly see what her life was really missing: gainful employment. A stake in the real world.

Her only worry is the twins. She's been so constantly available to them all hours of their waking lives so far, how would they take her sudden absence? This gnawed at her. But so did the notion of her idle self—a mother in yoga togs baking gluten-free nut–zucchini loaf. Is that how she wants her kids to remember her? Is that how she wants to remember herself?

On the drive downtown, she daydreams about the early days of her marriage, back when she and Nick were both struggling to get a foot in the door, hungry to prove themselves in their chosen fields. What a kick he used to get out of hearing the details of the trials she was working on, and how she'd laugh at his on-set anecdotes. She recalls with nostalgia how they'd meet up late for drinks and fill each other in on their respective professional dramas, making characters out of colleagues and crafting stories from the day's events. She suddenly realizes how much she has been missing that, and even more, how much she misses being *a person in the world*. A grown-up whom other grown-ups depend on for grown-up stuff. Stuff that doesn't include baking for the playgroup charity auction and overseeing laundry.

Maya flicks over to the public radio station and hears a story about the "plunging" divorce rate. According to the host, it's dropping, but not for the reasons his audience might expect. "The rate of divorce has gone down because fewer people are opting to get married in the first place," he says with a talk-radio DJ's air of mock surprise. His guest, a demographer, talks about how today's "younger generation" has lost faith in the institution of marriage.

"They see their romantic life in terms of serial monogamy rather than a single partnership," the demographer says in doddering consternation. "And a growing number of them are loath to make promises that the numbers have shown most of us can't keep."

The interviewer chuckles, seeing an irony. "So what you're

saying here is that by cynically refusing to marry, the younger generation has actually lowered the divorce rate."

The demographer agrees. "I guess if you don't try, you can't fail."

Maya turns the dial to find a pop song she likes and sings the silly words all the way downtown.

Gray is already seated when she arrives a few minutes late, apologizing and cursing the traffic.

"Save your sorry's," he says, rising from the table, a look of pure indulgence on his face. He stands there grinning as the waiter takes her coat and her flurry of regret subsides.

They both sink down into the booth, with its great velvet tufts, and Maya lets out a smooth sigh. "It's good to see you," she says, cupping her chin in her hands and studying his face.

"I couldn't agree more. How are my gorgeous godchildren?"

"Complete assholes. In the cutest possible way."

And so they make small talk for a while. She shows him photos of Foster and Isla in their Halloween costumes (a zombie Yoda and a princess zombie, respectively), and he tells a circuitous story involving a trip to Egypt, a spitting camel and his latest failure to quit smoking.

"So I'm covered in dust, sunburnt to a crisp, when the camel farmer turns to me and offers me a cigarette. What could I do?" Gray throws his hands up in the air as if to show it wasn't his fault.

Maya laughs, shaking her head in mock disapproval. "You know it would have been much healthier in the long run just to have punched him in face like you wanted to."

121

"I'm sure you're right."

"That's my new philosophy," she says impulsively. "Radical Honesty. Do what you feel and say what you want, and the universe will automatically answer."

Gray gives her a funny look. "And how did you arrive at this so-called theory?"

Maya shrugs and gives a noncommittal laugh. "I read it somewhere. But trust me, it *works*. It's amazing what you realize about yourself when you have the guts to admit what you want."

Silence descends. Gray stabs a straw at the ice cubes at the bottom of his Diet Coke. The waiter brings their food. Pizza for Gray and a salade niçoise with fresh tuna and no potatoes for Maya. Gray carves up his pie with a steak knife and eats it with his hands—something Nick would never do if a fork was available. Maya admires Gray's gusto. His greed. She reflects on how unusual it is for her to be eating a meal with a man who is not her husband. Then she remembers why she's here and a shiver goes through her. Maybe it was a bad idea to mention self-help when she wants to seem professional?

"Listen, Adam, I sensed you were apprehensive about meeting me, and I understand why."

Gray is motioning to the waiter for another Diet Coke. She reaches across the table and brushes the cuff of his suit with her fingers to secure his attention.

He looks at her warily. "You do?"

Maya nods. She wants him to understand she's no idiot. "It was pretty obvious," she says.

"It was?" Gray looks truly frightened now. Why is he taking it so personally?

"I hope you can keep this conversation between us. I haven't told Nick I was asking your advice. In fact, Nick has no idea I've even been thinking about it."

Gray has abandoned his pizza now and is shifting in his chair. How strange, Maya thinks, watching him fidget.

"Look, Maya," he begins. "I want you to know I'm on your side and I'll always stand by you. But I feel like you're putting me in a strange position here."

"It's really not the end of the world if they won't have me," Maya says quickly. "I just wanted to ask your advice on, you know, my prospects in the marketplace. I know you think I'm crazy to want to come back, but the truth is I miss it. I'm glad I had time with the kids, but now I'm ready to get back to work. Just like I used to. Much harder, if that's what it takes."

A look of comprehension floods Gray's face. He shakes his head and laughs to himself, as if at a private joke. Maya wonders if years of billable hours have actually driven him a bit crazy. He chews idly on a discarded pizza crust.

"Right," he says. "I get it. You're ready to come back. But you know times are tough, even in our relatively recession-proof profession."

Maya glances down at her fiddled-with salad. She wishes that for once she'd ordered something she actually wanted to eat.

"I know, of course. But I've got a whole new perspective to offer now. I'm experienced and committed, and I know exactly what I'm getting myself into."

"So why haven't you mentioned your plans to Nick?"

Maya pauses. She squeezes her hands together beneath her napkin. "I guess I wanted to gauge the situation first, before I put it to him. I think he may need some convincing, but I'm sure he'll come around."

"And what makes you so sure of that?" A strange smile plays on Gray's lips, then quickly vanishes.

"I'm confident that in the end, he'll support me in whatever I want to do."

Gray looks at her skeptically. "You know I love your hubby, but 'selflessness' isn't exactly his middle name."

Maya straightens up in a way that indicates she doesn't appreciate Gray's disloyalty. "That's where you're wrong. He's really changed. It's like something has shifted, internally. It's actually quite astonishing . . . But I'm not explaining it properly." She can feel her eyes shining, the blood rushing to the surface of her face. "Have you seen him recently?"

Gray regards her cautiously. "No. I mean, why would you ask?"

"I just thought maybe you'd had one of your secret afternoon drinking sessions. Not that I'd mind—I never did mind—it's just that if you had, I think you'd see that Nick's quite different than he used to be."

"You're blushing," Gray said.

"No, I'm not." Maya feels a hot rose bloom across her forehead.

Gray gives a dry cough and glances at his phone. "Just because he takes you out for a nice dinner doesn't make him a better man."

"You're such an old cynic, aren't you?" she says as lightly as she can manage.

Gray laughs and the storm passes.

"What happened to your romantic side? The power of love and all that stuff?"

"Do you mean the Frankie Goes to Hollywood song or the one by Huey Lewis and the News? Because if it's the latter . . ."

She gives him a swat on the arm. "I mean you used to believe in that stuff: the transformative effect of kindness. In university you were the most romantic guy on campus. What happened?"

Gray laughs bleakly and shrugs. "I guess that's what ten years of the law will do to you."

They spend the rest of lunch on easier topics—his apparently non-existent love life, her parents and their never-ending world travels, the coming election, whether their team would make the playoffs—and when the bill comes in its tiny tray, Maya swipes it, despite Gray's booming protests. She tells him to knock it off— it's her treat and was always going to be. *She,* after all, was the one who invited *him* out to lunch.

"But you're not even working, and I'm"—he pats his chest, looking around the room as if for the perfect adjective to describe it—"I'm *rich.*"

Maya sniffs and signs the bill. She stuffs the receipt in her purse, then looks up at Gray one last time. She is far too proud to mention the job thing again and finds herself thinking how much of a waste this lunch has been. How she might have spent the afternoon doing flash cards with the twins instead of indulging her fantasies of having a career again. What would a firm like Gray's possibly want with a bored housewife?

She mutters something about needing to get home and is relieved when the waiter quickly brings her coat. As she stands, Gray takes her by the shoulders and carefully studies her face.

"Don't be sore, old girl," he says softly—all the growly gruff-ness suddenly drained from his voice. "If you really want a job again, of course I'll do everything in my insignificant power to help you out at the firm. We can always use a talented mind like yours. I just want to make sure it's really what *you* want. Not what you think you should want. Not what your husband wants. Just your very own heart's desire. Does that make sense?"

Maya finds herself nodding fast, a brightness spreading across her face. She feels like a child on Santa's lap being told that in fact all her good behaviour *has* entitled her to a pony.

"Oh, Gray, that's wonderful. I mean, I don't want to jump the gun here—I know you can't promise anything—but it's just fantastic. I can't tell you how much your support means to me." She pauses and reminds herself to breathe. *Pull yourself together.* "And I do mean *me*. Not anyone else."

Gray smiles his wonderful wolfish smile and spreads his arms for a hug, which she falls into with an exhalation of tension, resting her head against his broad, suit-padded shoulder. They stand like that—old friends sharing an innocent embrace—until the moment passes and it's time to get back to real life.

CHAPTER 11

Nick

He wakes up in a lather—chest pounding, rib cage twisted in the bedsheets. For a moment, he has no idea where he is. He looks around, eyes flashing over the patterned wallpaper, the heavy drapes, the muted flat screen. There is a puff of lemon-scented steam and Shelley emerges from the bathroom, shower-pinkened and not wearing a towel. She drapes herself over him and nuzzles his neck like a sleepy cat. And he remembers: it is Tuesday afternoon and they are at the Plymouth. Two hours ago he met Shelley in the bar for lunch and explained why, despite an obvious attraction, it would never work between them. She was pouty enough to make him feel appreciated, but not too teary, thank God. Out of premature nostalgia, they ordered a second bottle of Chablis. And the second turned into a third. By then, the afternoon was shot and they were day drunk and so thoroughly enjoying each other's company that they decided they might as well have ex-sex to commemorate the affair they never actually got to have. Upon entering the room, Shelley slipped straight into the bathroom and shut the door. Nick has no idea how long he was passed out. Five minutes? An hour? Maybe more?

And that, roughly speaking, is how Nick ended up here—in bed on the fourteenth floor of the Plymouth, feeling as if he'd snorted several lines of ground glass and then gone for a roll in a cold puddle. Shelley, by the looks of it, is not suffering in the same way. She nuzzles and mewls and wriggles about in a manner that suggests one of two things: (1) she still wants to have sex, or (2) she is in love with him and wants to cuddle. Nick isn't sure which option he finds more alarming—though it's probably the first. At least if she's in love, he doesn't actually have to move.

Nick wants to be surprised he's ended up here but finds he can't be. When it comes to marital indiscretion, he's a novice— he's only ever flirted with the act, having never gone all the way. Instead he has a well-established pattern: It starts out with an exchange of numbers. This leads to texting. Texting leads to meeting for lunch, which leads to more texting, which leads to meeting up for drinks to discuss "what's going on here," which leads to Nick delivering his breakup speech ("I can't do this—I'm a happily married man," etc.), which leads to a feverish breakup make-out session. And there you have it: Nick Wakefield's guide to screwing around in two dates or less.

Shelley is now nibbling on the top of his ear and giggling to herself. "We're terrible people, aren't we?" she says. And Nick grimaces. He knows she's joking, but he suspects, at least in his own case, that it's actually true.

"I can't do this," he says.

She pulls back and looks at him, leaning back on her haunches like a rabbit rising to sniff the air for danger. Her hair is a jumble and almost as red as her nipples, which are right there, staring at him, asking for attention.

"Nick, you brought me here. This was *your* idea. Unless you've failed to notice, I'm actually *naked*." As she says this, they both look down at her breasts and she pulls up the cover of the duvet.

"I'm sorry," he says. "I've changed my mind."

Shelley's eyes fill with tears, and she smiles and shakes her head as if she was expecting this all along. Nick puts a hand on the soft curve of her hip, and without hesitating she winds up and smacks him hard across the jaw. His face sizzles with the impact, and the burn brings a strange kind of pleasure.

"I deserved that," he says.

Shelley just shakes her head and starts pulling on her jeans.

The rest of the day passes like an out-of-body experience. Nick feels as if he is dangling somewhere above himself and looking down, his psyche hanging on by a thread while his sluggish form drags itself through the office hours.

SoupCan is in pre-production for the CurvePhone job, which is ramping up to shoot in a couple of days. Usually at this point in a commercial gig, Nick is running on empty, tweaking with the life force, a deep well of pumped-up panic surging forward into the future. He gets these great geysers of energy that rumble up and out of him like Texas oil, gushing forth with terrifying force until the job is through. It's part of the reason he's stayed in this business—he's hooked on the gut-churning, ball-clenching mania that is production. He doesn't just ride the wave, he *is* the wave—a great, undulating superhuman tsunami of *will* that lifts everything and everyone in its path until the job is done.

But the rest of the day isn't like that.

Instead, Nick sits in his office, rubber spine slipping down his chair, as people he vaguely recognizes but doesn't actually know—wardrobe assistants, production designers, accountants, line producers, lighting specialists and agents—file in and out for meetings he should be taking control of but somehow isn't. Thank Christ for Larry, who presides on the big white sofa, greeting the masses, engaging in small talk, cracking jokes and, when the moment requires it, making the decisions Nick cannot muster the focus to make himself. Larry says they'll have the green filter, not the blue. Larry says the set design is too "chocolate box," a term Nick has often heard, and even used, but never really understood. Larry thinks the outfit for the male lead isn't swank enough—couldn't they find something a bit, I dunno, classier?

Nick listens to all this, knowing he should speak up, assert his so-called directorial vision, but he just can't bring himself to do it. Every once in a while, Larry glances at him and Nick offers a drearily authoritative nod of the head. He holds his chin in his palm and it is all he can do to keep from laying his cheek flat on the desk in front of him. This is pre-production, a long string of meetings stretching from early morning to night. After a couple of hours there is a lull, and Larry turns to him and asks, "What's your problem?"

Nick is taken aback. Larry is usually exceptionally tolerant of his moods due to his unassailable status as the "creative" member of the partnership. (He noticed long ago that most people who work in commercials actually prefer a bit of aberrant behaviour from a director—it makes them feel more artistically validated.)

"Sorry, dude, I'm going through a bit of a rough time at home. You know how it is."

This was pretty low, even for Nick—but there it was.

"Oh, man, I'm sorry to hear that," Larry says, giving his partner a sympathetic pat on the shoulder.

Poor Larry. His romantic woes have driven him into the arms of a long succession of shrinks, shamans, therapists, life coaches and lifestyle consultants. As a result, he's been conditioned to talk about feelings—his own and anyone else's.

Larry gets up and shuts the door. Then he sits down opposite Nick and looks at him in a way that says, *I am now making eye contact to facilitate honest and open emotional communication between men.* It's all Nick can do to keep himself from laughing or, failing that, throwing up.

"You know you can always talk to me," Larry says.

"Thanks, buddy."

"So what's up on the home front?"

Nick shrugs. His instinct is to shut down the conversation, but now that he's started it, he knows he has to throw the dog a bone. He offers Larry a plausible half-truth. "Ah, you know, just the regular family troubles. Maya's been on my case a lot lately. I guess you could say we've been going through a hard time. The twins are a lot to handle, and Maya's resentful that I don't spend enough time at home. She complains that I'm always working, and that when I'm not I haven't been particularly attentive. I don't think she's wrong, but I've found it hard to snap out of the pattern, you know?"

Larry nods solemnly. "I feel you, man. Loud and clear."

"I'm taking her on holiday next week, after the shoot's over," he says. "Beach holiday in Belize. I'm hoping we might be able to, I don't know, ride the wave into a better marriage. Does that sound totally cheesy?"

Larry's buttery expression of empathy has been replaced with a stricken look. "Dude, I am so sorry to put this on you right now, but have you not even been in the room today?"

Nick feels a jolt of alarm and his eyes drift down to the production schedule in front of him. He notices the shoot dates: November 1 to 4. The numbers have been crossed out and "5 to 9" has been written in their place.

"What the fuck?" Nick's hand is trembling as he picks up the paper.

Larry snatches the paper with a laugh. "The dates have changed. We were just discussing it with the production designer and the wardrobe stylist. Where the fuck were you, man?"

Nick drops his head into his hands. "I can't do those dates."

Larry sucks on his inhaler, then answers with all the air sucked in like a teenage pothead trying to get the most from a pre-class joint. "Why not?"

"Because those are the dates I've booked to go away with Maya." For a moment he imagines telling her the trip is cancelled, not even postponed (he can't get his money back now, and the resort was booked to the rafters for weeks afterward), and he has a clear vision of how it would go down: Maya's face would fall and harden. She wouldn't shout and cry or stamp her foot, but would simply finish whatever minor task she was performing—folding the laundry or peeling a tangerine—then remove herself from the room. After that the old marital gloom would descend, and more importantly, some crucial part of her, the part he'd spent these past few weeks coaxing open, would slam shut. All his hard work down the drain. Bailing on the trip was not an option.

"You've got to cancel," Larry says. He is now chewing his lower lip so hard it looks like he might actually break the skin.

"You're right, I do."

"She'll understand. She's a very understanding woman."

Nick shakes his head. "I'm not cancelling on her. I'm cancelling myself as director. I'm pulling out."

Larry stares blankly for a minute, as if he's just woken up from a disorienting nap. Then he springs to his feet and begins waving his hands in the air. "Nick, I know you feel like your marriage is in crisis, and I am *really* sympathetic to that—you know I am—but there's a lot riding on this job too. It's the first time we've worked with this client, and they're a big client. If we bail on them now, not only will they not work with us again but I'm afraid they might sue us."

Nick grimaces. "We're not bailing on them. I'm just pulling out."

"Which means they might pull out." Larry stares at him.

"Yes, but that's a risk we've got to take. Tell them I've contracted a mild case of Ebola. I can't do it."

As Larry rattles through all the pre-production costs—the insurance, the set bookings, the tens of thousands in deposits paid, the actors booked—Nick takes a moment to weigh the personal costs and benefits in his mind. Never before in his working life has he prioritized his family over his work. Not. Once. He's had good reasons—ones in keeping with his character and love of property and security and pretty things. Why potentially imperil a payout, he's always reasoned, when your family is going to be around either way? He knows other people think of their families first—or claim to—but Nick simply hasn't aspired to be one of these men. Whenever he hears of a politician or a CEO resigning in order to "spend more time with his family," he, like the rest of the world, assumes the man has been fired.

Despite this—or perhaps because of it—he finds he is keen to choose his family now. True, it's all about the long game, but Nick is surprised to discover that a part of himself actually welcomes the opportunity to act like the sort of man who cares about his marriage so much that he would risk his career to preserve it. *So this*, he thinks, *is what good guys actually do.*

"Larry, I know it's bad, but I'm not cancelling the trip. We're going to have to find another director."

Larry has his hands in his hair—his stubby fingers raking through and clenching at greasy brown curls. "But who? DeCarlo and Murphy are both booked for the season, and who else are we going to find on short notice? We need you, man."

Nick leans back and looks up at the ceiling. As he stares at the halogen lights, a sense of relief comes over him, as though he's just stepped out of an unbearable heat wave into a very pleasant icebox. The day drunkenness is suddenly gone. He can't begin to explain why, but he is back to being his crisp, sober self. He feels—there is really no other way to describe it—refreshed.

"You can do it," he tells Larry, who begins to shake his head.

"No, I can't."

"Yes, you can. And you will. And you want to know why? Because there's simply no other option."

Larry flips through production binders and file folders, pulling out script notes, schedules and budget breakdowns, as if one of them might hold the solution he's looking for. He riffles papers until he seems to forget what he is riffling for, and then he sets about riffling some more.

Nick stands and slips on his coat.

"Where are you going?" Larry, he notices, has a grey-green tinge under his eyes.

"There's not much point in me being here if I can't see the job through," Nick says.

"But what the hell am I going to tell the client?"

Nick considers this. His first impulse, of course, is to lie, claiming illness or a death in the family or both. But then he realizes to his own surprise that for once, he doesn't want to lie. He wants to tell the truth. And not only that, he *can* tell the truth. And he does. "Tell them I'm going to spend more time with my family." And with that said, he heads for the door.

CHAPTER 12

Maya

Maya loiters in the bedroom, teenage-gawky in her underwear, arms crossed, hip cocked, a heap of rumpled designer office togs at her feet. Looking at the pile, she feels slightly hopeless. All those "classic" suits now look off the mark—hems too high, sleeves too long, shoulders too boxy or not boxy enough. It all just reminds her of how much has changed since she actually worked for a living. She shivers and listens to Velma rooting around deep in the closet.

"I've found the perfect thing," she says, and clambers out clutching a black wool dress with a decorative rhinestone beetle brooch pinned to the chest.

Maya recognizes it as the dress she wore to Nick's father's funeral nearly ten years ago. It was an event that left him an orphan (his mother had had a fatal stroke just months before). Her own parents were there—tanned and lean and full of tales of their latest walking pilgrimage across Spain or riverboat trip through Cambodia. She sometimes wondered if their peripatetic retirement was some kind of grand avoidance technique—of boredom, of death. And most of all, of each other.

She makes an uncertain face, but Velma tosses the dress to her anyway.

Once on, it's not half bad. Cinched at the waist with elbow-length sleeves, it makes Maya feel like a political wife or a ruthless editor of a 1950s fashion magazine. She takes off the brooch (too fussy), slips on her best red heels and a tailored grey blazer, and lets Velma twist her hair into a topknot. And suddenly there she is: a lawyer.

Velma stands behind her, arms crossed, nodding, clearly pleased with her efforts. "They'd be crazy not to hire you. *Loco*," she says.

"You think?" Maya brushes a stray hair off her face and plucks some lint from her sleeve.

"I *know*," says Velma, pounding her chest. "I have a feeling for these things."

Maya smiles, amazed not for the first time at how comforting it is to hear people say the things you want to hear, even when you know they probably aren't true.

Velma sits down on the bed as Maya shimmies back into her jeans. "So have you told Nick you're going for an interview yet?" she asks with a twinkle.

"No. Actually, I'm telling him tonight."

Velma nods slowly. "Ah, that explains the nice dinner."

"And the bottle of Barolo. And the homemade tiramisu for dessert. I'm softening him up with food and dropping the bomb."

"Are you sure he won't be pleased? He should be proud to have a hotshot lawyer-wife," Velma offers.

"Let's not get ahead of ourselves—it's just an interview. I've been out of the game for three and a half years, which is like a lifetime in law-firm time." Maya smooths the dress on its hanger,

137

inspecting it for spots or loose threads. "They have no reason to hire me. And as for Nick, I think it makes him more proud to have me at home. He likes, you know, being the one who takes care of things."

Velma makes an incredulous face. "He can still take care of things when you're out working on your cases. That man Gray, he likes you very much. Maybe too much. I have a feeling for these things. I could see it at the twins' birthday party last year. You have nothing to worry about, dear."

Maya shakes her head awkwardly. There was a time in her life, not so very long ago, when people often said men were doing her favours because they were in love with her. She detested the assumption. "Gray's just an old friend," she says.

So much is riding on this job interview. That's why she's carefully planned how to tell Nick. She doesn't just need him to "let" her work—of course she can do what she likes. But the more she thinks about it, the more she deeply needs him to *want* what she wants.

Velma smiles knowingly. "Well, if you have trouble convincing him with the food, I guess it's lucky you have your bed back."

Maya covers her face in smiling embarrassment.

After the twins are asleep, she sends Velma home and goes about setting the table. She thinks about using the wedding silver and bone china but decides it would seem like she's trying too hard. When she hears Nick come in the front door, she arranges herself at the kitchen counter in a casual yet spritely pose—pretend-reading *The New Yorker* and sipping on a glass of red wine.

Seconds later, Nick glides in the kitchen door, looking a bit harried but glad to see her. He plants a soft, dry kiss on her cheek and then goes straight over to the oven and cracks the door. "Eggplant parm, my favourite," he says, looking genuinely happy. Maya grins and thinks how easy it is, actually, to please him. She feels a flash of guilt for all the years she didn't bother to try. Or was it that she *did* try and he simply wouldn't let himself be pleased? She tries to work it out, but her thoughts quickly tangle. Instead, she thinks of *The Way* and the law of Radical Honesty. *Ask the universe for what you want, and in turn you will be granted your heart's desire.*

"How was your day?"

"Great." Nick spins his wine in its glass and gives it an appreciative sniff. "Never better, in fact. How are the kids?"

"Oh, you know, the usual. Isla thinks she's a flying teapot. Foster bent back his friend Lola's finger at preschool. Apparently she was trying to steal his bucket at the sand station."

Nick sips his wine. For a moment Maya glimpses a flash of the old blankness, but then he seems to return to himself as if being dropped back into his body. He blinks. "Really?" he says. "Is there something I should do?"

"What do you mean, *do*?"

"I mean, do you think he'd benefit from a stern father–son lecture on the subject of sandbox etiquette?"

She smiles. The wine warmth blooms in her chest. "I think the teachers are pretty on top of it. Besides, Velma had him on the naughty step three times today, so he's feeling pretty contrite."

"Really?" Nick looks surprised.

"No."

They laugh and Nick goes upstairs to change out of his work clothes.

Alone again, Maya pours herself another glass of wine. She reminds herself that she's doing the right thing. That they are moving into a new place of safety, and that after all the pain and withdrawal of the past three years, the tension has somehow broken. She doesn't know how it's happened, and even though the how's and why's of it all still nag at her consciousness, she has decided not to question her luck. Maya pushes this rogue thought from her mind and tastes the sauce. It's one of her specialties, made with her own stock of preserved plum tomatoes (the canned ones are full of carcinogens), good olive oil, a splash of wine and a cheeky pinch of sugar. The sauce is tangy perfection, but she burns her tongue in the process of tasting it. She is pulling the pan from the oven as Nick returns to the kitchen, sits at the island and watches her work. When she bends over to take the plates from the oven, she feels his eyes move over her in an appraising way that makes her feel oddly self-conscious.

"You're a very lovely woman, aren't you?" he says in a voice that sounds almost on the verge of . . . what, exactly? Choking up? Breaking down? Hollow laughter? All of the above?

When she looks at him, his face is opaque. A mask. It's only when they sit down at the table and begin eating that Nick announces he has something to tell her. At first Maya worries he's going to steal her moment, but as Nick starts to talk, relief sets in. He is telling her that he's had to turn down a big job for SoupCan because the dates conflicted with their holiday. It's his own mistake, but he doesn't expect her to suffer for it.

When Maya hears this, she waves her hands and tells Nick that it's fine. Work is work. They can always have a holiday some other time. But Nick shakes his head firmly.

"Absolutely not," he says, in a way that lets her know he will not be moved. "I know I can shift the dates, but the point is something has to give. My whole life I've always let work take precedence, and I guess at some point that has to stop. We have to make the twins—and of course each other—the main concern. You've been doing that for years and now it's my turn." He puts a hand over hers in a way she finds almost unbearably earnest and oddly out of character. "Don't you think?"

Maya finds she's lost her appetite. She stares at her food, moving eggplant around the plate, trying to will it away like a naughty child at suppertime. "Yes, of course," she says quietly, giving Nick a sidelong glance. "You're right."

He looks at her carefully. "What's wrong, babe? You're not worried about money, are you? Because if that's the issue, I can assure you we're fine. I mean, of course it would have been nice to get the director's fee, but I'll still be cut in as a producer. And besides, since the Duracell job we don't really have to worry about . . ." He tails off as Maya holds up her hand.

"It's not that," she says.

"So what is it, then?"

Her chin wobbles then steadies itself. She will *not* cry. Crying is for the useless. "I'm afraid you'll think I'm a jerk if I tell you. Especially since your re-evaluation of priorities—which is wonderful, by the way."

Nick winces. "What is it?"

For a second Maya has a vision of them as one of those sickeningly supportive TV-drama couples who are always "checking in" with each other. She used to hate people who talked about how great their marriages were and how supportive their husbands had been through their pregnancy, illness, weight gain or whatever. She didn't just loathe them—she strongly suspected them of lying. Could anyone really be *that* happy? For years she doubted it. But now she glimpses that what they spoke of might actually be possible, a shimmering oasis in the desert. She still can't be sure how Nick is going to take her news, though, especially now that he's made a sacrifice of his own.

She forces herself to look at him and sees he is now officially worried, looking concerned not just for her but for himself. Does he think she's caught him out or something? Then she has a strange thought: *Maybe he's afraid I'm going to leave.* But why would he be? It didn't make any sense. She finds herself seized by the notion, and a part of her is tempted to say the words, just to see what it would feel like.

"What is it, darling?" he says, brow furrowing. "It's cruel to hold me in suspense like this."

Maya takes a breath. "I have a job interview tomorrow. At Gray's firm. I have no idea whether they'll hire me, but I've decided that whatever happens with this one, I really do want to go back to work."

Nick nods in a way that encourages her to keep talking, and the whole story comes tumbling out of her.

"It's just . . . the thing is, I'm going a bit crazy at home, and it's time I started bringing in some money again. I know you like the idea of me staying with the kids, being in charge of the household, but I feel like I've been losing myself. I think a lot of our problems in the past couple of years actually have to do with that—the fact that I've lost my sense of myself and my position in the world. I don't mean that the kids won't be a priority anymore, just that I want to have other priorities too. I'm really sorry. I know this couldn't have come at a worse time, with you passing on that job—"

As she talks, Maya feels Nick's grip on her hand loosen. His face remains unreadable, and she begins to think he's about to get angry.

But instead of saying anything, he reaches round and pulls her head toward his. Their foreheads collide with a gentle thunk, and for a moment Nick looks at her close up, eyes shifting from right to left to take in the whole of her face. Then he kisses her gently on the cheek, which turns into a kiss on the lips, which evolves into a kiss so deep and lovely it almost seems to have a language of its own. And what it says is clear: *I hear you and I understand you and everything you want is what I want.*

"So I take it you're not angry?" Maya says finally, once they've had a little giggle and resumed eating.

"Of course not," says Nick. "Why would I be angry? In fact, I'm delighted. Did you know that you delight me?"

A shiver runs up her spine. "No, I didn't," she replies. "But it's kind of you to say so."

Nick rises and opens another bottle of wine. He tries to pour her some, but she covers her glass with her hand. "Big day tomorrow."

"Of course," he says. He pops the cork back in, then looks at her quite seriously. "I want you to know that not only do I support you in this, but I will help out where help is needed."

"What do you mean?" Maya is confused. He wants to help with her work?

"I mean around the house. With the kids. If you have to work long hours or travel, or even just go out and get drunk at a strip club with clients—because I know you're really into that sort of thing—I want you to know that I'm going to be here, tending the homefires and all that. So you don't need to worry about the twins missing us, because I'll be here for them."

Maya is so startled by this speech she begins to laugh. The conversation could not have been going better if she'd scripted it herself in advance. She has a fizzy feeling in her throat and fights the urge to throw her arms around her husband. Instead, she stands up to clear the plates and bring out the unnecessary tiramisu. When she gets back to the table, though, she finds something is nagging at her—it's the *why* of it all again. Why now? Why has everything changed? Why is he suddenly so different?

She is about to ask him all these things, but before she can, Nick has plunged into the tiramisu and carved them each a great boozy slab.

He catches her look and says, "What is it?"

And once again she thinks better of things. "Nothing," she says, shaking her head. "I guess I just can't believe my luck."

The offices of Yeats and Goldblatt take up four buzzing floors of the city's highest office tower—a building officially named after the blue-chip bank that funded it but colloquially known as the Sword for the way it dominates the skyline with pointed phallic aggression. Maya has often gazed up at the Sword from the

ground and thought of all those years when she worked in a simi-
lar office, spending sixty, and sometimes seventy or eighty, hours
a week toiling away high in the clouds while the rest of the city
spread itself out beneath her. Amazing how quickly perfectly
normal things can become quite strange, because as familiar as
the business district is, she feels utterly intimidated—like a law
student out for her first job interview. She remembers what Nick
said to her as she was leaving this morning: "Remember who you
are." By which he meant that she must be confident in what she
has accomplished—all the cases she's won, all the clients she's
taken on, all the hours billed and the accolades in her classes at
school. Even the past few years of raising children. The sleepless
nights and diaper dramas and endless tests of patience involved
in caring for two tiny, needy humans. All these accomplishments
are hers and hers alone.

Maya tries her best to focus on *who she is* as she climbs the
grimy subway stairs and shoulders her way through the teem-
ing sidewalk of black-coated men and women toward the building's revolving doors. She can't help feeling out of place among
this army of professionals, their collars turned against the
wind, eyes to the pavement, minds churning over hidden tasks.
She joins them and is rushed along by the comforting current
of office life.

Gray is there to meet her at the front desk, an enormous takeout coffee in each hand. He gives her one and does a shallow bow.

Maya experiences a clutch of gratitude. "Thanks so much,
Adam. I don't even know where to—"

He motions for her to stop and she does.

"How long have you been waiting?" she asks.

"Not long," he says. "I figured you'd be early. And I've been here for hours anyway, so it was time for a coffee break."

She checks her watch. It's 7:45 a.m. and her interview with the partners is at eight o'clock. They take the elevator up to the twenty-third floor, and Gray ushers her into a waiting area with potted fronds and silent automatic glass doors she worries will close on her. He motions for her to take a seat and disappears down a beige corridor. She has been here once before—for her articling interview ten years earlier (they offered her a place, but she went with a competing firm)—and it all seems oddly the same. Same muted neutral walls and sofas, same softly typing twenty-something receptionist in a skirt suit offering water while she waits. Same smell of printer ink, coffee and freshly shampooed carpets. She plucks the *Wall Street Journal* from the periodical fan on the table and pretends to read it while trying to channel the crisp office energy. Two female lawyers clip past in identical black high heels and nude stockings, trailing rolling document cases behind them. Maya remembers what it was like to be in command of all those files and folders. The hours of research and case law and interviews that went into preparation for court, and the sensation of knowing your argument backwards and forwards, upside down and sideways. The wonderful feeling of being fantastically, ludicrously overprepared for an experience most people would find nerve-racking in the extreme. She wants to go court, to stand in front of a judge and present a well-reasoned argument—one so airtight that when her opponent tries to pick it apart, he will find himself blocked at every turn. Some people find the practice of family law depressing, but not Maya. She loves the transmutation of raw emotion into a settlement. The notion of taking a conflict and defusing it by nailing down all the lingering uncertainty. Divorce is ugly and ungainly, but her job was to simplify it by scrubbing it clean and trimming off the ugly bits.

Unlike most family lawyers, who tend to complain incessantly about their clients, Maya had always enjoyed the so-called human aspect of the job. Part of her role was to act as a sort of therapist to the client. People—particularly men, she had found—needed to go over and over the facts of the case, and indeed the breakdown of the marriage itself. They tended, on balance, to be mired in the past, even two or three years after the act of separation. The financial settlement, when it came, was a way for them to begin to digest the facts of a painful breakup. As a high-billing attorney at a blue-chip firm, she'd often found herself passing tissues to and patting the hands of executive alpha males as they dissolved into tears of despair and confusion while sifting through the ashes of their family life. In many cases, these men admitted that she was the first person who'd seen them cry for as long as they could remember. Instead of being uncomfortable with this level of emotional intimacy, Maya was invariably touched. Rather than approaching the job in a parasitic way, as someone who made money off other people's misery, she tried her best to be a fair and supportive facilitator of an otherwise painful process. She didn't just argue on behalf of her clients; she became their intellectual advocate and emotional rock in an otherwise cruel and impersonal system.

She is lost in nostalgia for the job when the receptionist says, "Come right this way, Mrs. Wakefield." For a moment she thinks of correcting her by saying "Ms." instead of "Mrs."—while it's true she took her husband's name, she still doesn't like the title that denotes her marital status. It makes her feel old.

The young woman leads her past banks of glazed glass office doors. When they reach the boardroom, Maya steps in on her own and lets the thick glass panel swing shut behind her. At the table are six men, all in their forties or fifties; she remembers a couple of them from her very first job interview and, later, court. She is surprised to see that one of them is Gray, but then she remembers that he's a full partner and as such would be involved in any new hires in the firm's family branch. A part of her is grateful he didn't recuse himself as he might have done, but another part is mildly annoyed. Whatever happens, she doesn't want any special treatment. As if to ensure this, she shakes the hands of all the partners at the table in exactly the same way, making eye contact and stating her name brusquely to everyone but Gray before sitting down in the empty chair at the other end of the table.

Roger Goldblatt, the son the of the firm's famously irascible, long-dead co-founder, doodles on a notepad with a slim silver pen as he addresses her. "So, Mrs. Wakefield, lovely to see you. I remember you well from your first interview. What makes you so sure that you want to practice law again after your—what?—two- or three-year hiatus?"

Maya takes a breath. She'd expected this question, of course, but finds herself unnerved by the lack of preamble. Hiatuses are for wimps in the rough-and-tumble world of law. She takes another breath and allows a calm, self-contained smile to spread over her face. She reminds herself to speak slowly, not to babble on like an anxious ninny.

"I'm glad you asked—and please call me Maya, by the way. Much as I love my family, it seems I'm not cut out for full-time cupcake baking." A ripple of laughter swirls through the room. She relaxes slightly. "It's not the status or the money or even the cafeteria tuna melts I miss." More laughter. "It's the *work*. I miss the cases. I miss the victory of avoiding court. And when that doesn't succeed, I miss working hard to craft an argument and laying it out in front of a judge. I miss dealing with clients and seeing the relief on their faces when I win. And as I'm sure you remember, I like to win. My record speaks for itself."

A couple of the partners glance down at the papers in front of them, and Maya realizes that they must have all her numbers right there—a statistical summation of her entire worth as a lawyer.

"But why Goldblatt's? Why not return to your old firm?"

"The parting was amicable"—Maya pauses to pluck a bit of lint off her cuff—"but you guys are simply the best."

She looks out at the table of open, attentive faces and feels a surge of confidence. One of the other partners asks what she can offer the firm now, compared to other potential associates "coming up through the ranks." By "coming up," of course, he means younger and unencumbered—and probably male. Like most old-world outfits, Goldblatt's is dominated by men. The partner doesn't mention that these associates are willing to work incredibly long hours, without the logistical encumbrance of marriage and children, but the implication is clear. Maya tells them not just what she thinks they want to hear, but what she truly believes: that she has worked and she has not worked, and after all is said and done, working is better. Better for her and better for her family. She can get up to speed on the case law in a matter of days. And the hours don't scare her. Unlike these young turks, she actually knows what she's getting herself into. She knows the circuit judges and the opposing lawyers. She's hooked up and tuned in and ready to plunge back in and give her entire brain and body over to the job.

The suits are silent as she talks, letting her state her case; some of them even smile and nod encouragingly. The words are tumbling from her mouth in fully formed paragraphs. As she talks about her love of the job, her past triumphs and her eagerness for future challenges—about how a firm like Yeats and Goldblatt can best drum up new clients and move seamlessly into the future—she looks over and sees Adam Gray watching her. And what she sees on his face is unmistakable: it is *love*. Not professional admiration, not loyal friendship, not a crush—it's the real thing. If anyone else in the room had glanced at his face at that moment, they would have seen it too, but luckily for Maya no one does. The realization is so disconcerting that she wraps up her monologue before her train of thought derails. When she is finished the men in the room all smile. They sip their mineral water and clear their throats and make upbeat small talk for a few minutes before the discussion of scheduling comes up. Roger Goldblatt himself poses the magic question: "When would you be available to start?"

Maya practically bounces out of the room; she would moonwalk in her heels if she could. She is on *fire*! She can *do* this. She's already down the elevator and nearly out of the building— excited to go home and make the twins lunch—when she hears Gray shouting her name across the lobby. She turns and sees with relief that the look from the meeting has left his face (perhaps she was just imagining things?), replaced by an expression of innocent affection.

"For all your talk of what a highly efficient, detail-oriented perfectionist you are, you left this behind." He holds up her coat.

Maya laughs, folding the coat under her arm. She can't stop laughing. She rises to the tips of her toes and grins. "So how was that?"

Gray reaches forward and actually chucks her under the chin, like a cowboy in the movies. "You done good, kid. I'll eat my hat if they don't hire you. Now let me take you out for breakfast to celebrate."

Maya hesitates—the twins. She'd been planning to rush home to do the nursery school run, but it was already too late for that. Then she looks at Gray—the tempting face of professional victory—and she shrugs and pulls on her coat.

"Why not?" she says. And they stride out into the square, overcoats buttoned against the icy early December chill.

CHAPTER 13

Nick

Ambergris Caye, Belize

The first day on the beach, Nick reads a magazine, drinks several sweet rum drinks and feels the tourniquet of muscle between his shoulder blades begin to loosen incrementally. "I haven't been this relaxed in years!" he tells Maya over his second plate of conch tacos, before falling back on the sand. On the second day, he reads some more, drinks some more, feels his body relax some more and his mind begin to wander. Not in a meditative way, but in a restless, muttering search. A loyal dog seeking its master or a junkie in need of a fix. By the third day, the thought of spending another minute in that lounge chair listening to the surf makes him want to pull his face off and howl at the blazing sun.

It's not that everything hasn't been perfect—the sun, the surf and the saltwater breeze are all around them in abundance. The hotel, a twenty-room eco-resort he'd found on a travel website recommended by his assistant, is just as advertised: secluded without being remote, luxurious without being ostentatious, simple without being austere. The beach is warm and white and devoid of hawkers selling cheap shell necklaces Maya would never wear. The $800-a-night room is airy and stylishly appointed in a crisp, hippy-chic fashion—bowls of bleached shells and a four-poster bed with billowing white linens. At night Nick lies awake in it thinking how great he feels, how fantastically *chilled out* he is. How if he weren't here, he'd be up all night on some awful set, sitting behind the first camera and stuffing his face with cheap sushi, drinking can after can of Diet Coke, wishing the script girl would just shut the fuck up so he could concentrate. Joking around with Mitch, his long-time first AD, and trying to convince a fretful Larry that a little bit of triple overtime never killed anyone—certainly not the client. Yes, thank God he isn't working. Better to be here, thousands of miles away, paying $800 a night to lie around and imagine what's happening on set.

Nick's thoughts of work carry over from night to morning as they eat their holiday breakfast of papaya, passion fruit and mango with lashings of yogurt washed down with black espresso. For the first time since they arrived, Maya seems just a tiny bit uneasy. She keeps glancing at him over her coffee cup and scratching at the hair at the nape of her neck.

Ever since she got the news about her new job, she'd been in an unassailable good mood. Chatty, easy, devoid of any silent neurotic gloom. There were still signs of the old Maya, though. In addition to the detailed menu plan and daily activity schedule for Velma, she'd created a hand-illustrated book called *Mommy and Daddy Are Going on Holiday* for the twins. It told the story—in coloured-pencil drawings—of how she and Nick were going to bid the kids farewell and hop on a plane that would take them to a beach filled with sunshine and palm trees. There were even drawings of Mommy and Daddy kissing over a candlelight dinner and later snuggling in bed, which was meant to convey, he could only assume, that these were the sorts of things that happened on holiday—not that this had been the case so far. If the lack of sex was bothering Maya, though, she hadn't given any indication of it. Perhaps she was still recovering from the flight.

"Are you okay?" she says now with a gentle expression intended to temper the question no man welcomes. Why, he's often wondered, do women continue to insist that their constant worrying is a form of love when all men sense its actual purpose: emotional control?

Nick notices that his knee is bouncing under the table like a rabbit on Dexedrine and he's been reading about the same cricket test match for the better part of half an hour.

"Of course," he says, throwing down the paper and spreading his arms in what he hopes is the sort of gesture an Incredibly Relaxed Man on Holiday might make. "I'm fantastic. Never been better. Can you believe how good this coffee tastes? And the sun! Who knew the sun could be that . . . well, that *sunny*?"

Maya is staring at him with open skepticism now. Trying hard is really not his style. She's no dummy, this soon-to-be-ex-wife of his, he realizes with a rush of premature nostalgia. She looks at him with concern and he looks back with curiosity. It's suddenly amazing to him that she can't see through his whole ruse, that it isn't entirely obvious to her what an asshole he is. Not just an asshole but a lying, selfish, pathetic excuse for a man, rather than the reformed "good husband" she amazingly, against all evidence, believes him to be. He experiences a wave of nauseating guilt before the old contempt crashes in to save him. Contempt for her self-serving guilelessness. How, he wonders irritably, could anyone be so wilfully blind?

Then he remembers: *People see what they want to see. They hear what they want to hear, editing the story in self-interested ways as they go along.* That's why it's so much easier to convince people of a comforting but obvious lie than a glaring but painful truth. People will find themselves drawn toward the story that makes them feel good, no matter how ludicrous it might be.

Maya goes back to reading her novel—a thick book club pick with a cover illustration of a freshwater lake at sunset—and Nick finds himself admiring her hair, which is unusually pale, some bits almost silvery white. At first he wonders if it's greying, but then he realizes she's gone blonder from the sun. Her skin is rosy despite her valiant efforts with umbrellas and coats of Swiss sunscreen. A faint galaxy of tiny brown freckles swirls into the V-neck of her T-shirt. Beneath it he can make out her red-and-white gingham bikini, which he hasn't seen in eons. His annoyance drains away and he feels excited to see the gingham. Under the table his leg is beginning to vibrate again, and Nick suddenly knows what he needs to do. And that is *something*. It's not that he's having a bad time—it's just that unlike his wife (and apparently the rest of the developed world), he finds it quite stressful to lie on a beach doing nothing, hour after hour, day after day.

"I'm going for a walk!" he announces a little too loudly, and then he leaps up from the table, sending his teaspoon clattering to the floor. He doesn't even bother to pick it up—the waiter is already moving toward him to do so—he just apologizes to no one in particular and shuffles off.

Nick decides to take a walk around the "grounds," which are not really grounds so much as a large garden of bougainvillea shrubs spreading out from a central fountain featuring a pair of burbling marble dolphins. He retrieves a penny from his pocket and tosses it in the fountain but finds himself unable, or unwilling, to make a wish. He walks barefoot, flip-flops in hand, across the coarse and prickly tropical grass toward an elaborate white bird-cage in the corner. Inside is Guido, the resort's forty-two-year-old talking parrot. There is a bowl of peanuts beside his cage, and Nick picks one up and presses it through the bars. Guido eyes him suspiciously, then sidesteps across his bar to accept the snack, ignoring Nick's attempts to start a conversation.

"Hallo, old chap," Nick says in his best English accent (yesterday he witnessed Guido doing a full routine of Monty Python quotes), but the scruffy green bird is evidently not feeling talkative.

Guido hacks open the peanut shell with his hooked beak and crunches down on the nut. Then he rotates his head, fixes Nick with his opposite eye and rubs his beak against the bars for more snacks. When Nick doesn't reciprocate, Guido leans back and says, in a distinct Jamaican accent, "You can't fool all da people all da time."

Nick is oddly disconcerted. Who would teach a parrot to say such a thing? Especially a hotel parrot. Whatever happened to Polly wanting a cracker? He fights the urge to reprimand the bird, then stops himself. He is about return to the breakfast bar for more thick black coffee when a poster on the wall behind the cage catches his eye. It's scrawled in bleary green ink and features a photocopied picture of a couple sitting on a beach having a picnic. "Get off the island!" it says. "Secluded snorkelling day trip for two. I will take you to my secret lagoon. $75 per couple—catch of the day and wine included. Call Ike."

Nick dials the number straight away. Ike, or someone with a Belizean accent he presumes is Ike, answers after seven or eight rings, just as Nick is about to hang up.

"Yeah, mon?" he says.

"Hi there, I'm calling about the secret lagoon snorkelling day trip?"

"WHA?" There is a crackling noise and Nick looks down at the phone to see if it's disconnected, then a few seconds later Ike returns. "Oh, right. Yes, my man. Of course."

Nick makes arrangements for a pickup the following day straight after breakfast. Ike will bring the snorkelling gear and Nick will bring his wife.

"Lemme guess—you two lovebirds are on your honeymoon, right?" Ike, a dreadlocked island native, leans back with a self-satisfied grin and continues to steer the boat. The rickety old tiller looks like it might snap off and there is two inches of seawater sloshing in the bottom of the cockpit, but Nick feels much safer since stepping off the dock. He is drinking a luke-warm beer and it's not even 10:00 a.m. They are finally off the island—going somewhere, doing something. He looks at Maya, who has her face turned against the wind, one hand holding a floppy straw hat. She is shaking her head and laughing, shouting to Ike over the sound of the motor that they've been married since they were kids themselves. She takes out her phone and shows him pictures of the twins.

"Good Lord, wouldja look at those gorgeous babies!" Ike laughs, waving his free hand. He reaches over and takes the phone from Maya, and as he does Nick watches it slip from his hand, bounce off the gunwale and fall into the sea.

Ike's hand flies to his forehead like he can't believe what just happened. Maya is frozen mid-laugh, her mouth hanging open.

"The kids!" she shouts, looking stricken, and for a second Nick wonders if she has somehow mixed up the pixelated images of Isla and Foster with the twins themselves. Then he realizes that the phone is her lifeline to them.

He reaches over and puts a hand on her seawater-dampened thigh. "I've got mine. It's all fine. It's just a phone." He reaches into his pocket and is about to fish his out out to show her when he realizes he forgot to charge it last night. It's dead.

Ike starts steering the boat around, but Nick knows it's just a gesture. The phone is long gone—a cellular burial at sea.

"No, no. Don't, please," Maya shouts at Ike above the waves. "I have insurance!"

Ike apologizes, shaking his dreadlocks and knocking on his skull at his own idiocy, but Maya implores him not to worry.

"It's not the end of the world," she insists. Then, suddenly emboldened, she adds, "It's probably a good thing!" She laughs into the wind and reaches into the cooler for a beer.

The lagoon, when they finally reach it well over an hour later, is everything Nick had hoped for. A small fan of beach furnished with clumps of palms and fine pale sand. The water is so blue it reminds him of a retro cocktail. The island is about the size of small city park and empty but for a few trees and a flock of lazily cawing birds Nick doesn't recognize. He's done shoots in places vaguely like this before—sunny, sandy and secluded—but never anywhere this remote or (dare he even think it?) magical. He's suddenly struck by the idea that this would be the perfect place to propose if he weren't already married. For a strange moment, he wishes he had another ring to give Maya. He's surprised by this strange thought and quickly writes it off as a director's instinct. He never could resist a good location.

Ike is handing them masks and flippers and talking mock ominously in his island patter of tides and reefs and the importance of not touching the coral. "It is razor-sharp—and blood attracts the hungry sharks," he warns with a grin that reveals the gap where his upper molars ought to be.

Maya drains her beer, pulls her hair into a ponytail and raises her arms above her head with an athletic flick as if to say she's ready for anything—even shark attacks. They pull on their masks and roll overboard.

Two hours pass in a silent aquatic dream. The reefs are shallow and full of slow-waving plants and tiny fluorescent fish that swirl and glitter like meteor dust from a distant galaxy. Nick loses himself examining a conch shell—complete with lurking conch, shrinking back into his house at a touch. Maya's long legs swish past Nick's head, propelled by oversized blue flippers, as she tails a lumbering blowfish. Time passes without sound or punctuation from the real world. The water makes Nick feel light and pleasantly helpless as he's pulled this way and that—a weightless waterbaby being nursed by the great mother current. He sees one of those flat, flapping creatures that look like the Death Star skimming along the seabed. At one point, Maya glides over and takes his hand, motioning for him to follow.

They round the corner of the reef and she points at a giant sea turtle, about the size of a small coffee table, floating sleepily from rock to rock. As he streams past, Nick sees the look on the ancient turtle's face and can only describe it as an expression of pure being. Soft focused eyes above a chinless half smile. When Nick looks up, Maya is making her way to the surface. Coming up for air, he hears her hoots of delight first. Then he feels her body against his, the slippery sensation of her treading water while pressing against him. She gives him a salty wet kiss, then vanishes back under the surface.

Later, when they are on the beach and finishing the whole bream and fist-sized prawns Ike has barbequed for them using his little gas hibachi, Maya pours them both more wine and lays her head on Nick's stomach. They lie there like that for a long while, bodies absorbing the sun, enjoying the skim of sand on their skin and thinking how lucky they are to have come here. Ike calls to Nick and says something about going to a neighbouring island to get more ice for the cooler, and Nick raises a sleepy thumb in consent. Ike places their bags and a big bottle of water on the beach and says he'll be back in an hour. Nick understands he's just trying to give them privacy.

When the sound of the boat's motor has faded into the wind, Maya shifts her shoulder in a way that tells Nick she's awake. Soon their hands are moving across each other and they are kissing. Not greedily like on the failed date night, but calmly and with purpose. Like they know what's coming next and understand exactly what to do.

And they are right to kiss this way because when sex follows—the first sex they've had in too many months to count—it is smooth and familiar. Something about the act reminds Nick of a summertime pop song, the kind that gives you a shiver and a nostalgic tug and a fleeting glimpse into the sweetness of life without weighing you down with insights or moral concepts. A perfect pleasure, Nick thinks, as they lie entangled under a palm tree after the fact. He's not even sure how they got from the beach into the shade. They stare out at the endless ocean and he sees that Maya is about to say something but then decides not to. Instead, she lays down her head and falls instantly asleep.

When Nick opens his eyes again, everything is different. The sun has sloped off their side of the island, leaving their private beach entirely in shade. The heat in the air has dissipated, but the sand is still warm. He looks for his phone to check the time, then realizes it's dead anyway. From the position of the sun, Nick figures it must be late afternoon at least. He scans the water for Ike and sees nothing on the horizon but a distant bobbing sailboat, out for a sunset sail. Maya snores gently beside him, her body curled under a towel, head cradled by a fallen palm frond.

Nick looks at her pale eyelashes, her small hand curled and trusting as a child's, and he feels a clutch in his stomach. *I love her*, he thinks. And then, more clearly, as if the words were written across the sky: *I will never leave her*.

And just like that, Nick knows it's true.

It's a revelation, of course, but one he doesn't have time to dwell on at the moment. Because now, he is suddenly and keenly aware, it's his job to protect her. To make sure they survive the approaching night. He gets up swiftly, careful not to disturb her, and gathers an armload of kindling from the nearby forest. By the time Maya wakes up, he has built a small fire using what's left of the gas in the hibachi. She rubs the sand from her face and looks down, suddenly self-conscious about her nakedness.

"How long did I sleep?" she asks, pulling on a billowy white bathing suit cover and hugging her knees like a teenage girl at a slumber party.

"Hard to say." Nick is poking his fire with a long stick, trying to get the embers to turn. "Couple of hours, I reckon."

"You *reckon*?" Maya snorts.

"Sorry, did that sound weird?"

She ignores this. "Where's Ike?"

Nick looks at her more seriously now. "No sign yet. But don't worry. We have lots of water left, some cheese and crackers, and I've started a fire, so we'll be fine through the night—if it comes to that."

Maya straightens. "The *night*?" Her eyebrows arch to a point.

Nick feels a hardness in his chest. He will protect her. That, after all, is his job. He moves close to her and puts a hand on her shoulder, looking her directly in the eye so she can sense his alpha dominance. Nothing can hurt her now. "I'm going to take care of you," he says. "If I need to, I can spear us a fish."

"Oh, really?" she says, biting the smile off her lips. "With what?"

Nick holds up a stick he carved to a point with his Swiss Army blade while she was sleeping. She looks suitably impressed, if skeptical. For a moment he feels an urge to pound his chest, carry her into the woods and have hungry, proprietary sex with her again. But he doesn't. For one thing, they need to keep a lookout for a rescue boat. For another, he's not sure he could perform again after all the sun and wine. But they have the rest of their lives to make up for lost sex.

While he is lost in this thought, Maya stands and begins packing their things into her straw beach basket.

"What are you doing that for?" he asks. "I laid them out so we would know exactly what supplies we have."

Maya shoves a celebrity magazine into the basket. And the water. He sees that she is in denial about their situation.

"Will you stop acting as if we've been left here to die?" she says. "I'm sure Ike is just around the corner. He probably got waylaid talking to his buddy at the bar—you know, island time."

Nick goes to her and wraps his arms around her. "Look," he whispers into her ear, "I want you to understand something, okay?"

He can see the nervous energy draining out of Maya and being replaced by something more sinuous and connected. They are on the same level at last.

"Yes?" she says.

He pulls back and looks at her face. "I love you and I am never going to leave you. Do you understand that? No matter what happens, we are together. The two of us against the world. Do you get that?"

She blinks. Nods. Then a peaceable smile spreads over her face. "Like on a desert island?"

"Exactly," he says.

And she leans into his chest, making him feel like one of those men on the cover of a romance novel—only there is nothing ironic or kitschy about the way he feels. He is filled with gratitude and relief—a man who has at the last second reclaimed the prize of all prizes: a beautiful, intelligent and loving wife. How could he have been so blind to her pricelessness? He is about to suggest that they do something out of character, like renew their vows or promise to come back to this very island once a year, when he hears the sound of an outboard motor over the waves. Ike and his battered dinghy round into view. He is waving two bottles of white wine, the tiller between his legs, and shouting apologies over the wind and a long, impossible-to-follow story—something about running out of fuel and his friend Mike at the marina.

Maya sighs and flops back on the sand, laughter bubbling out of her. Watching, Nick suddenly knows that everything is—and always was—going to be fine. In the end, the big lie was the big truth: his life really is perfect after all.

CHAPTER 14

Maya

"The navy or the grey?" Maya holds up two skirt suits, both freshly dry-cleaned and still in their plastic wrappers, for her husband to choose.

Nick, who has a squirming child on each knee and a sippy cup in each hand, considers the choice, bringing the entire weight of his directorial experience to bear. He closes his eyes and allows for a lengthy pause. "The grey," he says finally.

"Why?" Maya is suddenly unnerved by his certainty.

"Because it makes your ass look great."

"But I want to look professional, not sexy!"

"You'll look professional *and* fuckable," he says, reaching over to give her hip a good-natured thwack, which sends the twins into fits of giggles.

"*Language*, Nick!" She is grinning hard.

"Mommy's as naughty as you," Isla tells Foster, who in turn smacks her. "Foster, no hitting!"

"Am not."

"Are too."

"Am *not*. Spanking is different than hitting. Daddy spanks Mommy's bum-bum for fun."

"Does not."

"Does too!"

Instead of playing referee with the kids, Maya pours herself a cup of coffee. After one thoughtful sip, she shoots back upstairs to put on the grey suit, leaving Nick to break it up.

When she reappears twenty minutes later, hair ironed to a gloss, kitten heels clicking, Velma has arrived and is washing up the detritus of the weekend. Maya hugs her good morning, asks about her weekend, then feels a clutch of guilt at the state of the place.

"You look so *grown-up*," Velma says nodding, arms crossed.

Maya thanks her and proceeds to toast two English muffins, slather them in butter and honey, and push them greedily into her mouth, hardly bothering to chew.

And she does not feel the least bit guilty about that.

Where once she would have scrubbed the kitchen to gleaming on Sunday night (how else could she get to sleep?), now she's opting to let things go a bit. In fact "letting go" is her new mantra. Take last night. Nick came home from the grocery store with a MexiCasa taco kit, complete with oily shredded cheese, hydrogenated tortilla shells and pre-made, sugary salsa. A few weeks ago she would have had a full-blown anxiety attack at the thought of the twins ingesting such stuff, but last night she just shrugged and said, "Andale, andale! Ariba, ariba!" which made her entire family shriek with happiness. What difference was a couple of tacos going to make?

As it happened, quite a lot. The twins were ecstatic. Greasy tacos were clumsily assembled and messily consumed, a great pile of dishes accumulated. She laughed and ate and made googly eyes at her husband and children with salty ground-beef grease dripping from her fingers. Then she let Nick put the twins to bed and turned in herself, knowing full well that her husband would head downstairs to watch the basketball highlights and drink a beer, and that as a result nothing would be done about the dishes.

And apart from the moment when she had to go sit on the stairs and take twelve cleansing breaths, she was fine with that. Just as she was fine with the fact that the twins no longer asked to be breastfed—had in fact more or less weaned themselves from the moment they moved into their own beds. Since she and Nick got back from Belize, she hadn't offered and they hadn't asked. And she was fine with that. They all were. At least it was better than the alternative.

And now here she is, coat collar upturned, walking briskly down her street, heels hitting the pavement in perfect time, propelling her toward the rest of her career with each satisfying and efficient click. She feels, for the first time in months, as if she actually has somewhere real to go. It is a good feeling.

The streetlights are still on, casting a weird sepia glow over the neighbourhood. The street is shattered from construction trucks and diggers, a web of cracks and star-shaped potholes, as if it had been picked up by a giant and dropped from a great height. The damage is from home renovation work, a local obsession in the summer, now tailing off as the winter chill descends. This neighbourhood isn't just gentrifying—it's remodelling itself in the style of the one percent, tearing down postwar bungalows to make room for faux French regency mansions with hulking facades and ostentatious copper eavestroughs. Every time Maya sees a For Sale sign outside one of the few remaining little brick split-levels, she wants to rescue it from almost certain demolition. "Tear-downs" are what opportunistic real estate agents call these old houses, which are not very old at all—1940s at the earliest.

She grew up in a neighbourhood just like this one used to be, in a small brown stucco house on the east side of the city—a house her parents sold before retiring to a farmhouse in the middle of nowhere. She remembers her mother, a professor of architecture at the city's biggest university, telling her about these houses when she was a girl. Sturdy little houses, intended for middle-class family life, built for soldiers returning from the war. The houses of the postwar boom. Which became the turn-of-the-millennium boom. Which led to people buying perfectly good houses and tearing them down to build four-thousand-square-foot McMansions.

Usually such thoughts are enough to start the low simmer that Maya unconsciously sublimates into anxiety—an anxiety that's been with her for most of her adult life. A sense that something terrible is about to happen and she has forgotten to do something important to guard against it. Like not taking her vitamin D supplement (rickets!) or signing the twins up for Hindi classes (they will be left behind in the global economy!). The feeling, in essence, that the world is rapidly going to hell and she must do everything she possibly can to prevent its demise.

But today the waters are calm and cool, and as a result no such sublimation occurs. Instead, what Maya feels walking under the wet black boughs on this grey and snowless December morning is a sense of safety and well-being.

Maya is on her way to work, she thinks, narrating her life in the third person—a private game she used to play as a little girl. *She is wearing her best grey suit and her patent leather heels. At work, Maya will have her very own office with her very own desk. And a chair. And a drawer with pens and pencils. And a sign that says her name and position: Junior Associate. Maya is going to work very hard and earn her own money. And then at the end of the day, she's going to come home and have dinner with her husband and kiss her children goodnight. As she does almost every night.*

Except with the hours she's going to be working, the twins will almost certainly be asleep by the time she gets in. Or she'll be one of those mothers who rushes home for storytime and then puts in four more hours of work after the kids have gone to bed. And on top of the yeoman work required in her new job, there is also the obligatory guilt. She can feel it nibbling at the edges of her already. She pushes it firmly from her mind. Guilt, she knows, is her mortal enemy.

As she nears the subway entrance—a staircase into the bowels of the city that has always reminded her of a gaping toothless mouth—she notices other people like her, travelling toward the same destination. She can suddenly see all these people, the people in her neighbourhood, as if in a sped-up aerial shot, leaving their separate houses and surging toward the same fixed point: a tunnel that will take them to a train, from which they will all disperse into a different part of the city. They are all the same as her on the surface—professional people in their thirties, forties and fifties, wearing black and grey wool suits under black and grey wool coats, a dark brigade of middle-class professionals, the men carrying leather courier bags (briefcases, she notices, seem to have gone out of fashion since she had children) and the women gripping handbags the size of small arms carriers. Maya has one of these handbags herself, and for now it is empty of files. Inside is her phone, a package of aloe vera tissues, one lip balm, one lip gloss, a wallet containing $87.76 in cash, a package of tampons (to keep at work), a pair of foldable ballet flats (for the long walk home in the event of a terrorist attack), six black hair elastics, bobby pins, a granola bar, her keys and a copy of *The Way*. She finished the book weeks ago but still carries it with her everywhere. In case of what, she's not entirely sure.

Maya knows better than to start recommending *The Way* to everyone she meets, but she would if it didn't make her look like a crackpot self-help junkie. The fact is, all her problems with Nick evaporated as soon as she embraced the theory of Radical Honesty. When she told him of her desire to go back to work, suddenly he wanted it too. Amazingly, against all reason, the Law of Wanting actually worked.

Nick was returned to her by the universe, which, rather preposterously, turned out to be as all-knowing and all-hearing as *The Way* had promised. And then her wish to work again came true as well. Sometimes when she thinks about it too hard, her brain starts to fizz and she wants to run through the streets shouting the incredible story of what has happened. She was about to lose her marriage, but then some outside force of good returned it to her. She had no job and the universe gave her one. The only other time she had felt this way was when the twins were born. This strange realization that something completely regular and yet totally miraculous had just happened and she needed to tell everyone about it.

Except, of course, she doesn't. She doesn't shout the story of her resuscitated marriage to the other commuters on the subway train or to the young barista with the soul patch who makes her a non-fat half-caf latte. She doesn't shout it to the office mail guy or the receptionist or her new assistant or the other junior associate in the office next door. She doesn't shout it in the series of meetings she sits in all day with the lead litigator on the high-profile lesbian divorce case she's been assigned to. But when Gray convinces her to have a drink with him to celebrate her first day and let Nick do bath-and-bedtime, she finds it impossible to keep her giddiness from rising to the surface. In any case, he can see it.

"What's with the grin, gorgeous?" he says as soon as they are sipping a pair of enormous Manhattans in a booth in the new boutique hotel bar he has insisted on taking her to.

Maya can't believe how many of these places have opened and closed since the twins were born. At times she is amazed that people even do things like go to the movies or have drinks in hotel bars anymore; these pleasures of the unencumbered have become utterly foreign to her. Sitting in a bar having after-work drinks is like returning to a pleasant country she emigrated from years ago but has barely thought of since.

"Flattery will get you everywhere, my dear," she says with a twinkle. "Well, *almost*."

He flags down the waitress and orders "some of those spicy Szechuan peanut things" before returning his attention to her.

"So how was the first day back?"

"Fine. Better than fine, actually. Would you think I was a complete nerd if I told you it was absolutely thrilling? Not in the sense that anything particularly thrilling happened, but in the sense that I am completely thrilled to be back. I can't believe I was so ambivalent about the prospect for so long. I guess I felt like I wasn't entitled to have a life outside the home after the twins. They just needed me so much and Nick makes good money, so it seemed self-indulgent or something." She looks up at him, plucks the sour cherry from her drink, chews it twice and swallows. "Sorry, am I being boring? I promised myself no mommy talk at work, and here I am blabbing on about the kids on the first day."

Gray's face has taken on an oddly pained expression. "Not a bit," he says. "That's not mommy talk; it's just life talk."

Maya realizes that she knows very little about Gray's personal life these days. All their recent meetings have been focused on her. Feeling suddenly ashamed of this, she starts drawing him out gently at first and then dives in like a crack interrogator. Before long they've ordered another round and he's telling her the story of his last romance—a four-night stand with the pretty summer student a few months back—and how it all went tragically wrong.

"I honestly don't know why I get into these things in the first place when it's clear there's no future in them," he is saying. He tips another handful of peanuts into his mouth. "I mean, she was lovely—don't get me wrong. Still is, I'm sure. It's not like she's dead."

"Is she not at the firm anymore?"

"Thankfully, no. She was on a six-month secondment from New York." He unpeels a nicotine patch, loosens his tie, unbuttons his top two shirt buttons and smacks it directly onto his burly chest. "It hurts like hell to take off, but you get the best effect from putting it close to your heart," he explains.

"Right," Maya says, suddenly imagining Gray all alone in his penthouse loft with its concrete and glass and exposed ductwork. She sees him ripping off a nicotine patch and brushing his teeth alone before bed. "Are you lonely?"

He sighs. Perhaps he's sad that she'd even ask.

"Not really," he says. "I work too much for that. But I do wish I could have something . . . different. That I could find a person who I just . . . well, this is going to sound terrible, but a woman who I could really take seriously. Not as a person, but as a partner. You know, to actually share my life with. I think life is for sharing, don't you?"

"Of course. But what was wrong with whatsherface?" says Maya, relieved to be taking a turn as the empathetic one. "I mean, she was pretty and smart and presumably very nice, wasn't she?"

Gray nods dismally and waves a hand through the air. "Oh, Liza. Yes, yes, of course she was all of that. And because of that, she'll make some lucky man a fantastic wife and mother someday. But that man just wasn't going to be me. For one thing, I'm too old."

"Old! But you're not even forty yet!" Maya leans across the table, her hair sweeping over the peanuts, and hisses. "And by that I mean *we're* not even forty yet. Which for your information is *not old*. Besides, I thought all single guys your age dated women in their twenties now. I didn't know it was even a big deal anymore."

Gray leans back and laughs. "It's not a big deal! Whoa, whoa, touched a nerve there, did I?"

"Not really. I just . . . as a friend, I strongly think you should be able to date whoever you want and not worry about it. At least from my point of view."

Gray looks at her and snorts. He presses his forehead to the table in a gesture of exaggerated exhaustion, and when he lifts his head he is red-faced and laughing mock tragically. "If only I could."

"Could what?"

"Date who I want."

"Well, why can't you?" Maya tries a peanut and is surprised to find that it is wildly spicy. She drinks the last half of her second Manhattan in one go.

"Are you okay?"

Maya waves her hands in front of her face. Gray reaches over and pats her on the shoulder. Then the pat turns into a gentle squeeze. It's the sort of squeeze a high school football coach would administer to his star quarterback. Not a creepy squeeze but a collegial one. To Maya's surprise she finds it very soothing. No one has rubbed her back in ages, not even Nick. She finds it so pleasant, in fact, that when Gray orders another round of cocktails, she doesn't even bother to object. She just smiles and then narrows her gaze at him, as if to say, *You tricky bastard*.

"So . . ." she says, a rogue thought suddenly swimming into her head. "Is this where you and Nick used to come on your man dates? Or did you go strictly to strip clubs?"

Gray raises his eyebrows and flattens his tie, which, Maya notices for the first time, is printed with tiny geometric wasps. "I have no idea what you mean."

"Whatever," says Maya, reaching for her next drink before the waitress has even pulled it from the tray. "I don't care what you guys got up to. It was probably nice for Nick to have, you know, someone to confide in. I'm sure you know we went through a pretty rough time. It was actually touch and go there for a while."

"Oh, yeah?" Gray mumbles, suddenly craning his neck to study the menu board as if it were the Rosetta Stone.

Maya feels self-conscious about confiding in Gray—he clearly doesn't want to hear it—but at the same time she feels compelled to tell him everything. He is, after all, the only friend still in their lives who has known them both since the beginning. The person who introduced them, in fact. She suddenly needs to present him with the incredible recovery they have made. Their marital tragedy narrowly averted—but why? Under scrutiny, she's still not sure. Was it really *The Way*? Maybe. Or maybe the change wasn't in her but in Nick, unprompted. Gray may be the only person who understands the evolution of Nick. The change and where it came from. She realizes it is this—not the new job or the whisky—that's causing the humming in her veins, that accelerated feeling she has had for the past few days of hovering slightly above earth, moving just above the legal human speed limit.

"Nick's completely different."

"Mmmm?" Gray gestures to the menu. "They have tacos here, you know. Pork belly or tuna?"

"None for me, thanks. Are you listening to what I'm saying, Gray? It's about Nick. He's changed. Like completely."

Gray looks up and places his chin in two hands. His eyebrows are raised as though he has just now computed what Maya is saying.

"Really? Completely changed. Like how?"

"Well, for one thing he doesn't work all the time anymore. And when he is at home, he actually seems engaged. He acknowledges the twins as something other than small angsty marsupials."

"You mean he doesn't play with them?"

"No! I mean he plays with them *more*. And he seems to want to get to know them—young children have a lot of character, if you take the time to notice."

"I'll take your word for it. You know I adore my godchildren."

Maya glowers slightly. "I'm just saying, Nick's like a new man. He's been incredibly supportive of me coming back to work. Our sex life is better. And, I dunno, he's just more *present*. It's like for years he was anywhere other than with me, and suddenly one day he just returned. I don't know why but he did, and now everything's completely different. If that makes sense."

Gray drains his drink and searches through his wallet. He finds some cash and slaps it on the table. "Well, congratulations, I guess. It sounds like you two are very happy."

"Sorry, have I said something annoying?" Maya tries to meet his eyes but the bulldog is back, glowering out into some invisible field in the middle distance.

"No, no, not at all." Gray is standing up now, pulling on his coat. "I've just got to go home and get cracking on this file. It's always a pleasure, my dear."

"Adam"—Maya's tone is sharper than she intends, but she goes with it—"it's your old friend Maya talking here. What's the problem?"

Gray, a heap of a man in his big wool overcoat, suddenly pauses and deflates. He looks at her and considers something. She can see him considering it, and she wants to know what it is he's considering.

"Tell me," she urges.

"No."

"Are you . . . is that you're jealous?"

"No."

"Not of *us*, I mean. But of the fact that, you know, we're so happy? God, I sound like a jerk saying that."

"You do." He extends the handle on his wheelie folder with an officious snap.

"Gray!"

"Maya."

"I need to know. I *deserve—*"

He leans down and kisses her goodbye. The kiss lands half on her cheek, half on her mouth, silencing her instantly. She can feel his lips, warm and slightly parted. Or maybe it's just a lingering trace of whisky.

"See you tomorrow," he says, and goes.

CHAPTER 15

Nick

Nick is in the editing suite when he gets the call.

"Excuse me, boys," he says to Larry and the editor—a Dane called Henrik whom they've flown in just for the job. The three of them are squeezed onto a single low leather sofa in a dark, windowless room, which, Nick is increasingly aware, smells of microwaved ham. For the past three hours they've been hunched over the footage for the CurvePhone spot, cutting and splicing images of a preposterously good-looking young couple in various states of semi-clothed argument, intimacy and repose. He pulls his phone from his pocket and steps into the hallway. After a large intake of fresh air, he answers.

"Talk to me, Gray."

"Hello." Nick is instantly aware from the depth of the gravel in Gray's voice—a certain throaty barely-awakeness—that he is in a foul mood.

"What can I do for you, my friend?"

"You've been ignoring me," Gray says evenly.

Nick fights a powerful urge to pretend that the call's breaking up and switch off his phone for the rest of the day—something he's done with Maya in the past. He's about to start the crackly voice ("Hel—? Are y—? Can hea—? Hel—? You're bre—" *click, dial tone*) when he remembers there's always text. And email. And the landline.

"Not so. Not ignoring you at all, dude. I've just been insanely busy. This CurvePhone job is eating up all my time."

There is a pause in which Nick can hear Gray's ragged inhalation. He's smoking again. Not a great sign.

"That's not what Maya says. She tells me you've changed. She says you've become the perfect husband."

"Does she now?" Nick tries to affect a jocular manner. A sort of "Heh, heh, who can figure women?" tone. He is suddenly desperate to keep the conversation light, the dialogue upbeat.

"So your plan is working out," says Gray. "Well played."

Nick flinches. "Hey, it wasn't *my* plan. It was *your* plan. And in fact, I thank you for it, because it's changed my life. I'm not just acting different—I actually *feel* different."

"I'm happy for you," Gray says in the same robotic tone. A tone that sends a queasy murmur through Nick's intestines. "But you can't run from the truth, Nick. You still are who you are."

"What's that supposed to mean?"

"It means when are you planning to leave her?" Gray's voice strains slightly at the seams.

Nick ducks into his office and closes the door. He wants to shush Gray even though there's no one there to hear him. He is grimacing and his free hand is flapping at the air like a wounded water bird. He catches a glimpse of himself in the frosted glass wall and is not surprised to see that he looks like a doofus sitcom dad.

"Look, Gray, I don't know. The truth is, I'm really confused right now. Everything we talked about in September . . . I don't know. It's not that anything's changed, materially speaking, but maybe *I've* changed. I feel different—about everything."

"So you're not going to leave her, then?"

"No. I mean, yes. I mean . . . I don't know what I mean. I need some time. What does it matter to you, anyway?" Nick feels a thrust of indignation under his sternum.

"Well, as your friend and sometime legal adviser, I just thought you should probably break the news to her sooner than later. I feel—in my professional opinion—it's gone far enough."

There is a beat. Then Nick says quietly, "But you said six months. Why now?"

"It just seems cruel."

"So this is your *professional* opinion?"

"Well . . ." Gray clears his throat, searching. "I guess it's more of a personal one, now that you mention it."

"I'll take that under advisement."

"All right, then."

"All right."

And they hang up without saying goodbye, just like busy men in the movies.

Nick doesn't go straight back to the editing suite. He is surprised to find that he has been sweating. There is hot dampness on the back of his neck and in his underarms. He unbuttons his shirt and dabs himself with the cloth napkin he keeps in the top drawer for the rare occasions he has lunch at his desk. As he is doing so, his assistant walks in.

"Oh, sorry!" Ben says, wincing at his boss's state of undress. He starts backing out of the office, but Nick waves him back in.

"What is it?"

"I just wanted to remind you that you have your wife's office Christmas party tomorrow night, and as you know there's a Secret Santa and you're in charge of getting the gift."

"Did I actually tell you that?"

"You forwarded me an email from her. You said it was part of your attempt to 'pick up the slack' now that she's back at work."

Ben looks to the ceiling as Nick finishes buttoning up his shirt.

"The price limit was twenty dollars, but I know you always like to go a little over—just to be on the safe side—so I've purchased three items for you to choose from: a black faux suede iPad mini case, a silver-plated picture frame and one of those giant jasmine-scented candles with three wicks. Everyone loves all those things, right? Anyway, you can pick one and the other two can be returned. Do you have time to look at them right now?"

Nick shakes his head and tells Ben to wrap up the silver-plated picture frame. Then he returns to the edit suite for the rest of the day.

By the time Maya walks in the door that night, it's nearly ten-thirty. Nick is half-asleep on the sofa in front of a reality show about house flipping. The twins are in bed, bellies full of pesto pasta, bottoms pink from bathwater and heads full of dreams cinematically enhanced (Nick hopes) by his bedtime reading of *The Paper Bag Princess* and *Walter the Farting Dog*. He is amazed at how exhausting he finds those two hours—5:30 to 7:30 p.m., the time of day he once thought of as playtime. The flirting-over-a-cocktail hours. No longer. In past few weeks, he has learned to approach this daily transition with military precision. When it comes to small children, the trick, he has discovered, is to be present and in the moment, while also keeping a hawk-like eye on the clock—to indulge in an all-consuming game of fairy-princess-and-Spiderman-having-a-picnic, while simultaneously wiping down a high chair and filling a bath. It's imperative not to rush—if the twins detect hurry, they assume an automatic passive resistance, slowing down the schedule to a treacly pace. If prompted, a toddler can transform the simplest daily acts into epic dramas. Getting into and out of the bath becomes a suspense thriller complete with inciting incident, agonizing build, denouement and dramatic twist ending.

This is why, when his wife walks through the door, Nick is curled on the sofa under a quilt with his shoes still on, numbing himself with bad television. He can hear Maya clattering around in the kitchen, popping a cork, pouring herself a glass of Chianti.

"There's half a cheese omelette in the pan," he says by way of greeting. Now she is sitting beside him, drinking her wine, eating the omelette with a children's spork. She is wearing the navy skirt suit today—form-fitting with a crisp white shirt and a silk scarf he brought her back from a job in Paris. She looks a bit like a sexy airline stewardess from the 1970s, he thinks. The sight of her in tailored office clothes should not be a surprise—he saw her off at breakfast, after all—but he finds it still gives him a nostalgic pang for the early days of their marriage. He considers slipping a hand up her shirt.

"How was your day?" she says, leaning over and giving him a kiss on the head, eyes on the TV screen, where a heavily pregnant blonde woman is crying because something has gone wrong with her kitchen renovation.

"Fine, fine. Good." He wants to elaborate but fails to think of how.

"Thanks for putting the twins to bed."

"My pleasure. They still get a bit weepy and ask for you, especially at storytime."

Maya winces. "Still?"

"It's only been a couple of weeks—I'm sure they'll be used to it by Christmas."

Maya's eyes glitter with emotion and he sees he's said the wrong thing.

"But what if I don't want them to 'get used to it'?" she says. "What if I—oh God, what have I done?"

She covers her face with both hands and Nick strokes her hair, careful to give her space and permission to have a good sob. He sees now that it's okay when she cries, that it's not an accusation.

When Maya's breaths grow even again, he says, "You made the right decision to go back. I know it doesn't feel like it now, but your having a career is as important for them as it is for you. And me. Let me do bedtimes for the next while."

"Really? Velma can always—I mean, thanks. That would be really nice." For a moment, she looks as though she might start crying all over again.

"Of course."

Maya nods, wiping her nose childishly on her French cuff. Then she says, "Are you doing the voices?"

"Yes, darling. I'm doing the voices."

"Even the sad ostrich voice?" She lengthens her neck and pinches her features together in a surprisingly successful imitation of an ostrich.

"Yes. I mean, I try. I can't promise an Oscar-calibre performance. Maybe I have a shot at a Golden Globe or a SAG Award. But I'm trying."

"I know you are. And I appreciate it. I really do. And you're right: they'll get used to it soon."

They stare at the television for a moment. Not really watching but not talking either. Then Nick puts his hand on Maya's knee and clears his throat.

"Babe, I need to talk to you about something."

"Mmm?" Maya continues to stare at the TV with pink, unfocused eyes.

"It's serious. I have a confession to make."

She hears the change in his voice and turns to look at him. "What is it?"

He leans over and strokes her hair, feeling the bump of her ear under a curtain of corn silk.

Her face takes on the old worried expression. "Seriously, you can tell me," she says. "Whatever it is, we'll get through it."

Nick pauses. "The wipes," he says finally. "I forgot to get unscented ones. The twins' asses smell like bubblegum."

Maya gives him a troubled look. "Is that all?" she says. "I have an extra case in the linen closet."

"Oh." Nick gives a hollow little laugh. "Thank Christ."

If Maya is unconvinced, she doesn't show it. She puts her plate on the coffee table, then lies down beside him, her head nuzzling his neck, two pairs of knees nestled into each other. They lie like this for a while, two tired people contentedly not talking, until it's time to go to bed, together.

CHAPTER 16

Maya

·

Of all the kit required for the competent and efficient practice of family law—access to credible reference materials, a closet full of suits, a degree from a reputable law school, a labyrinthine filing system and a very thick skin—a box of tissues is probably the most easily overlooked. Ideally a jumbo box, hypoallergenic and aloe-infused.

Now here she is, at two in the afternoon on the day of the office Christmas party, in a court-ordered mediation with a major client, watching her client's ex-wife weep. The other lawyer, David Whatshisface, is a small, sweaty man with rat-like features whom Maya vaguely remembers from the debating society at law school. He pats his pockets, looking for a tissue, and when he doesn't find one, he looks at her pointedly as if to say, *It's your house.* And it is. They've gathered in her office boardroom, at her behest, in the hope of settling out of court. She fishes a crumpled handkerchief from the bottom of her bag and pushes it across the table.

"No, no, I'm fine," says the ex-wife, sniffling and daubing at the corners of her eyes.

Maya's client, Jacob Brooks, offers no response to his ex-wife's theatrics. He sits staring at the back of his smooth, pale hands as if in a meditative trance. A slim, elegant man with a whisper of a voice and intelligent eyes, he rarely speaks, but when he does everyone leans in to listen.

The ex-wife's name is Victoria, but Maya thinks of her privately as Uptown Girl, for the way her story so closely resembles that of the 1980s Billy Joel song. Insect-thin and manicured, she is in her late thirties, has a bottomless supply of family cash and has spent the past three years burning through a prodigious amount of it in a bitter and protracted divorce with Brooks, her third husband, a moderately famous novelist with a background as humble as hers is grand. Their court case has lasted nearly the entire duration of their three-year-old son's life.

"Take as long as you want," says David Whatshisface, laying a soothing hand on his client's arm. "We all understand how difficult these things can be."

Uptown Girl nods and flicks at her face with her fingertips, the whites of her eyes floating up toward the ceiling and back down again. A pair of very expensive false eyelashes give her the look of a psychedelic-crazed, 1960s beatnik model. Maya wonders vaguely if she has a personality disorder—undiagnosed psychological illness being one of the key reasons seemingly functional people end up in court, trapped in intractable battles of will. She glances over at Jacob but he is still deep in his trance—a state Maya recognizes as a common refuge for the unwilling victims of ongoing civil litigation. Between the original settlement and his legal bills, he is almost broke; he hired Maya on his line of credit in a last-ditch attempt to maintain joint custody of his son.

It's the only thing he ever asked for when they split, and the one thing his ex is determined to wrest from him.

Uptown Girl is wearing a chaotically printed fluorescent-yellow dress and matching shoes that Maya registers as designer-something. A woman like this would never buy anything so hysterically loud without the safeguard of great expense. "It's just, you know, he hates me and my family," she is saying of Brooks, as though he were not in the room. "He always resented my father's success as a banker, and he used to make fun of my wealthy friends—he thought he was better than them because he'd gone to college on a scholarship and, you know, *made his own way in the world.*" She says this last bit with a tiny sneer, as if she's pointing out some eccentric piousness on his part. "But in reality he's just bitter. And all the more so because I was awarded the house and support payments. But as you know, that's for the simple reason that I don't actually have an income—I gave up my party-planning business to take care of Baxter, and my family pays my rent and legal fees. I'm *literally* a broke, unemployed stay-at-home mother. Not full time, obviously, since Baxter still has his nanny, whom he loves—another thing he resents paying for. The point is, the loathing and resentment he has for me, I can see that hate in Baxter's eyes when he comes back to me after spending time with his father. And the things he says—" She starts to choke up again.

Her lawyer, who's taking notes on his laptop, pauses. "Just take a breath," he says. "And when you can, I want you to tell me what it is in your son's behaviour that's led you to believe that Jacob is engaging in a campaign of denigration."

Uptown Girl composes herself and takes a breath. "Well, for instance, last week when I was trying to take away his iPad before bed, Dexter said, 'Mommy's stupid. I'm going to poo on Mommy's head.' And then he said he wanted his daddy."

Maya interrupts. "And . . . sorry, what exactly did you take from that?"

The client huffs slightly, to indicate that Maya isn't getting it. "My ex obviously told my son to defecate on my head. Can't you see? It's a clear-cut case of psychological and emotional abuse. We have to get him out of that house. He doesn't belong with his father; he belongs with me. I'm his *mother*."

At this, Jacob Brooks springs up and slams both palms down on the table inches from his ex-wife. She gives a little shriek, but on her face Maya can see a flicker of pleasure mingled with fear—the adrenaline shot of finally getting the desired reaction. She sees how it must have been between them: the spoiled, beautiful rich girl and the up-from-the-bootstraps boy with his cleverly concealed temper. A hot, toxic and volatile combination that was doomed before it began.

"How," Jacob Brooks begins slowly, looking not at his ex but at some fixed point in the middle distance, "do you live with yourself? Or is that the whole problem? That you can't? So you invent conflicts to distort and deflect your own feelings of self-hatred? Or . . . ?" He seems to lose his train of thought and falls back into his chair, limp and silent again.

Maya clears her throat and commences with a speech she's made many times before—about how sometimes it's necessary to take a step back from the situation and weigh the emotional cost of legal conflict against the tangible gains, but before she can begin, Uptown Girl leans in and hisses, "I want you to know that my family and I are willing to throw any amount of money at this. We are committed to getting Baxter back."

She looks at her lawyer, who opens a new file and slides it across the table. "In light of this, my client is willing to offer her ex-husband a very generous deal: she will forgo the support payments and reimburse him for his share of the marital home in exchange for full custody of Baxter, including all major holidays with the exception of a week in the summer and over Christmas, but excluding Christmas Day itself."

Maya watches Jacob Brooks contemplate the woodgrain in the boardroom table. Finally he says, "If you're offering to buy out my portion of our son—and it seems that you are—the answer is a categorical no."

He nods at Maya and she pushes out her chair with a definitive creak.

"Well, then," she says. "I guess that settles it. Or not, so to speak. We'll be seeing you in court."

Back in the office she checks her work email, scanning a long stream of messages flagged "Urgent," most of which are anything but. It is, she reflects, almost as though urgency has become the regular state of being at the firm, a cruising speed well over the limit. She feels the old feeling—the gut-clench of panic, followed by the fizz-pop of stress hormones in her blood—and recognizes it almost fondly. For the first time in years, she feels genuinely under the gun. It's not such a bad thing.

Amid all the work emails is a note from Nick asking what time he should meet her at the Christmas party in the atrium of the natural history museum. The party is the first "with spouses" event she's been invited to since returning to work. Back in the old days of their marriage, before the twins, she and Nick had a "no social drag" policy, which meant they didn't bring each other to work events, since it was a drag for everyone involved—the date (who felt uncomfortable and out of place), the invitee (who would rather just hang out and talk shop with colleagues), and the other guests (none of whom really wants to make small talk with a co-worker's spouse).

She'd assumed the same rule would apply now that she was back at work, but apparently not. When she'd mentioned the party in passing, Nick jumped on it. He'd filed it and dialled it before she was able to dissuade him from coming. Not only that, he'd booked Velma for the night *and* had insisted on buying the Secret Santa gift when she grumbled about being too busy to do it herself. So it was a good thing, right? A good and perfectly normal thing to attend one's own office Christmas party with the husband to whom one is very happily married. Except now that the night is upon her, Maya finds herself inwardly backpedalling for reasons that are a mystery even to her.

She looks around the office anxiously, eyes scanning stacks of bursting folders, copies of depositions and affidavits waiting to be filed. She is tempted to claim that she has to work, or that she feels the old strep infection coming back. But instead she forces herself to reply to Nick's note.

"See you at eight." And that is that.

Two hours later, Maya is struggling to zip up the strappy silk cocktail dress she's changed into when Gray materializes in her office doorway in a dinner jacket, looking like a handsome vampire waiting to be invited in.

"May I?" he says, with a dapper flourish of his winter gloves.

"Of course."

She turns her back and he zips up the dress as nimbly as a tailor. When she turns back to look at him, she is relieved to see that the strange tension from their drink her first day back seems to have evaporated. She considers saying something along this line, then thinks better of it.

They get on the elevator together, whooshing down twenty-three floors to the cool marble echo chamber of the lobby, trading notes on the cases they're working on. Maya tells Gray about Uptown Girl—her half-cocked case against Brooks and her callous offer. Gray laughs at her impressions but cautions her to handle her client with care.

"Divorce makes people crazy," he says, "as you'll soon be reminded."

"What's that supposed to mean?"

Maya stops in her tracks so that people around them have to swerve to get by. Gray looks surprised.

"Because you're working in the family law division?" he says slowly.

Maya bridles slightly and drops it.

Gray gives her a slap on the shoulder. "Take it easy, kid," he says. She chews her lip.

The party is held a few blocks away, in the museum's sprawling new atrium—a thousand tiny candles twinkling under the brontosaurus bones. Fresh versions of familiar colleagues fill the room. Maya looks for Nick but doesn't see him.

She is overwhelmed by a powerful thirst just as a waitress with a brassy red bob slides a tray brimming with champagne glasses under her nose. She smiles, feeling almost as if she conjured this young woman and her tray of chilled, fizzing glasses. "Thank you *so much*," she says to the girl, who smiles at her beguilingly. Seconds later the glass has half-vanished.

She looks around for Gray but finds he's evaporated into the crowd. One of the junior associates, a twenty-something named Mike Nash who was hired at the same time as her, strikes up a conversation. He's telling her about his "all-consuming addiction" to the eucalyptus steam room at their corporate gym, which Maya hasn't yet bothered to visit. ("It's effing amazing. *Way* better than sleep, which I don't really bother with anymore. Who's got the effing time?") All at once, a familiar voice whispers in her ear, "Is this your work husband? I really hope not, because he's not worthy of you." Maya spins around and kisses Nick, then gratefully introduces the two men. Nick and Mike immediately fall into an easy man-patter about the city's new soccer club, in that way that only men who are strangers can.

Maya touches Nick's arm and motions to indicate she's heading to the bar. Once in line she finds herself immediately behind Roger Goldblatt, who, to her mild horror, puts an arm around her and slaps her on the shoulder in a "Hey, old buddy" kind of way. She judges him to be at least four or five Scotches to the wind. "Maya Wakefield, our newest oldest associate"—he pauses to chuckle at his own unfunny joke—"have you met Peter and David here? They're on the board, so we're forced to invite them to the Christmas party."

Two bulging white-haired men in identical navy suits offer

their hands to Maya and make disingenuous jokes about how unimportant they are. Roger hands her a glass of champagne that he seems to have pulled from his pocket.

"So how is our loveliest new associate getting on? Have you had the taste of blood yet?"

Maya coughs. She's terrible at accepting compliments, especially weird ones.

"Not yet," she says. "But I have my first hearing next week, so I'm sharpening my teeth." She mimes filing her incisors, but no one seems to get the joke.

Roger peers at her through a pair of greasy tortoiseshell glasses. A single wiry hair has sprouted from the bridge of his nose. Maya racks her brains for his wife's name, then decides to take a flyer.

"Is Michelle here? I'd love to see her again." Even Roger looks impressed.

"'Fraid not," he says. "She's exhausted. You know she has one of those mystery diseases, the ones that make you sleepy all the time. So she never comes out to parties. Either that or she just hates me!" He pauses. "Speaking of marriage, I heard you're working on the Jacob Brooks divorce. Awful business, isn't it?"

Maya thinks of Uptown Girl with her Day-Glo silks and her ocean of self-pity and feels a crumbling sensation deep in her pelvis. "Oh, yes," she says but declines to elaborate.

Roger puts a clammy hand on her shoulder. "And extra important you win, of course, after that business with her father."

"What, uh, business?" Maya knows she should conceal her ignorance but doesn't.

"You know her father's a very powerful merchant banker.

Owns the second biggest in the city. He pulled all his corporate business with the firm when he heard we'd taken on his former son-in-law as a client. I tried to explain there would be no conflict, but he was enraged and not in the mood to be damage-controlled. The Heathfields are used to getting their own way—you might have noticed. I hope you make sure they don't in this case."

Maya nods. Swallows. "I'll do my best."

"Do better," Roger says. "It really is an unfortunate falling-out. Her father and I have known each other since school days. We were both on the rugby team."

"Rugby, really?" As Maya says this, she realizes she sounds more surprised than she should. Roger probably weighs less than she does.

"It was a small school," he says. "Anyway, the point is we'll be watching that case with interest."

Maya nods, her body edging toward the other end of the room. "Message received. Loud and clear."

She is about to bolt when Gray appears and gives Maya a knowing look that says, *Tread carefully*. She shoots him one back that says, *Please fuck off and get me a drink*. Roger is oblivious to all this suggestive flickering, as he tries and fails to pluck a half-melted ice cube from the bottom of his whisky.

Gray puts a hand on Maya's elbow and turns to his boss. "Do you mind if I steal away our protégée to meet some of her new colleagues?"

Roger waves his hand in dismissal, and Maya and Gray are released into the crowd. She finds herself following him as he pushes through the sea of half-drunk lawyers to the food table, where he fills a plate with tiny beef burgers and begins eating them, one per bite. For a while Maya just stands there like a spectator in a pie-eating contest. Finally she grabs one off his plate and pops it in her mouth. She feels instantly better, as if all her wandering brain cells had suddenly congregated back where they should be. Grease. Salt. Fat. So that's what she's been missing all these years.

"I need to talk to you about something important." Gray says this very quickly, as if he has to get it out before he thinks better of it.

"I'm all ears," she says, plucking up another beef burger in a brioche and giving it an appreciative sniff. This one, she's pretty sure, has melted Gruyère on top.

Gray waits for her to swallow. The champagne envelops her like warm gauze. It occurs to her that she hasn't seen her husband in quite a while.

"Spit it out, then," she says.

Gray exhales and runs a hand through his hair. A bit of litigator's theatre. "Nick is planning to leave you," he says finally. "He's been planning it for a while now. That's why he's changed. He's hoping to get a better deal."

Maya has that sensation she used to get at parties when she was in her early twenties—she thinks of it as "the Bell Jar feeling," as if she is looking at her life from the wrong side of the telescope and things that were far away are suddenly dramatically closer. Her eyes drift woozily across the room, the sound going in and out like a radio feedback loop in her head. She sees all the people, but she doesn't actually register anyone until her viewfinder comes to rest on Nick. He is standing at the bar, half-obscured by the crowd, speaking urgently to the catering girl with the brassy red bob. The waitress says something Nick doesn't like and he backs away, the old blank expression like a blind pulled tight across his features. Maya has no idea what's happening between them, but it's clear they have met before this evening. She decides then and there that she will never ask him how.

"I don't believe you," she says to Gray, keeping her eyes on Nick. Her voice is a cold, dead thing. "Why should I?"

"Because I'm your friend. And because it's true."

"Prove it. You know if I ask Nick about this, he'll just deny it and I'll be inclined to believe him—he's my husband and the father of my children—so if you're going to drop a bombshell like this, for God's sake I hope you're fucking well able to prove it."

Gray heaves in obvious discomfort. "All right, then," he says, closing his eyes. When he opens them, he is staring deep into the crowd. "Your house has an estimated market value of $1.8 million; the cottage is worth about a quarter of that. The cars are worth somewhere between thirty and forty thousand each, factoring in depreciation. You pay the nanny just under forty, cash, though that was Nick's idea and you're not comfortable with it. Last year Nick earned in the region of half a million. This year he stands to earn about one hundred grand less, mainly because he's taking fewer jobs in order to spend time with you and the kids. Now that you've gone back to work, the income and domestic labour imbalance is beginning to correct itself. You've been away on holiday and your sex life is coming back. Nick listens and is attentive to you—more than he has been in years—and the same goes for the kids. Everything feels different because it *is* different. You are married to a different man. A better man. A man who has made you into a better, more independent woman.

But your life is not what it seems, Maya. In fact, it's the opposite of that. The problem is, when he petitions you, the court won't recognize that. The court looks only at surfaces, not at deeper motives. It isn't fair, but you know it's true."

She reaches out and finds herself putting a hand on Gray's forearm for support.

"Careful now," he says, looking around for a chair and not seeing one. "Are you okay?"

Maya nods. She feels as if a physical trauma has been done to her. In one minute-long monologue, Gray has just unravelled her entire world like a cheap ball of string. She looks down at the floor and imagines it lying there, the limp remnants of her formerly enviable life.

"Why are you telling me this?" she asks, and as she does so, she feels the familiar anger welling up. The rage, she knows, is a way of displacing the sadness that is the thing that will take her under, never to resurface. The anger, however misdirected, can at least be used to power her through this party, the rest of the night and tomorrow. And the next day. There is energy in the rage.

"Because I was the one who talked to Nick in the first place. It's the advice I give all my clients."

"I get that. But why are you telling *me*?"

Gray takes a thoughtful sip of his cocktail. "Because I couldn't live with myself otherwise. I couldn't be an accessory to your betrayal."

"But you betrayed Nick by telling me. He's not a client—he's your friend. Just like me. We're your *oldest friends*." She says this with a kind of bereft wonderment. When she looks up she notices

Gray is actually trembling. Not just his hands but his whole person. This enormous man, who has argued his case in a hundred courts and won, is fluttering like a sheet of paper.

"I know," says Gray. "And it was wholly inappropriate. But I think in this case I was somewhat subconsciously motivated."

Maya stares at him. She is gripping her champagne flute and wonders if she has the strength to break it. She clenches it as hard as she can, craving the pop of glass and the puncture of flesh. Hard as she tries, it doesn't give.

"What are you talking about?" She spits out her words with distaste. "What do you mean, *subconsciously motivated*? Why would you encourage my husband to leave me?"

Gray pries Maya's glass out of her hand and sets it down. He keeps her fingers pressed in between his own.

"Because I'm in love with you, Maya," he says. "And I always have been."

CHAPTER 17

Nick

Nick sits alone at the kitchen counter watching Mr. and Mrs. Fish floating in a slow spiral on the surface of their marital bowl. It's all his fault. The night before, after one too many vodkas, he'd decided they looked lonely. Forgetting the carny's warning about Vietnamese fighting fish, he'd scooped out Mrs. Fish and plunked her in with her feather-finned mate. Then he passed out on the couch with Letterman blaring, feeling slightly better for this good deed. Now they are both dead. Dead because of him.

It's been six weeks since Maya left with the twins and he is going to miss his fish friends, however unstimulating their company might be. The events of that night have played through his mind so many times that he can fast-forward them now: Him at the law firm Christmas party, sharing a bad joke with Shelley while lifting a glass off her tray. His wife across the room, sharing an intense exchange with Gray. Then suddenly Maya is there beside him, looking the opposite of flustered. She is very still. Very sure. Her lipstick is perfect. She gives Shelley a smile that could flash-freeze the living. "I have to go," she says. The twins have come down with something. Apparently they are inconsolable and need her. She feels guilty for working so much. "But you stay," she adds—emphatically, not passive-aggressively. He looks at her face and can see that she means it. It's the only thing that will make her happy. "Stay and enjoy yourself. Please?" He protests weakly—offers to take her home. He almost insists. But in the end, he stays. And when he gets home, his family is gone.

He's made some futile attempts at seeking comfort. Left a couple of messages for Gray, only to receive apologetic texts about being "utterly swamped" by a "life-sucking mega-case." Apparently his oldest friend is too busy for one of their epic nights out. And in truth, Gray's scarcity provides Nick with a glimmer of hope. According to the optimism bias, it can mean only one thing: Maya hasn't mentioned their separation at the office. She isn't telling people yet. If she were, Gray would have called him. And since he hasn't, perhaps she's not entirely sure.

So it's just been Nick and the fish. Round and round they went in their separate bowls, looping past the decorative underwater ornaments nestled in the artificial blue pebbles at the bottom of the tank. Sometimes they'd stop to nibble the flakes he crumbled like a dusty, unappetizing snowfall on the surface of the water, but mostly it was just the same loop in their parallel glass bubbles. Swim, swim, swim, castle, treasure box. A world on endless repeat. Nick has spent a great deal of time getting inside the heads of Mr. and Mrs. Fish, and even in death, he feels a strange pang of envy. They may be dead, after an excruciatingly boring life, but at least they're together.

He looks around the house and experiences the familiar undertow—a kind of dull, self-loathing enervation that has, to his vague surprise, turned him into a complete slob. Maya didn't take much when she moved to a corporate hotel suite—that's all she will reveal, despite his repeated inquiries into her whereabouts. Apart from some clothes, books, toys and the organic, fair-trade contents of the fridge, she left the place untouched. But the house has rapidly devolved without her. It is as if, unbeknownst to Nick, her presence was beating back the creep of primordial filth, and now that she has gone the native bacteria, empty beer bottles, crumpled newspapers, sticky marks and sink stubble sense their occupying enemy has withdrawn. At first they crawled out slowly, sniffing the air, blinking and timid in the light—a coffee ring here, a toilet-seat dribble there. But now that they know the coast is clear, the agents of filth are laying waste to the place, shouting at each other, getting drunk and rioting in plain view.

The mess is a mockery of his authority. He knows he should hire a cleaner now that Velma's gone, but somehow he can't bring himself to do so. Hiring a cleaner would mean having a stranger in the house, and having a stranger in the house would mean showing someone around, and showing someone around would mean explaining why none of the people who should be here—who clearly resided in this large four-bedroom family home until very recently—are here any longer. He could make up a story about a death in the family, a cross-country trip for a wedding or a funeral, an event that he, as the man and the breadwinner, was unable to attend, but that wouldn't entirely solve the problem. What if—he could barely bring himself to contemplate the thought without his stomach constricting into a rotted walnut—they never came back? What if he has to put the house on the market and move to a miserable downtown loft like Gray's, with concrete floors, exposed ductwork and icy industrial lake views? No, he can't get a cleaner. A cleaner would make the situation real. And it goes without saying that he can't clean.

He thought about calling a friend but then realized he'd actually have to tell someone else the story. How Maya left quickly, without argument or discussion, after the office Christmas party—at which she treated him coolly, and rather strangely, but not like someone she was about to abandon. How he came home and found the house empty and cold, the lights off and the heat turned low (even in her exit, she was fastidious), and it wasn't until he received the tersely worded text half an hour later that he had any idea what had happened. He's pretty sure that Shelley's appearance at the party was the reason, but he's still in the dark about Maya's thoughts.

Since leaving, she'd refused to answer any of his calls or emails—had refused even to acknowledge him the morning he waited, in complete desperation, outside her office building. Eventually she appeared, looking wonderful, he thought, in a new shearling coat, collar turned against the wind, blonde hair swept up into a tidy knot, tiny ears pink with cold. He'd staggered up to her raggedly, in the manner of the sick or insane, a cup of coffee clutched in his raw hands for warmth, and had spoken her name low and at close range. She'd turned and looked at him, quite pointedly, as if she had no idea who he was. There was not even a glimmer of recognition. It was like her memory had been erased, or she had been expecting his appearance and had steeled herself against him. Whatever the case, she gave him a single unreadable glance and then swished into the revolving doors, leaving him standing there in the cold. He considered following her but then had visions of raised voices, flying hands, commotions and security guards. Real life, he reminded himself, does not operate according to the rules of a romantic comedy.

Every day for weeks now he's dragged himself from bed, head thumping from another night of restless, broken sleep, to drink a pot of black coffee in the increasingly disturbing spectre of his kitchen. There is, he realizes with a chill, a part of him that wants to see just how far it will go. Will he become one of those people who have to be rescued from under a pile of newspapers and pizza boxes by paramedics and a TV crew from the Lifetime network? In a feeble attempt to guard against this possibility, he pours the floating bodies of Mr. and Mrs. Fish down the garbage disposal and flicks the switch beside the sink.

At least Christmas is over. What a horror that was. At first he thought the worst thing would be to spend it alone in the house semi-drunk, as he'd planned to. Maybe check into a railroad motel just to complete the vision of despair. So when Maya called him up on Christmas Eve morning and offered to bring the twins around for the day, he'd jumped at the chance. Now the memory of them both running to him—squealing with delight, then looking back uncertainly at their mother—makes him almost physically ill. Maya arrived at the house in the same black shearling, the one he didn't recognize, covered with a skim of snow from the walk from the car to the front step. He asked her to come in but she refused with a thin smile that hardened to neutral as soon as the twins disappeared into the house.

"I was hoping we could talk," he said.

"You hoped wrong. There's nothing to talk about." She handed

him an enormous bag of presents, all of them wrapped and rib-
boned and looking irritatingly jolly. "I assume you have a tree?"

"Sure," he lied, his heart sinking because now he definitely
couldn't persuade her to come in. She would see the state of the
place and take the kids back again.

He looked at the bag and noticed a gift tag with his name on
it. "You got me something," he said. "You shouldn't have."

"Well, I did."

They stood there in silence.

"I should have got you something," he said finally. "I was
afraid you'd refuse it."

"And I would have, so you were right."

Nick looks uncertainly at the parcel with his name on it.
"Should I refuse this?"

"No, Nick. It's all yours." She nodded and took a step back,
letting the screen door swing toward him to bring the conversation to a close. "I'll be back tomorrow at noon, so please have
them in their coats and boots, okay?"

And with that she got in her car and drove off into the blizzard.

Christmas Eve with the twins was not the comfort he'd
hoped for. He'd forgotten, somehow, that he was there to entertain them, not the other way around. It was all he could do to
keep the cartoons blaring and the fish sticks and curly fries in
the oven. After a few hours of TV and kiddie computer games
(Maya had relaxed the screen ban in this time of crisis), Isla and
Foster began to squabble from boredom and restlessness, so he
gave them their presents a day early in hopes of mollifying them
in the hours before bed. It didn't work. As if sensing his lack of
patience, they ripped through the lovingly wrapped packages

from their mother and resumed their moans and low-level discontent. They seemed like small, angry people irritated by their own skin, perpetually on the verge of crying, creating endless tiny conflicts over nothing. Watching them fight over the last curly fry, Nick had a horrible vision of them as spoilt, jaded and perpetually unhappy children of divorce. *They are mirroring the misery I have created*, he thought. A few wretched hours later, once they were in bed and finally unconscious, he sat at the kitchen counter and poured himself three fingers of Scotch.

"What now, Mr. and Mrs. Fish?" he'd asked the happy couple, then still swirling in their mindless loop. He felt the whisky begin to blossom out from his chest and spread to his cheeks and forehead, pleasantly numbing him, putting distance between him and the pain. Maybe Maya was just going through a temporary bout of madness, much like his own period of discontent a few months back—at least this is how he'd come to think of it. He reminded himself how close he was to leaving her, and how differently he feels now. People really can change. They can even pretend to change, and somehow in the pretending real change occurs. He knows this because it's happened to him. He remembered reading in a book once that character and habit are essentially the same thing. If you persistently act like a responsible person, you will eventually become one because your actions will meld with your being. *The mask shapes the face. You are what you do.* This is what happened to Nick. He evolved into the man he was pretending to be. For a few glorious weeks, the inside and the outside of his life matched, and he thought he could get away with it.

As he is thinking these things, his eyes slide over the sticky, milk-splashed counter to the last wrapped gift, the one with his name on it. It's a thin, rectangular parcel, meticulously bound in fine tissue paper dotted with sleigh bells and holly. A silver ribbon, curled at the ends, pulls it all together. Nick pictures Maya sliding the ribbon over a pair of scissors to get the curl just right—something he has seen her do dozens, if not hundreds, of times but has not fully appreciated until this moment. *I married a woman who curls ribbons*, he thinks, hot tears springing to his eyes. He opens the card. On the front there is a photograph of a kitten in a Santa hat, and inside it says, simply, "For Nick." A bit cool, he thinks, wishing for "love" or at least an *xo*, but any communication is progress. Throwing back the final swig of Scotch for courage, he rips the present open.

Inside are three things. The first is the familiar yellow folder, the one he gave to Gray labelled "Wakefield Family Assets." The second is Gray's note, the one guesstimating the asset breakdown for the split he couldn't face. The third is from Maya—a petition for divorce.

CHAPTER 18

Maya

Statement of Claim

Victoria Ottoline Everton Heathfield
and
Jacob Michael Brooks

TO THE DEFENDANT: A LEGAL PROCEEDING HAS BEEN
COMMENCED AGAINST YOU by the Plaintiff. The Claim made
against you is set out in the following pages.

IF YOU WISH TO DEFEND THIS PROCEEDING, you or a
lawyer acting for you must prepare a Statement of Defence in
Form 18A prescribed by the *Rules of Civil Procedure*, serve it
on the Plaintiff's lawyer or, where the Plaintiff does not have
a lawyer, serve it on the Plaintiff and file it, with proof of service, in this court office WITHIN TWENTY DAYS after this
Statement of Claim is served on you.

The Plaintiff claims:

The Defendant has breached the terms of their divorce agreement, which granted shared custody of their son, Baxter James Heathfield Brooks (referred from herein as "Baxter"), and in which he promised to "co-parent kindly, openly and cooperatively."

In September of this year, shortly after Baxter started attending preschool, the Plaintiff noticed a change in her son. He became bad-tempered and angry, and would call her "nasty" and say, "I'm going to poo on your head." When she asked him where he got such ideas, he would say, "Daddy told me to."

The Plaintiff was distressed and took Baxter to see a play therapist (see attached report), as well as several other mental health specialists (see attached social worker report and child psychologist report), and she determined that her young and impressionable son was having his mind poisoned against her by her ex-husband, who is and remains bitter, following the fallout from the divorce.

The Plaintiff believes this denigration is tantamount to a form of child abuse, as it "confuses Baxter and makes him unhappy." She is loath to see a small child's loyalties tested by divorce and wants her son to have as happy, secure and stable a life as possible. So long as the Defendant persists in denigrating the Plaintiff in a manner that is emotionally abusive to their son, this is impossible.

BACKGROUND

The Plaintiff and the Defendant were together for eight years and married for four. The Plaintiff describes it as a difficult relationship in which she tried to make peace and the

Defendant "was consistently distant and resentful of her family's money and success." The Defendant's anger, she says, was mostly centred on his bitterness about her privileged upbringing and his resentment of her father, a successful entrepreneur. After the Plaintiff had her son, she felt compelled to provide him with a more stable home and resolved to leave the Defendant. Once she had done so she felt things were better, but after their divorce settlement—in which the Plaintiff, a full-time homemaker, was awarded the family house and support payments—she felt things begin to sour. This period of difficulty culminated in her husband's alleged campaign of denigration and abuse, where Baxter is concerned.

REMEDIES

The Plaintiff asks that:

The court amend the custodial portion of the divorce agreement, granting her sole custody of Baxter so she can provide him with a fit and stable home, free from abuse, denigration or conflict, and in which he will feel secure, confident and loved.

She be granted sole discretion over every major aspect of Baxter's life, including education, healthcare, nutrition and extracurricular activities and lessons.

The Defendant be granted a thirty-six-hour window of access (Saturday morning to Sunday evening), every other weekend until Baxter reaches the age of consent.

Maya takes a breath and then bends down and rests her forehead on the cool varnished cherrywood of her desk. She is tired. More tired than she has ever been. She tries to remember what she felt like in the sleepless days and nights after the twins were born (a time she can only remember as a colour—a fleshy, bewildering pink). She must have been tired then, but it was a different sort of exhaustion, one buoyed by hormones and a sense of powerful, goddess-like accomplishment (two people had just come out of her, after all). Today, six weeks after leaving her husband and hours before her first big hearing, she is tired in an entirely different sort of way. She is scooped out, empty, like a dried-out and discarded corn husk. There is nothing left where her old self used to be. And yet as she lies there, bent over her keyboard, breathing in the clinical smell of toner and carpet cleaner, she knows what she has to do. She takes a deep breath in, gets up, puts on her coat and leaves.

Twenty minutes later she is at the courthouse. The hearing isn't for half an hour, but she has booked a private room to meet with the client first. When she gets there, Jacob Brooks is already waiting. "Thank you," he says with a slight bow, as if he wasn't sure she would come, despite having prepaid her court fee of $17,000. She carefully pushes the money from her mind.

She hands him the counterclaim—which simply asks that the custodial arrangement be left as is for Baxter's welfare—and watches Brooks quietly absorb it. He doesn't smile, but she can see his relief in reading his own case laid out clearly and reasonably before him. "Mr. Brooks is a model citizen and a loving father who never asked his ex-wife for anything apart from joint custody of their son." Maya sometimes suspects that half the job of a lawyer is to offer solace in the form of such documents.

Brooks closes the file and shuts his eyes for a moment before looking up and out the window. Although he is calm and immaculate in his slim navy suit, Maya can feel the anxiety radiating from his body in waves.

"What a mess I've made," he says finally.

Maya shakes her head. "Not you, *her*. You didn't bring this case. And what was your option but to fight? You've got to remember that there are some things worth fighting for in life, and this is definitely one of them."

He nods and clears his throat to indicate he's ready to begin.

"Now remember, when the judge asks you to speak, try to keep your comments focused on Baxter's well-being, rather than your ex-wife's faults," Maya says.

Brooks dips his head to say yes, he understands. She wishes she could promise him natural justice, rather than the official kind to which he will be subjected.

A clerk calls their number and in they go.

The judge, a burly, white-haired man in his fifties with a yellowing Santa's beard, calls the hearing to order and then asks, in that brusque, half-irritated way that almost all judges have, "So what exactly is going on here?"

The opposing counsel begins to speak on behalf of Uptown Girl, but Maya interrupts.

"Your Honour, it is abundantly clear that Ms. Heathfield is a vexatious litigant. This is the seventh action she has brought before this court in two years, and my client is simply a committed father who wishes to be a part of his son's life."

The judge swivels his great big bear head and studies Uptown Girl through a pair of bifocals. She's had her highlights brightened for the occasion and is wrapped in a coat that appears to have been made of thousands of sheared animal tails woven together and dyed purple. Maya notices a well-thumbed copy of *The Way* sticking out of the top of her handbag.

"And what does your client have to say to that?" the judge asks whatshisface, who snaps to attention.

"My client is here only because she is concerned, as any mother would be, with the welfare of her son, Baxter. It is her opinion—backed by a small team of psychologists and social workers, as we have documented—that he is exhibiting distressing behaviour which is the result not just of his unsettling custodial situation but also of his father's pernicious influence."

The judge's eyes flick to the other side of the room, where Jacob Brooks sits trembling with badly concealed rage. He is sitting bolt upright and staring straight ahead, hands clenched into white-knuckle fists. Looking at him, Maya feels her stomach flip like a dying fish.

The judge is churning through documents, sliding papers this way and that across his desk. When a stack falls from the bench in a flutter, Maya jumps up and beats a clerk in handing them back to him. He adjusts his glasses again and sighs.

"You two," he says, pointing a thick sausage finger at one side of the court and then the other. "Come here where I can see you both."

Maya glances at Uptown Girl, who blinks her watery eyes wide and stands, smoothing down her skirt before clipping up to the bench. Jacob Brooks soon joins her, and they stand there, side by side, both pairs of hands clasped behind their backs like naughty children awaiting punishment.

The judge closes his file before reluctantly resting his eyes on the couple before him. "What I want to know," he says slowly, "is what exactly is wrong with you two that you were able to stay together for—what?—eight years and have a child together, but you are incapable of resolving even the simplest dispute about your son's future? Why can't you just . . . I don't know, go have a glass of wine and talk it over?"

Jacob Brooks clears his throat and begins to speak. His voice, to Maya's surprise, is soft and low, and the judge has to lean in to hear him. "Your Honour, if I may. My ex-wife has made normal relations impossible. She communicates with me only through lawyers and has refused my repeated requests for mediation. She does not have the best interests of our son at heart. She will say or do anything to get what she wants, and in this case that is our son. She will stop at nothing and has the funds to use the court system to her own ends indefinitely."

The judge nods. "And you, Ms. Heathfield? What do you have to say for yourself?"

Uptown Girl is silent, and for one hopeful moment, Maya thinks she may be too nervous to speak. Then she sees her shoulders quivering and realizes she is silently weeping—or affecting to weep, because when she speaks her voice is calm and clear.

"Your Honour, all I want to say is that I love Baxter more than the world and I am simply doing what's right for him. It's my belief that any responsible mother in my position would do the same."

The judge shifts and settles, allowing his girth to reassemble itself on the bench. He jots down a few notes before scooping the papers before him into a pile in a manner that indicates he has come to a decision.

"Ms. Heathfield," he says, looking at Uptown Girl, "I have no doubt you are a loving and responsible mother, but the amount of litigation you have brought before this court is shameful. You need to take responsibility for the marriage you made and deal with your ex-husband in a more humane and adult way. The civil courts are not a family counselling service or a forum for you to play out your interpersonal melodramas. They are here to resolve disputes when private citizens cannot. In light of this, and despite my lack of sympathy for Ms. Heathfield's crocodile tears, I am amending the original custodial agreement to grant full custody to the mother with fortnightly weekend access visits to the father. I am sorry, Mr. Brooks, but I do not feel that you and Ms. Heathfield have the tools required to successfully co-parent your son. Therefore I must make a difficult decision, but one that I hope will bring a swift conclusion to your endless legal disputes."

Jacob Brooks rocks back on his heels, blown as if by an invisible wind. When he turns, Maya can see a terrible blankness in his expression. It's the face of a man who has not yet grasped the events that will change his life forever. Uptown Girl spins on her kitten heels and gives Maya a wincing smile, her fists crunched into little balls of joy. "Thank you, Your Honour," she squeaks.

The judge watches all this without amusement.

"You do realize that you've rewarded her bad behaviour?" Jacob Brooks says plaintively, loud enough for the entire court to hear. But the judge is already banging his gavel and gathering up his robes to leave.

Maya pleads, "Your Honour, my client is being punished for his ex-wife's refusal to seek mediation or come to an equitable solution. Surely the existing custody agreement best reflects the needs of the child: to have both parents fully involved. Studies show—"

But the judge, who is now standing, cuts Maya off with a raised hand. "You can keep your studies, Ms. Wakefield." He pauses to look at Jacob Brooks, who is standing limply before him, unmoving, as if he might stay there until reality sets in. "I'm sorry to disappoint you, Mr. Brooks. Your lawyer here is certainly determined to earn her keep. But that's my final ruling, and nothing will change it. Now the two of you go home and do your son a favour by never showing your faces in this courtroom again."

And with that, the judge sweeps out. Once he is gone Uptown Girl makes no secret of her celebration. She shrieks and throws her arms around her lawyer, oblivious to her ex-husband's despair. Three feet away, Maya and Brooks pack up their files as if in a parallel universe. As they leave, Maya feels the energy draining from her body and the old exhaustion crashing in.

"Don't worry, we can challenge this once the dust settles," she begins, but Jacob Brooks is already shaking his head.

"I'm broke," he says. "And tired."

"I'm so sorry" is all she can think of to say.

He shrugs, back under control now. "You did your best. No need to apologize."

They shake hands grimly and go their separate ways.

In the public bathroom, Maya retches once at the sink before splashing her face with cold water.

That night, in her furnished hotel suite, Maya orders the twins a pizza from room service and then puts them both down in her king-size bed. They're all back to sleeping together since leaving home. She wakes up a little after nine with a start—lights blazing, still in her office clothes, a copy of *Walter the Farting Dog* open on her chest.

The suite is comfortable enough, with its triple-ply carpet, ruffled drapes and regular maid service, but she just can't relax there. She stares at the garish damask wallpaper, wide-eyed and disoriented, then wanders into the adjoining room and tries to read a magazine. Minutes later she finds herself creeping around the place, checking behind potted ferns and chintz draperies. She's not even sure what she's looking for. Every time the phone beeps with a text message these days, she has the same sensation of dread—a premonition that terrible news is heading her way. Now that she's had her own bad news and acted on it, she supposes the dread is just a rational reaction to a world in which nothing can be trusted.

Because of all this, the knock on the door both startles and makes sense to her. She looks at her phone. It's not even ten, so it's probably the maid asking to turn down the beds. Either that, or it could be Nick. She thinks of the last time she saw him, standing in his bathrobe on the steps of the house on Christmas Eve, and it makes her dizzy with anger and guilt. She smooths her hair with her palm and opens the door.

Gray is standing outside with a bottle of champagne. He is wearing a snow-dusted overcoat with hulking shoulders, and in the narrow, wallpapered hallway, he looks even bigger than he actually is.

"Hey, kid," he says, squeezing her shoulder firmly. "My condolences on your first big loss. It happens."

For a moment Maya is confused, but then she realizes he's talking about court today. She smiles a weary thank-you and looks down at her outfit: a skirt suit accessorized with a pair of UGGs and a ratty cardigan. "I'm not really in a state to entertain," she says.

In truth, she's been studiously avoiding Gray ever since his bombshell at the Christmas party—taking the fire stairs to avoid passing his office and arranging to be in court during the weekly partners' meetings. She's angry and deeply unnerved. Some days it feels as if Gray reached in and rummaged through her insides. The information about Nick was difficult to process in itself, and Gray's subsequent declaration of love was—and is—just too much for her. She feels that if she focuses on it even for a second, the centre will not hold. She wants to let him in—the company of an old friend is just what she needs—but to do so would risk sundering her entire, Scotch-taped-together world.

Gray holds out a green glass bottle fogged from the cold. She sees that it's good champagne, the proper French kind with microscopic bubbles. "It's important to mark these occasions, I'm afraid. The losses as well as the wins. They're all the same. There's some Buddhist saying about that, I'm pretty sure. Anyway, let's drink. Firm tradition."

Maya lets him in and they sit on the overstuffed sectional in front of a muted episode of *Law and Order*. Gray goes to the kitchen and fills two tumblers with bubbly. Then he unzips his enormous briefcase and pulls out a plastic bag with several Styrofoam containers that he lays out on the suite's dining-room table. "Barbequed Peking duck from Hoo Lee Gardens—best in Chinatown, if you ask me," he says.

Maya watches the feast being laid out and feels her stomach clench. In the past few weeks she hasn't really eaten much other than cheese sandwiches from the firm vending machine and chicken Caesar salads from room service—all dietary rules have gone out the window—so the sight of a proper dinner overwhelms her. "You didn't have to do this," she says. "It's all kind of wasted on me anyway."

Gray turns her by the shoulders and frogmarches her to the table. Then he scoops rice on her plate, followed by glistening mouthfuls of sweet, fatty duck and garlic-steamed greens, while she sits gratefully sipping the cold stream of French bubbles.

"Thank you," she says numbly.

But Gray barely looks at her. He's busy topping up their glasses. Finally he sits down and smiles.

"I'm so proud of you," he says.

Maya waves her hand in front of her face. "Why? I'm a fool. And now a loser."

He shakes his head so hard she thinks his ears might come flying off. His hair is wet with melted snow and he looks like a Labrador fresh from the lake.

"On the contrary, my dear girl. You are as clever as they come. You just have an open heart."

They are eating now, both of them. Maya is suddenly ravenous, inhaling great mouthfuls of duck, relishing the crispy bits, trying to cram as much as possible onto every forkful. Gray pauses to watch her with obvious pleasure. He takes a long draught from his glass.

"Losing that hearing really had nothing to do with you. The judge just sided with Heathfield for prejudicial reasons that were entirely beyond your control. Sometimes justice ain't fair."

Maya lowers her fork.

"I worked my ass off and my client deserved to win—and we *still* lost."

Gray serves himself more rice. "As Clint Eastwood said, 'Deserve's got nothing to do with it.' Especially in family law."

"Perhaps not, but I still don't feel particularly good about it."

"The system's skewed. But you knew that."

"I still feel foolish." Maya pauses her eating and breathes through the pain in her shrunken stomach.

"Well, maybe you won't when your own divorce comes through."

She puts down her cutlery with an irritated clatter. "I suppose deserve's got nothing to do with that either?"

Gray puts a hand on the table, a strangely papal gesture. "I've tried to leave you alone lately because I thought you might want some space. But I'm done now. I'm officially back. How are you?"

Maya thinks of the past few weeks and finds she can't remember most of it. There was work and the kids, and then there was more work. Mostly there have been long, grey nights of broken sleep in a hotel bed that felt like a cage.

"I'm okay," she says. "Trying to make sense of the world ever since you took it upon yourself to shatter my naive illusion of happiness. How are you? And please don't say you're in love with me, because I really can't hear that right now. I swear if you say it, I will stab you with this fork. I won't want to, but I will."

Gray frowns. "I wasn't going to mention it."

Maya stares at her hands. "Good."

"Look, Maya, I know it's a lot take in, but please don't shoot the messenger."

"Why would I do that?" She's irritated at his cliché.

"I dunno. People tend to. You know I only ever wanted good things for you and Nick. You were my idols. I thought your marriage was an example to live by."

There is a long silence in which Gray's email alert goes off twice. He doesn't check it.

"I just feel so . . . duped," Maya says finally. "I thought we were in a completely different place. I thought that I'd changed him. Can you imagine that? Like I was the first woman in the history of the universe to have successfully changed a bad man into a good one. That's how in denial I was. Unbelievable."

Gray puts down his plate and leans back against his chair, letting out an enormous whoosh of breath. "Maya—" he begins, but she stops him by leaning on his arm. It's not a sexual gesture but an act of submission. Maya is the puppet who has had her strings cut, and Gray catches her as she falls. He puts an arm around her and strokes her hair. He kisses the top of her head. She is surprised to find she doesn't mind him doing this. Maybe it's the champagne. Or the loss in court. Or just the feeling of total confusion. But whatever it is, she finds it comforting. "Maya," he says again. "We need to talk about it."

"Talk about what?"

"The thing I said. About my . . . about how I feel."

She is still, the whole of her weight leaning into him, taken up by him.

"No," she says. "No, we don't."

"Well, what are you going to do?" he says.

"I have no idea."

"You can't stay here forever."

Maya shrugs as if to say, *Why not?* But her eyes are not convinced. She knows he's right. A corporate hotel suite is no place for three-year-olds. And Velma can't do the commute to preschool much longer.

Gray cranes his neck to catch her eyes. "I know I don't have to tell you this, but you should be the one in the family home, especially since you have the children. It's important, not just as a place to live but for your protection. Legally. Down the road."

"Possession is nine-tenths of the law?" she says weakly.

"I don't have to tell you that half that house is yours. Half of everything is yours—all things considered, probably more. I know you don't want to think about this stuff, but you should."

Maya sits up and presses her knees to her chest. "You know what the funny thing is? After all that, I don't actually care about the house. If he wants it so much, he can have it. If that's what's important to him, I hope he enjoys it. All that stuff—all the stuff we accumulated over those years—it just doesn't matter to me anymore. I thought after I moved out I'd want to fight over it, but I don't."

Gray looks at her with dubious sympathy. His eyes say he understands, but the rest of his face says he's heard it all before. "I understand you feel that way now, but remember you need to provide a home for the twins, so that may change. In fact, I'm almost certain it will."

Maya presses her chin down on her knees and considers this.

"In the meantime, you need a more comfortable place to stay.

A place with, I don't know"—he looks around the hotel suite, with its plush carpet and patterned wallpaper—"a kitchen that isn't a hotplate."

She nods. "You're right. But I just don't have the energy to look for an apartment right now. I don't even want to talk to Nick, let alone put the house on the market or whatever we're going to have to do. I can't face it yet. I just wish . . ." She drifts off, and for a second it seems she might be falling asleep, but Gray prompts her with a rub of the shoulder.

"What do you wish?"

"I wish I knew what to do."

Gray picks a grain of rice off her collar. "What if I told you what to do?" he says. "Not in a bossy way, but as an old friend who has your best interests at heart?"

Maya smiles uneasily and blows a piece of hair off her forehead. "Sure. I'd love that. Boss me around."

"I think you and the kids should stay with me for a while."

Maya begins to speak, but Gray covers her mouth as a joke.

"Look, before you say no without thinking about it, consider this: I've got lots of space, and Velma can move in too if you like. Everybody would have their own room. The twins' school isn't too far. There's tons of parking space in the underground garage, and frankly, I feel somewhat responsible for all of you, given the way this whole mess played out and my small but essential part in it. Honestly, nothing would make me happier."

Maya is now making strange trumpet noises into Gray's palm, half-laughing, half-struggling. She tries to pull his hand from her face, but he easily overpowers her.

"I'm not letting you speak until you say yes," he says.

They keep up this strange game until Maya's protests turn into eye-rolling acquiescence. She doesn't come around to the idea of staying with him so much as give in to it. She is just so very, very tired. When he takes his hand away, she is nodding.

"All right, fine," she says, wiping her mouth and laughing. "Have it your way."

And he does. They move in the very next day.

CHAPTER 19

Nick

The weekends with the twins are the hard part.

The rest of the time he is able to coast—to take refuge in that numb, unquestioning place where there is neither happiness nor pain, only joyless work, automatic banter and alcohol-aided deflection. He lived so long in that place before the change that the blankness almost feels like a homecoming. He is surprised when it doesn't make strange with him. Instead, it ushers him in like a hotel concierge, smiling and doffing its cap ("Welcome *back*, sir!"), and showing him to his blandly furnished but familiar room. This time, he lets himself go deeper into the blankness than he's ever been. He wouldn't take notice of an actual emotion if it sat on his lap naked and squirming. He feels like there is a hole in his chest the size of a fist and the wind whistles through it. He can see people looking at the hole, their eyes flitting from his face to his chest. Their eyes say, *Whoa*, and he finds to his surprise that he is well past caring. Where he used to mind about appearances, now he finds he doesn't. Instead, he just listens to the wind and feels it go through him like nothing at all. In this, at least, there is progress.

He takes up smoking—not in the house, of course (he's not *that* far gone), but standing on the back stoop, staring at the melting snow, the half-thawed layers of ice and shit and soil. He knows there is a point in every winter (usually around the end of February) when everyone in this city believes the cold will never end. But this time the feeling is a religious conviction. It reminds him of that children's book where they go to the land of perpetual ice and meet the evil white queen. The threat of darkness is perpetual. The sky is clamped over the city like the lid of cast-iron pot. The polar vortex has settled. He dreads the day it lifts and lets the sun shine on his new life. At least as it stands, his internal and external worlds are well matched in their frigid gloom. Any evidence of beauty, of warmth, of hope, he feels, would only make things worse. He has heard of depressed people who had to leave California for this reason—the sunshine was making them more depressed. He thought that was stupid at the time. Now he believes it.

The thing about the twins is, he misses them terribly when they're not around. A kind of missing he doesn't experience as longing so much as a kind of low-level anxiety that eats at him like rot. He connects this dreadful sensation to his children because of the way he feels at the sight of toddlers in the park, babies in arms or even commercials for orange juice. He can mostly hold it together, except when other children are around.

And yet when they're with him—all fat, sticky cheeks, starfish hands and pleas for "Up, up, UP!" and "PLAY with ME!"—he finds he can't enjoy them. Her absence, the lack of her, the terrible misunderstanding between them (which he knows is not really a misunderstanding per se, but a lie that turned into the truth, then got misrepresented as the original lie), looms over all his interactions with Isla and Foster now.

Still, he is learning. Doing the single dad weekend dance—a pathetic, unsophisticated two-step he used to pity in others. He used to see those men, sitting in family-friendly brunch places, checking their phones as the kids eat eggs smothered in ketchup. Wandering cluelessly through the park or standing silently by the sidelines of the playground as the mothers trade gossip and jokes. He feels badly for them now in the same way he feels badly for himself. A great big pity party is what he's throwing—self-pity-palooza, with an exclusive guest list of one.

Take today, a Saturday. The twins have been here since dinnertime last night, when Velma dropped them off, but she put them to bed while Nick worked late. He's taken the day off so they can spend some "quality time." He would like Maya to see them together, doing wholesome family-type things—proof that he is an earnest husband and father, not the selfish, deceptive bastard she believes him to be. But there is no chance of this. Between Velma and the nursery school, Maya has arranged it so they never see each other, not even to hand off the children. And needless to say she's ignored his increasingly desperate and stalker-ish pleas for conversation. Lately he's eased off, the hope draining out of him.

Nick stands outside on the back deck in his bathrobe and a pair of old boots, drinking coffee and smoking his first cigarette of the morning. He sucks hard, trying to get as much nicotine in his bloodstream before the kids wake up. He hears them before he sees them, through double-paned French doors, their weird morning singing. Playgroup songs he doesn't know the words to. He tries to slip back in the room without them noticing, but the blast of cold fills the kitchen along with the grim whiff of smoke.

"Why are you playing outside, Daddy?" asks Isla, barefoot and ratty-haired in her flannel nightie. "Are you making a snowman? What's that funny smell?"

Nick ignores this and heads straight to the sink to wash his hands, but the soap dispenser is empty. The household supplies have dwindled in Maya's absence—even the stacks of frozen organic butter and the club packs of Kleenex he used to tease her for stockpiling in happier times. For some reason, he is paralyzed over what to do about this. To buy more things would be admitting she's never coming back, so instead he makes do. Blows his nose on dirty T-shirts, breakfasts on dry toast. This morning, he washes his hands with dish soap. He does this even though his children are so innocent they don't know what a cigarette is, let alone understand what one smells like.

Isla is tugging on his robe now and Foster is punching his butt cheeks one at a time like a prizefighter in training.

"Waffles?" Foster asks uncertainly.

Isla shrieks in support before Nick has time to put a damper on the idea. "Yay! Waffles! With booberries and maple!"

"But Daddy can't make waffles, you know that," Nick says, mainly to Isla because Foster's returned to his bottom pummelling.

Isla pokes a thumb in her mouth and looks at him with imploring eyes. She pulls it out again and says, "But we never get waffles at Mommy's, 'cause she says the waffle thing is at Daddy's. It's no fair. No waffles, and they are our most favourite food in the whole world."

She begins to sob quietly, just as Foster starts his howling chant: "WA-FULS! WA-FULS!" Isla's face brightens—her younger brother has hit on a winning strategy. "WA-FULS! WA-FULS! WAAAAAAA-FULS," they shout—until Nick cuts them off with a booming surrender. "Oh, all right. FINE," he barks, beginning to root through the pot drawers to see where the waffle iron might be.

He is amazed—not for the first time—to see evidence of Maya's spectacular levels of household organization in places he's barely, if ever, bothered to look before, like the pantry drawers. Inside there are three white plastic tubs lined with paper towels and labelled "Kitchen Gadgets We Never Use," "Kitchen Gadgets We Rarely Use" and "Kitchen Gadgets We Sometimes Use." He reaches into the last one and finds the waffle iron, a heavy cast-iron thing with a long and menacing cord. The twins cheer at the sight of it and begin pelting each other with Lego pieces.

Nick sets out the iron, then opens the fridge to look for waffle ingredients. At first he is stumped. Then he sees a carton of eggs, which looks promising. He even remembers buying it, in a rare trip to the corner store about two weeks ago. He checks the expiration date: yesterday. Totally fine. In the lazy Susan he also finds spelt flour, baking soda and baking powder. He's not sure what the difference is between the last two but figures it can't hurt. Emboldened, he starts pulling out ingredients at random and adding them to his batter bowl: ground almonds, quinoa flakes, cinnamon and something called kamut. He throws in some powdered formula, because there is no milk, and adds water. Then he stirs it all together, thinking, *How bad can it be?*

Foster is lost in a Lego freestyle trance, but Isla, ever the hawk-eyed critic, is observing him closely. She drags a stool over and watches as he tips the bowl of goop into the heated waffle pan and watches it sizzle and begin to smoke. He shuts the lid before anything else bad happens.

"I think you're supposed to put oil on it first," she says.

"Why didn't you tell me that?"

"Because I'm not even four yet," she says.

She has a point.

When he ejects the waffle from the pan, it is less a familiar breakfast food than a sodden cement plank with messy cross-hatching. Undeterred, he makes two more and sets the table. They all sit and take turns drizzling maple syrup from a sticky bottle scavenged from the back of the fridge. Foster, who hasn't entirely recognized the direness of the situation, picks up his waffle and takes a large bite, which he immediately spits out onto his plate.

Nick pulls out the box of Cheerios and slams it on the table. "Sorry, kids. Daddy tried but Daddy failed, okay? No waffles."

To his amazement, the twins don't immediately start to howl. Instead they silently contemplate the cereal box. After what feels like a minute but could only have been a few seconds, Isla starts to cry. Not a whiny, wheedling sobbing, but a tragic, wide-open-eyes, glistening-tears-rolling-down-her-cheeks sort of weep.

"What's wrong, kiddo?" says Nick, who is reluctant to scoop her up for fear she might push him away.

Isla sniffs and stares at the cereal box. "My heart misses Mommy's waffles."

At Big Papa's Waffle House, breakfast arrives covered in clouds of whipped cream, berry goop and chocolate sprinkles. Definitely no kamut in there, Nick thinks grimly, sipping his bottomless cup of stale black coffee. When the kids beg for Sprites he says yes, even though it's only ten in the morning and he knows it will make them wiggy. By the time they leave the restaurant and trudge to the sledding hill, the twins are fractious with sugar. They whine over snow-filled mittens and fight over who will pull the sled. Nick has to stop several times and make empty threats about "going straight home" to even get them to the park, but once there they fling themselves face first down the hill, giving him a moment of peace. He is losing himself in work messages on his phone when he feels a mitten-buffered tap on his shoulder. He turns around and sees a small dark-haired woman standing before him. She's wearing a fur coat. He can tell it's not fake but a real sheared mink, and she also wears a woolly orange hat that matches her lipstick.

"Oh, Nick," she says, offering him a silky hug. "I heard about you and Maya. It is the saddest thing. Are you okay?"

Nick staggers slightly. He can't think of anything to say. Feels like he's been sucker-punched. This is the first time anyone has mentioned Maya's leaving to him. He looks at this lady in her mohair mittens and her snow-dusted furs and he senses that she is familiar, but not necessarily in a good way.

She sees him squinting and says, "It's Rachel—Rachel of Rachel and Glen."

"Oh, right. Of course, Rachel," he says. Rachel and Glen-the-entertainment-lawyer, their so-called couple friends. "How are you?"

"Oh, I'm fine," she says batting the air with her mitten. "But you . . . Look at you all on your own with the kids. I'm so sorry to hear about all this. It's funny because I was saying to Glen just the other day that I always thought of you two as a sort of golden couple. You're both so successful and good-looking, and I mean, *twins*?" She motions down the hill to where Isla and Foster are wresting a Thermos of hot chocolate from the hands of another child. "It's just so perfect, you know?"

Rachel pauses and Nick smiles and nods. He has a flashback of being at a barbeque at this woman's house a few years back, a pool party in the suburbs. Drinking craft beer and making small talk with a bunch of lawyers, including her husband, beside a grill the size of a rocket launcher. All the energy drains out of his body just looking at her.

"Yeah, well, it is . . . what it is. I guess," he says helplessly.

She gives a sympathetic pout and squeezes his arm before turning to shout at her daughter.

"Verity! Put your hat back on or I'm counting to ten!"

When she looks back at him with the pitying look that is meant to be empathetic, Nick wants to slap himself. And then her. Instead he searches the hill for the twins and spots them snapping icicles off tree branches and licking them. He smiles remembering the taste.

"You look like you're doing okay, considering," says Rachel.

Nick nods. "Yeah, it's not so bad, I guess."

"Let me know if I can do anything to help. If you ever want me to watch the kids . . . I mean it. *Anything*."

"Thanks, Rachel. It's fine. Honestly. It's good."

"That's good you two are being amicable about things then, for the kids and everything."

Nick murmurs something about everything working out for the best and watches as Rachel's eyebrows creep up her forehead.

"So I take it you're fine with the situation, then? Because just between you and me, people we know at the firm were a little surprised about it. I mean, obviously she and the twins needed somewhere to stay, but it seems a bit inappropriate to move in so quickly, whatever's actually going on between them. I mean, who knows?"

Nick shakes his head in confusion. "Sorry," he says. "Sorry?"

Rachel takes a panicky step back in her fur-trimmed mukluks. "Oh, God, I can't believe you didn't know. I thought—"

"You thought what?"

"I thought she would have told you. Or he would have. How could you not know? Aren't you and Adam Gray, like, old friends? VERITY, I'm serious. Put it on now OR ELSE!"

"So you're saying they've . . . moved in together?" Nick says quietly.

Rachel puts a mitten on his forearm. "I'm sorry, I thought you knew. Are you okay?"

Nick doesn't answer this last question because he is too busy looking for his kids. He scans the hill and then spots them hurtling along in a sibling embrace, the flying saucer spinning out from underneath their bums as they scatter apart at the bottom of the hill, screeching with laughter. By the time they stand up, he is there, tucking one twin and then other under his arm, leaving the saucer where it lies. The children scream, thinking Daddy's playing a funny joke, horsing around with them like the other dads on the hill. But Nick is not one of the other dads. And he's most definitely not horsing around. He walks back to where Rachel stands, poking a straw into a box of pear juice for her runny-nosed daughter.

He puts the twins down in front of her. They jostle in their snowsuits, a pair of tiny Michelin Men tipping over then righting themselves, giggles dissipating. Verity eyes them suspiciously and sucks her juice.

"On second thought, Rachel, you *can* help me out," Nick says as brightly as he can manage, trying to shave the aggressive edge from his voice. "Do you mind watching Foster and Isla for an hour or two?"

Rachel is visibly shocked. Although she is known for her offers of help, she is clearly unused to being taken up on them. She sputters something about short notice and the busy day ahead.

The twins are starting to whimper about the cold and Nick knows he needs to make a quick exit. As soon Rachel has nodded an ambivalent "Sure, but wait—" he is off at a sprint across the icy park path and back to his car. He jumps in the Audi and points it toward downtown, flooding the engine with gas and causing the sedan to fishtail at more than one intersection along the way. He parks in the basement of the building, not bothering to get a ticket for guest parking, and rides the elevator up to the enormous chrome-and-glass lobby. He's upping his game this time. But it doesn't occur to him to devise a strategy.

He dials Gray's number on his cell, knowing he'll be in the office on a Saturday (they all work weekends), and sure enough his assistant, Mandy, answers. Nick puts a scarf over his mouth and says the name of a man he knows to be one of Gray's biggest clients, a captain of industry who is going through a messy divorce from his second wife. "I need to see him immediately. It won't take a second," he says. "I'm down in the lobby, had some other meetings today."

Mandy asks him to hold, then comes right back on. Which means Gray's there.

"Come right up, Mr. Penfold. Twenty-third floor. I'll call down and have security give you a pass. Mr. Gray is busy today, but he can happily fit you in for a coffee."

Nick hangs up and feels the blood pounding in his head. What exactly is he here for? He's not even sure. In the elevator he feels the stern tug of gravity in his stomach, and for a second the force is so strong he feels he might be pulled through the floor and down the shaft, lost forever in the bowels of the city's second-tallest skyscraper.

The elevator stops once, to let on a pair of young women dressed in weekend jeans. They stand on either side of him, casually discussing holiday plans, before getting off two floors later. Nick feels like a coiled spring of terrible potential, and he is amazed strangers don't notice it.

He gets off at the twenty-third floor—the ironically named "Family Division." He stands for a moment in between the banks of elevators. A moment of frozen uncertainty. Then he knows: for once, Nick stops *thinking* and just *does*. He strides boldly past the receptionist, who calls after him, like a secretary in a movie, "Excuse me, sir. Do you have an appointment? The office isn't actually open to—"

"Penfold to see Gray!" he shouts over his shoulder without breaking stride. This must placate the receptionist because she doesn't rise from her desk. Rounding the beige-carpeted corner into an empty glassed-in hallway of locked office doors, Nick finds what he's looking for: the partners' offices, each with a gleaming brass nameplate. He finds Gray's door and pushes it open, but he isn't there. Mandy, who sits directly outside, seems to be on lunch break. He takes his opportunity and enters the office, shutting the door behind him and scanning around to see how it's changed since he came here with a bottle of good Scotch the day Gray made partner four years ago—the beginning of one of their more epic nights on the town. The large, light-filled room is dominated by the view of the lake—an undulating grey skin that sprawls out to meet a matching sky. The place is a mess—towering piles of paper and case law volumes teeter on every surface. There is a wine-coloured leather sofa upholstered in file folders, empty Coke cans and Styrofoam takeout containers. Nick takes the only available seat—a swivel chair behind Gray's desk, which is an L-shaped expanse of teak with a desktop computer and two sleeping laptops. Every inch of the desk is covered in papers, business cards, paper clips, candies, pens and unstuck Post-it Notes. Nick counts three staplers of different colours and sizes. Amid the jumble is a single framed photo in a cheap translucent plastic frame. Nick is surprised that Gray has anything personal in his office. He squints, rolling forward on his Danish wheels, then recognizes the image with a start: it's a picture of the three of them, taken the weekend when Gray introduced Nick to his future wife. A fateful day. The two young men stand with the woman between them. Nick is tanned and startlingly thin, his neck rising out of a buttoned-down blue-striped shirt like a stem. His sleeves are rolled up at a self-consciously jaunty angle, his hands shoved deep into the pockets of his pleated khaki walking shorts. He cringes at the sight of a raspberry pocket square, folded just so. Gray, by contrast, is all hulking hippy scruff—a sullen, heavy-lidded smile peeking out from under a bushy student Afro, topping a Peruvian-knit sweater so authentic Nick feels itchy just looking at it. They are two young men, ungainly and obnoxious each in his own special way, but it's the woman between that gives him real pause. Maya looks slightly off balance in a pair of bright white Keds, both hands clasping the handle of an old-fashioned picnic basket, one that Nick suddenly remembers well, full as it was of wonderful things he'd never seen or tasted before that day: samosas, spanakopita, licorice allsorts and a bottle of cherry schnapps. She stands between them, close yet entirely on her own, touching neither. Her skin is pale and yet somehow seems to reflect the golden afternoon light, blonde hair tucked up under a Blue Jays baseball cap. She wears the cut-off denim shorts that were popular among university girls at the time and peers at the camera, a sunny-day squint, her expression in its in-between state, features about to break into a laugh or a frown. He knows that face so well, yet he can't quite work out which is coming—the clouds or the sun. Maybe he never could.

"The first day of the rest of your life."

He looks up and Gray is there, standing in his own threshold, hands full of file folders. It's only one in the afternoon, but his tie is already loosened. His Afro has thinned with age, but it's still characteristically tousled. *A great big gorgeous mess*, as Maya used to call him in her half-mocking way. Nick recalls this, as he recalls almost all his memories now, with a stab of regret. *Why didn't I see it coming?*

"That's what I used to think," Nick says, glancing again at the picture in his hand before setting it down gently on top of a dusty legal text. "But maybe it was just the beginning of the end."

Gray puts down his folders with a grunt, letting them slide across the floor in a sloppy fan. He clears a bit of space and sinks down into the sofa, conceding the desk chair to Nick. He doesn't look up while he's doing this, but mutters something incomprehensible and work-related to himself. When he's finally settled in he locks eyes with Nick, who is staring at him hard—harder than he's ever stared at any person or thing in his life. He is trying to look through Gray's thick skull into his brain to determine his motivations, to understand his level of strategy or deceit. Instead, all he gets back is a dead-mackerel stare.

"To what do I owe this unexpected pleasure?"

Nick puts a hand on each knee and squeezes. "At first I wasn't sure. But now that I'm here, it seems pretty obvious. I wanted to look you in the eye. I wanted to see the man who destroyed my family up close."

Gray leans back and raises two hands in a gesture of passive defence. "You know I'm not that guy, buddy. I can see how you might think—because of the way things have worked out—that I haven't had your back these past couple of months, but don't forget you were *both* my friends. I had to choose who to help. And Maya . . . well, we work together. I see her every day."

Nick hears the blood pounding in his ears like a distant but fast-approaching drumbeat.

"I know you do. Because she's living with you. Along with *my kids*. Every day and every night. And every morning after." Nick's volume stays the same, but his tone hardens.

Gray stands. Nick can see he is doing that thing people are

supposed to do with bears—where you make yourself seem as big and imposing as possible to scare away the riled-up animal. It's all he can do not to raise his arms in the air and shout, "Ooogah-boogah!" back at him.

"Maya is my friend," Gray says evenly. "She needed someone to talk to her—honestly, I might add."

At this, Nick suddenly finds himself standing too, but he's not trying to look big—he *feels* big. Heavy and monstrous with barely suppressed rage. "Honestly, huh? If what you thought she needed was honesty, then why did you suggest deceiving her in the first place? Have you told her that? That it was all your idea and I was following your counsel?"

"It wasn't my counsel. I just told you what previous clients had—"

"And did you happen to mention what happened when you urged me to proceed? How I essentially told you to fuck off? Did you mention that to her? How I changed, for real, without even knowing I would, just by behaving like the man she needed me to be—*the man I actually AM*? Did you mention any of that to her when she was crying on your shoulder late at night with your bottle of unoaked fucking Chardonnay?"

Gray pulls his phone out of his pocket and starts keying the password, but Nick bats it out of his hand with a single swish of his arm. The phone flies, hits a bookshelf and falls face down on the floor with a definitive crunch of glass.

"I just upgraded last week," Gray says, but he makes no move to retrieve it.

Now they are standing chest to chest, like a couple of puffed-up teenage boys. Gray puts his hand on Nick's shoulder.

"Listen, buddy, why don't we just call it a day and go for a drink? Maybe hit the lunch buffet at For Your Eyes Only? It's Saturday, so I haven't got any meetings. We can talk it out, just like the old days. Whaddya say? Should we simmer down, take this discussion outside?"

Nick stares at the floor, feeling the energy drain from him, and he knows Gray is right. They should talk it out. That's the adult thing to do. His shoulders drop. He rubs his face, suddenly dizzy from all the adrenaline surging through him. "Maybe," he mutters, more to himself than anyone else. "Yeah, you're right."

Gray keeps on slap-patting his shoulder, almost rhythmically as they talk.

"Hey there, old buddy." *Slap, slap.* "You okay?" *Slap.* "You've been through a hell of a lot, but it's for the best, you know." *Slap, slap.* "I've seen this sort of thing before, and crazy as it seems, one day you'll look back and say, 'That was actually the best thing that ever happened to me.'" *Slap, slap, slap.*

And then, without hesitation, Nick winds up and punches Gray square in the face. It's a direct hit and he feels the skin split under his knuckles, bone connecting with bone with a crack that is both sickening and delicious. He knows that this will be the end of something—perhaps of everything—but he does it anyway because he is past the point of caring about consequences. What he needs now is some semblance of closure. A punctuation mark at the end of the tragic sentence. With a single blow, he's made his position clear in a way no amount of talking or writing or battling in divorce court would ever do. He might have had his family taken from him, but he did not take it lying down. Even in his addled mind, Nick is sure his children will respect him for this—one day.

Gray falls to his knees, holding his face and cursing through a mist of blood. Nick's first impulse is to help him, but he sees that would be awkward, so instead he sits back down in the desk chair and waits for the inevitable. First Mandy rushes in, shouting at the sight of Gray's face, which is smeared in fresh blood. Despite his less-than-convincing protests, she calls security. All three wait together in an almost companionable calm for the guards to arrive. Gray snuffles as Mandy dabs his nose with tissues. Before long two paunchy ex-cops in polyester trousers arrive, grumbling into oversized walkie-talkies. And then Maya joins two weekend cleaners and a photocopier repairman who have gathered at the door to gawk at the scene. She pushes her way past them and looks bewildered as Nick allows himself to be clumsily handcuffed by the guards, who have clearly never made an arrest in their lives.

She doesn't bother to ask what has happened. The guard moves to perp-walk Nick out and she orders him to wait.

"I got a call from Rachel Katz," she hisses in his ear.

Nick opens his mouth—to say what, he's not sure—and then looks down at his handcuffed wrists and stops.

Maya continues, her voice so soft and even it terrifies him. "She was beside herself because she didn't know how to reach you. She said you just abandoned the twins with her. Just left them there and ran away. She said you didn't leave a phone number or anything. She didn't know what to do. Is this true?"

Nick tries to think of something breathtaking to say. Something that will explain everything and show her that all of it was meant in good faith—an attempt to sort out everything that's gone horribly wrong. He searches for it like an actor who's forgotten his big line. But the line never comes.

"Maya," he says.

But it's too late. She's with Gray now, taking over from Mandy, tipping back her old friend turned lover's head to staunch the nosebleed.

"Maya," he repeats as the fat men prod him along, threatening worse if he doesn't hurry up. He says her name once more, but she doesn't look up. It's as if she can't hear him at all.

CHAPTER 20

Maya

Maya drives to the police station early the next morning. It's just like a movie, with a lady cop drumming her fingernails behind the bulletproof glass of the cashier's window as Maya counts the cash, crisp fifties straight from the bank machine.

She knows that Nick could post his own bail, but he is still her husband and the father of her children. Because of this, on a strange and irrational level, she still feels responsible for him.

What she tells herself is this: *I need him not to fall apart for the sake of the kids.*

They leave the station together and stand for a while in the parking lot. It's early and the streets are deserted. It's snowed overnight—possibly the last blizzard of the year—and everything is covered in a fine dusting of icing sugar. The snow has a muting effect and the city is quiet, cars and streetcars skimming silently past. They stand apart. The only people in the parking lot. Possibly the world.

"Where are the twins?" says Nick. It's the first thing he's uttered since he zombie-shuffled out of the cell, eyes red-rimmed, a haze of stubble across his jaw. He carries his parka under his arm, seemingly immune to the cold. Maya flinches at the sight of his pale blue cashmere V-neck flecked with Gray's blood. Nose blood, she reminds herself, which somehow doesn't seem quite as bad as blood blood.

"They're at home," she says, then corrects herself. "At Gray's."

And now it's Nick's turn to flinch.

She sighs. "What would you have me do? Abandon them in the park?"

"I didn't abandon them."

"They don't even know Rachel—it was upsetting for them. All of this is upsetting for them, even if they don't show it." Maya thinks of their confused little faces when she went to pick them up from Rachel—how they ran to her and jumped up, climbing her coat to get into her arms.

"I'm not the one who left," he says.

She feels a terrible urge to unleash on Nick right here, but immediately tamps it back down. She's not going to let herself fly to pieces. Not here in this parking lot. She will not give him that. She sucks in cold air through her nose and feels the sensation subsiding.

"You need to pull yourself together," she says.

He looks at her incredulously, forehead puckered. "You're kidding, right?"

"No, not at all. You can't go around like this. You need to talk to someone or start doing something. Take up cycling again or . . . I don't know, just get your head sorted out. You can't go around punching people. This isn't the movies."

He looks at the slow-falling snow. "It's funny you should say that," he says with a heartbroken almost-smile, "because it *feels* like the movies."

To her surprise he keeps talking, an ache in his voice.

"I know how I must seem to you, but you have to believe me when I tell you it's not what I want. None of it. I want us to be together. As a family. That's what I want. I think it's what I always wanted—I just didn't know it. I got . . . confused."

Maya hears herself laugh. It's a thin, joyless sound.

"What's funny?" he says.

She shakes her head and presses the key to unlock the driver's door. The car bleats and clicks, its lights flashing on and off, an invitation to enter. Nick touches her elbow and she flinches. Because of course she *has* been burned. All those years she lived and breathed the atmosphere of his unspoken contempt for her, his vacant self-regard.

"You are such a liar," she says. She knows it's not a very sophisticated thing to say, but she says it all the same. She wants him to know she thinks it. Not just thinks it, but believes it.

"No," he says. "I *was* a liar. But then I changed. The change was real. It started out a lie, and then it became the truth."

Maya looks to the sky and opens the car door. "Nick, I've *seen* the notes you made on the asset file. Gray *told me* your plan. I'm not an idiot—I'm a fucking divorce lawyer. I know what people are capable of, and now I know what *you're* capable of. You wanted to be free of us, and now you are. So I'm giving you that, okay? You need to stop with the lies now—both to yourself and to all of us. You wanted your freedom and now you're getting it."

She opens the car door and begins to duck in but stops when a terrible thing happens. She hears it before she sees it—a great wracking inhalation that can be only one thing: the sound of a grown man crying. Not just any grown man, but Nick. The King of Cool, the Master of Distraction, the utterly unflappable father of her children. She has seen him cry before, but not like this. Which is to say, not *really*. She stands with the door between her and her sobbing husband. He is gulping for air now, his face a flushed, snot-smeared mess.

"Oh, Nick. Please don't."

He covers his face and mutters into his bare, chapped hands. "Is there nothing? Nothing at all?"

She shakes her head, and even though he doesn't see her do it, the gesture is implicit in her silence. "Why should I take you back?" she asks. "Give me one compelling reason."

Nick looks up, his face churning with thought.

"The money," he says finally.

"What money?"

"If we don't break up, we won't have to divide the assets. Everything can stay as it was."

"*That's* your reason?" she says, almost laughing the brittle laugh again. "That's your big clincher?"

He sniffles. "I thought I'd try a more pragmatic tack. The emotional plea wasn't working."

Maya gets in the car, slams the door and starts the engine. Before she pulls out of the parking lot, she lowers her window and looks one more time at this gaunt, unshaven apparition of her former husband.

"Nick," she says, "you'd better get yourself a lawyer."

For the next few weeks, their work schedules out of sync, Maya and Gray barely see each other. They move past each other in the loft like ghosts, getting up at odd hours, leaving separately and coming home late, eyes circled and brains fogged with case law. Maya works in bed while Gray pulls a few all-nighters at the office, sleeping on his sofa and changing his shirt and tie for the next day's meetings. The last time they spoke at length was the night Gray asked Maya to move in with him. They have become experts at avoiding what's going on and why she is there and what the plan is, if there is a plan. And all this is fine with Maya. Or if not "fine," it's better than the alternative—talking about her feelings. These days she would rather eat a glass omelette than talk about her feelings. She's even stopped seeing Judith—a strange decision in a time of crisis, but there you have it. Maya's decided she's just going to have to let things get messy and then see what happens.

One drizzly Friday evening, she rushes home to relieve Velma and put the twins to bed. Sprawled on the polished concrete living-room floor she finds Gray, still clad in one of his vast collection of rumpled navy suits, head and feet sticking out from under a pile of nubby Scandinavian sofa cushions. Isla props a bolster on his chest and straddles it triumphantly.

"Look, Mommy! We're burying Uncle Adam alive!"

Foster, who has been dragging an L-shaped cushion across the room, runs to her, howling with joy, and she picks him up, burying her face in his silky curls. He smells like a shampoo she doesn't recognize, and she realizes it's been a long time since she bathed him herself.

"Are you going to read me stories tonight, Mommy?" Foster

asks, sucking in his lower lip in a way that suggests he is managing his expectations about the answer.

"You bet I am, baby," Maya says, giving him a love bite on the ear. "As many stories as you want."

At this, Isla perks up. "Five stories?" she says.

Foster is dismissive of his sister's math. "Five stories isn't even a lot. It's for babies. I'm getting thirty stories. And maybe a hundred extra too. And then infinity after that!"

"Okay, then. Deal." Maya laughs and covers his face with kisses. Then she peers down at Gray, who is still prostrate under a jumble of upholstery with a goofy, exhausted smile on his face. "Can I fix you a cocktail?" she asks.

"God, yes," he says, releasing a great breath as Isla resumes straddling his chest.

A pizza is ordered for the children and sushi for the adults, and once the chaos of bath and bed and storytime is over ("That's *not* infinity, Mommy—I counted!"), Maya and Gray find themselves flopped out on the semi-disassembled sofa, debating whether it's too late to start a movie.

"Ooh look, here's one," Maya says, clicking through the dial. "It's about a guy who pretends to be a girl so he can seduce the hot office lesbian he's in love with."

"If you're going to waste ninety minutes of your life, it may as well be on quality trash," Gray counters, grabbing the remote and scrolling down the menu. "Okay, I've got it. A jealous husband tests his wife's loyalties by contacting her online and pretending to be an old flame. As their 'affair' escalates, he's not sure whether to feel jealous of or wildly excited by the new passion he's incited."

Maya groans and pours them both more wine. "That's completely unbelievable. Who would bother having an affair with his own wife? And how could she be so easily manipulated?"

Gray shrugs. "I'd believe anything now. There's no romantic comedy set-up that's too outlandish, if you ask me."

Maya gives him a skeptical squint. "Why? There's nothing outlandish about *this*." She gestures around the room to indicate the situation they are in.

"Of course there is!" Gray hollers this, then lowers his voice for fear of waking up the twins. The loft is huge—nearly three thousand square feet. There are no walls to speak of, just three smallish bedrooms partitioned off like giant office cubicles, their walls barely reaching halfway to the cavernous eighteen-foot ceilings. He continues, "You and the twins moving in here is the most surprising and wonderful thing that's ever happened to me. It's completely changed my life."

Maya laughs. "But you're always working. You're never here."

"That's because I'm trying to give you some space," says Gray. "If it were up to me, I'd just hang out at home with the three of you every day. I feel like the luckiest man in the world." He leans over and takes a piece of Maya's hair and runs it between his fingers. She feels suddenly self-conscious, like an unwilling audience participant in a pantomime magic show.

"Adam, I . . . don't know what to say. I'm grateful, obviously, for your generosity, but in the long term, I'm really not sure it's appropriate for us to stay here."

He tucks the lock of hair behind her ear and leans back. "Why not? You know you can stay here as long as you like. I'd prefer it if you stayed for good. That's not a formal invitation—I don't want to put you on the spot here—but I do mean it. I want you to stay. It's what I've always wanted."

Maya sits with this for a moment. She lets it settle over her. "It all feels a bit sudden," she says after a while. "I guess just I figured that, you know, once the settlement with Nick comes through, I would get a place of my own and start my new life."

Gray smiles at her in his slightly hopeless, open-faced way—a smile so far from the bullish courtroom litigator she can't help being flooded with fondness at the sight of it. It's not attraction she feels, exactly, but more like a deep familiarity. She feels *safe*, and she knows she feels this way because she has known Adam even longer than she's known Nick. He's been smiling at her like this since they met in residence in first year. They'd study together, and every once in a while she'd turn her head and catch him with that face. It is a smile she can trust. But also one that makes her feel ever so slightly guilty.

"That's a very lovely offer," she says finally. "Just let me think about it, okay?"

Later that night, after the wine and the so-bad-it's-good romantic comedy, Maya accepts a different offer, and that is an invitation to sleep in his bed. The sex is not what she expected. They are silent because of the twins—though in truth Maya knows an air-raid siren couldn't wake them mid-cycle—and Gray is very serious about it all, as if he's attempting to scale a mountain he has been training for his entire life. Maya keeps wanting to burst out laughing, not at the act itself, which is surprisingly enjoyable and easy, but at the fact that she's doing it—having actual sex!—

with a man other than Nick. And of all people, that man is Gray. She feels guilty and ridiculous by turns. But in the end they find a sweet and timid groove, like two teenagers just managing their first slow dance. It's really not bad. Not terrible at all.

Afterward they snuggle under the duvet in his low-slung king-size bed and talk about the cases they are working on—his a custody suit between two married lesbians and a single gay man, and hers a good old-fashioned empty-nester's financial settlement.

Gray opens the bedside table drawer and takes out a small Cuban cigar box. "Joint?" he says with a twinkle.

Maya opens her mouth to say she really shouldn't—the twins might wake up, and besides, pot disagrees with her—but instead she hears herself saying, "Why not?"

Later, after they have whispered a giggly goodnight and turned out the lights, Gray wraps his arms around her, one strong hairy forearm over her waist, the other looped under. He clasps her to himself in a way that Nick—always a private sleeper—never did. Despite the strength and weight of his embrace, or perhaps because of it, she feels the bed pinwheeling under her like a plate in a circus act. She waits until she can hear him snore, then wriggles free and slips back into the spare room, where the kids will find her in the morning.

CHAPTER 21

Statement of Case

Name: Maya Helen Wakefield

DOB: 20.11.1975

I, Maya Helen Wakefield, of Penthouse B, Cannery Lofts, Toronto, Canada, make this statement in support of my divorce petition.

I married my husband, Nicholas Thompson Wakefield, on 14 August 2001 at my parents' farm in rural Ontario. Nick and I met at university, and afterward I attended law school while he started his advertising business, SoupCan Productions, now one of the most successful commercial agencies in the country.

After the marriage, Nick and I cohabitated happily for a few years. Having tried unsuccessfully to get pregnant for several months, we decided to do a round of in vitro fertilization three years ago, and I quickly became pregnant with twins. We were divided by the news. I was overjoyed, but Nick was far from happy. From the outset, he had been against the IVF, and when we learned we were having twins, he made his resentment strongly felt in opposition to my joy. Although we rarely argued, a tension built up between us during my pregnancy, and that was key to the eventual disassembling of our marriage. As I wound down toward my maternity leave, Nick began ramping up, working longer hours and travelling more. As I nested, he withdrew. The more I stayed in, the more he went out. Before long it felt as though we were living separate lives.

After I gave birth, I threw myself into motherhood wholeheartedly. I was breastfeeding two tiny infants, and for the first few months, I could barely discern between day and night. Nick, to his credit, did try to help at the beginning, but his attempts at hands-on fatherhood seemed increasingly inept and half-hearted, and only served to frustrate me in my sleep-deprived state. This learned helplessness has long been a tactic of Nick's, and it certainly served him well when it came to caring for our children. He drifted further away, though I hardly noticed at first. Soon the children were in my sole care. I may as well have been a single mother for all I saw of my husband. Sometimes it felt as if we were living in different time zones in the same house. I think it is safe to say that while he certainly loves Isla and Foster, Nick has left the lion's share of their care to me.

Six months into my maternity leave I was barely able to function from sleep deprivation, so Nick and I hired a nanny, Velma Gonçalves, who remains with the twins to this day.

Initially, Velma's arrival eased the tension in the house significantly. Finally I was able to go to the gym or get out of the house on my own occasionally. But over time, as Nick continued to keep himself scarce, I felt the tensions begin to surface again. The chasm that had opened up between us wasn't closing. If anything, the opposite was happening. Several times during this period, I suggested to Nick that maybe he could come home earlier in the evening or cut down on working weekends so we could spend some time together as a family, but he simply ignored these requests. In any case, things remained the same. We had one major argument, which occurred when Nick purchased, without telling me, two tickets to Paris for my birthday. Given that the twins were still breastfeeding around the clock (they were eight months at the time), there was no way I could have gone on holiday for a week, and had he paid any attention to his family's routine he would have known this. I believe Nick felt I was sexually rejecting him during this time, and it's true that our sex life had withered. However, rather than discussing this reasonably (my suggestions of couple's counselling also went ignored), we simply continued to avoid the issue and drift further apart.

When the twins were nearing a year and my maternity leave was almost up, Nick and I made the decision that I would resign my position as a junior associate at the law firm where I worked. I had been agonizing about going back—I did not want to fail my children or sacrifice my career, the classic professional mother's double bind—and Nick persuaded me to give up work. He felt strongly that, now that we had two children, we needed someone to run the household apart from Velma, and I agreed. Though I was deeply ambivalent about the decision to give up a job I loved, I knew that the children would grow up quickly and if I wasn't careful I'd miss their entire childhood in a flurry of trials and paperwork. I hoped my becoming a full-time mother would bring us closer together, but it seemed to push Nick even further away. We no longer socialized together, which I suspected had to do with my lack of a career (it's hard to make small talk when your days are spent in yoga class and Gymboree), and instead of feeling better about my situation, I developed what I now recognize was a crippling anxiety about the safety of my children. I became obsessed with protecting their health and purity, carefully monitoring all food that passed their lips and making sure everything they came into contact with— from the toys they played with to the clothes they wore to the shampoo they used—was completely free from parabens, dyes, chemicals and toxins. The more I obsessed in my domestic loneliness, the more Nick avoided me, until it became a vicious circle of unhappiness.

Over the first couple of years of the twins' lives, I would occasionally wonder if Nick was having an affair. I have no idea if he did, but he certainly had plenty of time and freedom to do so. It is also true that he spent most of his rare time at home on his phone. I'm not saying he did stray; I'm just saying it would not surprise me in the least to learn he had, especially given what happened next.

In the fall of last year, Nick contacted our old university friend Adam Gray, who also happens to be a family lawyer with my firm and the godfather to our children. He told Adam

Gray that he wanted to divorce me and retain at least joint custody of the twins. He disclosed all our financial records and asked what the likely settlement would be. When Adam told him that he would, under the law, have to compensate me as a stay-at-home mother as well as hand over a majority portion of our assets, Nick became distressed. He searched for a way to circumvent this deleterious financial situation while still bringing about the end of our marriage and family life, and eventually he found one.

Shortly after hatching his escape plan, Nick jumped into action. I watched my husband transform before my eyes. Almost overnight, it seemed, he went from being a remote, aloof, uninvolved and workaholic father and partner to one who prized his family and marriage above all else. He encouraged me to return to work, which I did quite happily (I have resumed my position as a family lawyer). He began coming home earlier, spending a great deal of time with the twins, cooking and generally taking up the slack that resulted as I juggled the demands of a full-time career and motherhood. This was one of the happiest times in our marriage, and indeed my entire life. The fact that I feel like a dupe admitting this only exacerbates the shock and sadness I have experienced since our marriage fell apart. The false Nick I experienced for those few months was more real to me than any of his previous incarnations, except perhaps the man I originally married. I was devastated and humiliated when the truth emerged.

Late last year, just before Christmas, I moved out of the family home and took the twins with me. Since then I have moved in with Adam Gray, who kindly offered to take us in. Over the winter, Adam Gray and I grew close, even closer than we had been in the past, and recently we have begun "seeing each other" in a more formal sense. This new relationship has allowed me to move on in a way that is both stable and familiar for the twins and for me. Nick has retained visitation rights and sees the twins every other weekend and on Wednesday nights.

On March 1, after learning that I was cohabitating with Adam Gray, Nick came to the office where Adam and I both work and, after a discussion, assaulted Adam. He was taken into custody, but we asked the police not to press charges, mostly for the sake of the children.

It has become ever more clear to me that there is no hope of salvaging our marriage. Nick and I have been apart since before Christmas, and there is no prospect of reconciliation. Although we don't speak with regularity, I'm sure he will agree that divorce is unavoidable. I would like this process to be completed as soon as possible, to enable us both to move on with our lives separately.

Statement of Truth
I, Maya Helen Wakefield, believe that the facts stated in this Statement of Case are true.

Signed: _____

Dated: _____

CHAPTER 22

Nick

Nick rides his bike downtown.

It's the second day of the first spring thaw and the city is just starting to emerge from under itself. People are peeling off layers and rolling down windows and stepping out of shops just to tilt their faces up to the sun in disbelief. The city exudes a collective sigh of pleasure.

He takes the long route, cutting across the beltline trail, through the big cemetery and down the ravines, and out into the wide valley road that leads him to the centre of town. There is mud spattered on his jeans and a skim of sweat across his face, and he feels, for the first time in months, as if he's absorbing the world. He locks his bike—the basic three-gear commuter—and gazes up and down the street in wonder. Only a year or so ago, this corridor was nothing but dollar stores and sleazy karaoke joints. Now it's awash in cocktail bars and new restaurants. Usually he feels a mild indignance in the face of this kind of gentrification, especially in neighbourhoods hipper and younger than his own. But he doesn't feel this way today. Today he is glad. Not just that it's sunny out, but that things can change. And sometimes for the better.

Shelley suggested they meet in a dive bar. Not a real one, of course, but one of those self-conscious places that used to be a hardware store and is now called the Hardware Store, even though it's really just a place where people in their thirties can feel comfortable swearing, drinking musty draft beer and smoking on the pavement outside. It's supposed to be authentic, but it makes Nick wonder: What's any more real about getting drunk in a place that used to sell hammers and nails? What if it had been a tanning salon instead? He considers this as he swivels on his diner stool and orders a mineral water and lime.

The guy behind the bar grimaces behind an Abe Lincoln beard and mock bifocals. "Is soda water okay?" he asks.

Nick nod-shrugs to say it's all the same to him.

He peers through the tiny rectangular window on the bar door—a pane of glass embedded in quilted red vinyl, the kind of door they have in seedy nightclubs or small-town peeler bars—a door meant to keep all funny business safe from prying eyes. There was a time when he would have been relieved at the presence of such a door. Back when he was a disenchanted husband on the prowl, a man with secrets and things to hide and lose. Now none of that matters. He is entirely free and could meet with Shelley on a crowded patio or his own front porch if he wanted to. He is free to kiss her, or even take her home to bed, for he is a separated man.

Separated.

It is, oddly enough, one of those occasions when the legal term and the internal emotional response perfectly match. Nick feels separate—from his wife, from his family and most of all from himself. Not the man he is today, but his old self. The scared and desperate man who clung to the clean and shiny aspects of life, skimming along the surface like a terrified speed skater on broken ice. Now he is in the muck of it. It is as if he's moving through the world halfway below ground, like a bulldozer pushing a wall of debris before him with every step he takes. The energy it takes to get anywhere is monumental, but at least the progress is real.

He catches a glimpse of himself in the fogged mirror over the bar and is startled. He has lost weight, but it's not the leanness that unnerves him. It's the beard—a grizzled muss along his chin and cheeks streaked with two lightning bolts of grey. He didn't decide to grow one—it just appeared, as if of its own accord. When he came home after his night in jail two months ago, he found he'd run out of razors. It was the first morning he hadn't shaved since high school. The next day he didn't again, and so on. And now he is changed. Not just the beard but his posture and something in the set of his eyes. They are deeper in his head, anchored and watchful. His old leather jacket from university, hardened from years of disuse, is starting to soften up around his shoulders. He's wearing it again because he likes the way the leather smells, like dust and forgotten campfires—old age and youth in a crumbled embrace. Nick can look however he wants since he began "running the company remotely"—which is Larry's euphemism for his indefinite leave of absence. In the one meeting they had about it, neither mentioned the words "nervous breakdown" or even "stress leave," though Nick is aware that both probably apply.

Shelley arrives ten minutes late and trips into the bar blinking, eyes blinded from the early spring sun that's melted the snow outside into puddles, bringing in with her a hopeful whiff of springtime dog shit. "Hi," she says, stumbling back a little at the sight of him. "You're early."

Nick goes to look at the time on his phone, then remembers he intentionally left it at home. "It's the new new me," he says, half joking.

They embrace, doing the peck-on-each-cheek thing, foreheads banging together, and Nick is startled once again at how awkward he suddenly feels doing stuff that once came naturally: extravagantly tipping doormen, giving other drivers the finger, air kissing. He's like a child who's gone through a sudden growth spurt—none of his old mannerisms fit.

Shelley perches on the barstool and swivels around to peer at the drinks menu. Her hair is longer than it used to be, and the Christmas ball hue has darkened to a subtler aubergine. She tucks a curl behind her ears and primly smooths down the front of her flower-print dress. It occurs to him that she looks a bit like an errant schoolteacher from the 1950s, and that it's not unappealing.

"I'll have a blood orange margarita," she tells Abe Lincoln, who nods by pushing his chin out like a rooster without the comb. He brings them a small bowl of those pink Styrofoam shrimp chips that come with cheap Thai takeout. Nick, who has barely eaten all day, puts one on his tongue and lets it dissolve like a giant fishy lozenge.

"I heard about you and your wife," Shelley says, fingering a shrimp chip of her own, not actually looking at him, adjusting her glasses with her other hand. "I'm really sorry. That's super harsh."

"Who told you?" Nick asks, then reconsiders. "Actually, don't tell me. It doesn't matter."

Shelley looks at him. "It was someone in the industry. You don't know them."

Nick nods. He realizes that she means it to be comforting. There is a beat of silence and they stare at each other's reflections in the mirror above the bar. Shelley wobbles on her barstool and some of the tension dissipates.

"This is kind of a weird question, but did it have anything to do with us talking that night at that Christmas party? Do you remember?"

"I wanted to apologize to you," he says slowly.

Shelley accepts her cocktail from the bartender and puts the straw to her lips. Her eyebrows rise as if to interject, but she lets him continue.

"I wasn't great with you back in the fall. I was ... I don't want to say confused, because that sounds like a cop-out, but I know I wasn't any good. I didn't know what I was after, and I think I led you on—romantically and professionally—and I want to apologize for that, for what it's worth."

Shelley takes off her glasses. Without them she looks a bit sleepy, her eyes somehow bigger and smaller at the same time. She cleans them carefully while considering her answer, working the napkin in tiny circles with a tight pincer grip.

"I didn't think you were that bad," she says. "Just a bit confusing. I mean, I've certainly been treated much worse. Not by a guy your age, but still."

She says this not as a way of absolving him but as a plain fact. Nick is sure it's true, and it doesn't make him feel any better.

"Hey, my food blog is going really well," she says, brightening. "A small publisher has asked to make a book out of it, a guide to how to eat well in the era of social media. How to do a pop-up restaurant in your house and blog your food travels—that kind of thing."

"That's fantastic," Nick says and he feels genuinely happy for her, as if this good news is somehow meant for them both. "I knew you'd do something like that."

"Like what?" she says warily.

It strikes him that she is still a bit defensive. He doesn't mind, but he desperately wants to put her at ease.

"Something original. You just struck me as a person who was going to go off and follow her own path and do interesting stuff that no one else had thought of. I liked the fact that you had ideas."

"You didn't seem very interested in my ideas when we had lunch that time. You just looked at my boobs."

Nick drains his soda water. Takes it on the chin. "You're right. I did look at your boobs. I'm sorry about that."

She laughs. "And I'm sorry I wore a see-through top and no bra. You see? You're not the only dirtbag."

They are laughing like friends now, and Shelley orders another margarita. When the bartender looks at Nick, he shakes his head. She watches this and says, "Not drinking?"

"Nah. Thought I'd give the old liver a holiday. Spent Christmas at the bottom of a vodka bottle, and then things kind of spiralled out from there."

She chews her straw. "Yeah, I know what you mean. I didn't have a drop for most of last year for kind of the same reason."

"Really?"

"Well, that and the fact I was travelling through Africa and it can be hard to find booze in tiny Muslim desert villages."

Nick can't believe how easily it's come up—the reason he invited her out in the first place.

"That's actually the reason I wanted to talk to you today," he says.

She blinks, surprised. "You wanted to talk to me because you quit drinking? Is this like one of those AA apologize-to-every-one-you-know dealios? Because it's really not necessary."

"No, no." Nick shakes his head as if to clear it of a bad smell. "I mean about Africa. I wanted to talk to you about that charity bike trip you volunteered for. The one from Cairo to Cape Town."

"Really?" Shelley adjusts her glasses. "Your company wants to sponsor it?"

"Not exactly," says Nick. "But something like that."

CHAPTER 23

Maya

The day before court, Maya leaves work for an extended lunch hour and takes herself divorce dress shopping. She wanders into a tiny boutique in the underground mall beneath her office, a place she walks by every day but has never been in. The shopkeeper is a small woman with an enormous red beehive. She welcomes Maya calmly and without enthusiasm, as if she understands the gravity of the occasion. Maya goes directly to the changeroom and the woman brings her dress after dress, in sombre colours and conservative cuts, dresses in grey and blue and black. They all look very nice, or at least perfectly acceptable, but somehow she knows they aren't quite right. She tries them on obediently, one after another, until her shoulders are itchy from wriggling in and out of new fabric. Finally, as she is standing in the change-room in her underwear and tights feeling sweaty and defeated, the woman appears with something different: a black pencil dress with tiny red polka dots that is demure but figure-skimming, sober but cheerful.

The shopkeeper does up her zipper silently and Maya stands

for a long time, staring at herself in the three-way mirror. She isn't preening but truly staring, her body eerily still, like one of those living statues in the touristy parts of every town. The salesperson, who had been almost entirely silent, now speaks in a thick Scottish accent. "Y'just know when ye find the right one, dontchye?" she says.

Maya nods slowly, still looking at herself in the mirror. Her body is fuller, less bony than it was in the stay-at-home-mom days, when she was working out with Bradley and subsisting on kale and quinoa. These days her main exercise comes from dialling the Persian takeout place from the office at 9:00 p.m. as she works her way through the files that never stop collecting on her desk. Work has added a new convexity of cheek, a curve in her upper arms and weight to her breasts that she hasn't seen since she was pregnant, and then only briefly. To her surprise, the new flesh comforts her. It means she is not going to be one of those whippety divorcees, with their hard, lean faces and lemon-sucking expressions—women who look as though they are holding on for dear life.

The dress helps Maya to appear the way she wishes she actually felt—the way she both wants and needs to look in court tomorrow—and that is *absolutely sure*. Standing there in the three-way mirror, she has a sudden flashback to ten years ago and another three-way mirror, in another tiny boutique, with another dress altogether. She squeezes her eyes shut and sees herself then: in her early twenties; wasp-waisted from cigarettes, Diet Coke and membership in the law school running club; hair highlighted a little too harshly and nose sun-freckled; and the dress, a gloriously clichéd confection of butterscotch taffeta and Victorian lace that tapers at her middle then floats out around her like a cloud. What had she felt then, apart from slightly on edge and giddy with attention? She'd felt completely certain. So certain that she'd never even thought to stop and question how certain she felt.

Maya comes to and nods to the shopkeeper, who is watching her from a distance, looking quietly alarmed. "It's perfect," she says. "I'll take it."

Five minutes later she is back at her desk and Gray pokes his head in the office. It appears first, hovering sideways, then the rest of his body joins, only to stumble to the floor at the last second like an unrehearsed vaudeville act. "Howdy," he says. "How's the un-bride to be?"

Maya finishes typing an email and presses Send. "I'm fine," she says. "A bit wobbly, but can't complain."

Adam smiles a wolfish smile. His polished left toe taps out a soft-shoe on the industrial carpet. "I've made a special reservation for dinner tonight. I hope you don't mind. At that new Japanese steak place you've been wanting to try."

Maya opens her eyes wide in what she hopes is a pleased expression. "Oh, that's really lovely, but I was kind of hoping to get home in time to put the kids to bed and then maybe catch up on some work."

Gray furrows his forehead like an elderly basset hound, gives a defeated nod and turns to go.

Maya sighs, wondering how many things a working mother can feel guilty about at once? (Answer: unlimited.) "Okay, okay," she calls after him. "What time's the reservation?"

Gray spins on his heel. "Eight. I'll meet you in the lobby and we can take a cab together."

As soon as he's gone, Maya dials Velma. She answers with

a laugh. At first Maya's confused (Does Velma think it's funny that she's bothering to call? Surely she hasn't been *that* negligent lately?), then she realizes her nanny is laughing at the children.

"Hahaha . . . Hello? Oh, hang on a sec—Isla don't put Cheerios in your brother's nose. It's not nice! Hi? Maya?"

"Hi. Is everything—"

"No! Foster, WE DO NOT THROW SAND. Sorry, we're just at the playground, and the twins were taking off their clothes because the weather's so nice. It's hard to stop them once they start, you know?"

Maya does know. She looks out the window, sees the sun and imagines the first warmth of spring on her skin. She can almost smell the trees budding twelve storeys below. The playground. The screaming pit of glee. The date bars being doled out by carers. The cool mothers texting on their phones. The safety-net dads lurking beneath the jungle gym, arms outstretched to prevent an assortment of imagined potential injuries. It's been ages since she's been to the playground, but Velma takes the kids every day after preschool. She can hear them begging in the background.

"Are you at the wading pool? Let them go in if they want, Velma. It doesn't matter if they get their clothes wet."

Velma laughs again. "No, no, that's the problem. They want to go in the pool naked, but there's no water in it—too early in the season. Isla, dress back on, PLEASE!"

A loud clatter as the phone drops and then the scuffle of feet on pavement. "Velma?" Maya asks after a bit.

When Velma finally picks up the phone again, she's out of breath. "Sorry about that. They are on the swings now, so is fine. Sorry, is there something important?"

"Yes, just that I need to work late again. Are you okay to stay with the kids tonight?"

"Of course," Velma says, but Maya can hear the pause in her voice.

"Velma, what is it? Do you have something else? If so, just tell me and I can make other arrangements."

"No, no, it's not that. It's just that I was wondering how long you're going to stay here, because for me, being in Mr. Gray's house . . . I must be honest. It is not the same."

Velma has made no secret of missing the old house, and Maya can hardly blame her.

"Not long, Velma. I told you we're going to get our own place as soon as the financial settlement is done. And the lawyers meet tomorrow, so soon."

There is a muffled silence on the other end of the line. Then Maya hears Velma proffering juice boxes to the twins.

"You know I'm here for you. As much as you need," Velma says. "But are you sure?"

"About what?" Maya suddenly feels sick. All of it—the guilt, the uncertainty, the stress—hits her like torrential gust out of nowhere. It blows her down.

"You know, about Nick. Have you heard from him lately?" Velma says this gently but with real urgency in her voice. "I'm sorry to ask. It's just that when I do the weekend drop-off, he seems different. He has a beard and it's really cute. But it's not just that. He seems better, you know? I mean, maybe you should at least talk to him."

Velma waits for a response and Maya can hear her waiting. Her eyes prickle and she throws back her head to prevent the tears from spilling over the rims. She adopts what she hopes is a breezy, business-like tone.

"Nick always seems changed, Velma. That's the whole point. He alters himself when he needs to. He's a shape-shifter. He gets what he needs from people and then he discards them. Do you understand?"

She can hear Velma release a defeated breath. "Yes," she says finally.

Maya knows she should stop there, but suddenly she needs to continue. "So whatever you think you see in him, the so-called new him, you need to step back and consider if what you're seeing is real. Because I can tell you, it isn't. He's not a person to be trusted."

"But, Maya, before you walk away completely, think of the twins. They—"

"Don't!" It's the first time Maya has ever raised her voice at Velma. "I'm sorry, but you have to understand this isn't about our marriage. It's about money. That's all Nick really cares about, or at least it's what he cares about most. Do you understand me?"

"Are you sure?" Velma is quiet. "Really? Nick?"

"I know it's surprising, but yes. Don't worry—everything's going to be fine. Adam is on it."

"Mr. Gray is your lawyer?" She can hear the wariness in Velma's voice. "But isn't that a conflicting interest?"

"No, it's not a conflict of interest. I'm being represented not by Adam himself, obviously, but his best associate. It's going to be fine, Velma. We'll all get exactly what's fair."

Maya and Gray sit at the bar at the Japanese steak place, their faces just inches away from a man in a white paper hat who just chopped a pound of seared meat like it was made of soft butter. They share a beer from a giant silver can, so cold the metal bites their fingertips as they tip it into glasses. Gray orders another can, and then a mountain of steak and tempura and other Japanese things involving seaweed, while Maya sits dazed by the flashing blades and sizzling static of the grill.

It occurs to her that Gray has something to say, something big—why else would he have brought her to this strange place with all its noise and distraction? She feels a sharp twist in her stomach and pushes the thought away. "Thanks for ordering," she says. "I'm not very hungry."

He smiles. Everything she says makes him smile. She has no idea why.

"That's okay, I'm starving. I'll eat whatever you can't."

He reaches into his briefcase and takes out a file labelled "Wakefield Divorce."

Maya grimaces. "Really? Are we going to go through this here? Over dinner?"

Gray shrugs his broad shoulders. "The hearing's at nine and I want you to be briefed. We might as well do it with a drink in our hands."

Maya gulps but Gray is too busy leafing through documents to notice.

"Gulp," she says, to draw attention to her gulp.

"Don't be nervous," Gray says. "We're going to get you exactly what you're entitled to. The law is very clear."

"Fifty-fifty. That's all I ever wanted. I told Allison that, so I'm sure it's reflected in her statement of claim."

"Actually, that's what I wanted to talk to you about." Gray pops a soybean pod in his mouth. "You're entitled to a lot more. When we consider. . . all the relevant details."

Maya leans back and sighs. "Such as?"

"Such as the fact that you gave up your career for several years to raise his children—"

"A career that I have resumed—and by the way they're *my* children too."

"Not to mention the mental and emotional humiliation involved in his deception—"

"A deception I'd really rather not drag through the courts, because it doesn't make any of us look good."

Gray closes the file. "And by 'any of us,' I assume you mean me?"

Maya lets her head fall into her hands for a moment. "I just— the point is not to take him to the cleaners but to prevent him from leaving me and the kids high and dry. I just want what's fair, okay? Half. No more, no less."

The meat arrives. A thousand slivers of Kobe beef. Maya looks at it and feels her stomach flip. She takes a draught of icy beer as Gray tucks in, smacking his lips like a cartoon villain. She watches him put away half the plate before the side dishes arrive, marvelling not for the first time at his ability to consume. Gray is like a furnace, a burner of energy and creator of heat. The thing that makes him a great lawyer is also his greatest burden: the constant and unquenchable thirst for *more*.

Without asking if she wants one, he orders them another beer.

Maya chews a prawn, thinking of bed and the sleepless night

ahead of her. Gray wipes his mouth and throws his napkin down on the plate. Then he looks at her and begins what she immediately understands to be a speech he has worked on in private. *Here it is*, she thinks. *Here it comes*. Though she has no idea what "it" is, she knows something heavy is imminent.

"You are a woman of principle, and I respect that," he says, resting his hands on his upper chest. It's an odd gesture, one that makes him look as though he is gearing up for a gorilla-like chest pounding. Instead, he keeps talking. "But the reason I want you to consider the nature of the settlement is because it will affect your future security. It's really none of my business, of course, but I would like it to be. Officially speaking."

"Officially?" Maya is confused. "You know you can't act for me, Adam. That would be a conflict—"

He shakes his head vigorously. "No, no, no. I mean officially in a personal capacity. Look." He opens his briefcase again and pulls out another folder, which he hands directly to her. Inside is a glossy real estate brochure featuring pictures of a large yellow-brick house on an uptown street not far from where she used to live with Nick. There are photos of a sunny kitchen trimmed with marble and butcher's block, and a large garden filled with flowers and trees and an old-fashioned swing set.

"I don't understand," says Maya. "You're looking for a house?"

Gray takes the brochure from her and gazes at it, clearly entranced. "I bought a house," he says. "I made the offer today. They accepted. The loft is going on the market tomorrow."

"Well, that's great," she says. "I'm happy for you. It's a beautiful house."

Gray takes her hand and unfolds it in her lap, then he presses the brochure into it, as though it's a talisman. Maya can feel the glossy paper stick to the dampness of her palm.

"I'm not quite sure you're feeling me here, Maya. I bought the house for you. For *us*. For the twins. Now that the divorce is coming through, I want us to live there together. As a family."

She feels the back of her neck start to prickle, and instantly black bars emerge at the edges of her vision. She breathes in through her mouth and out through her nose, the way Bradley taught her to do.

"What are you doing?" asks Gray. "Are you okay?"

She nods and speaks through the fleshy Darth Vader mask of her fingers. "Mmm, fine. Just getting some, uh, carbon monoxide to the brain. Or is it carbon dioxide? Whichever doesn't make you pass out. I can never remember."

When the black bars recede, she takes another sip of beer and looks at the brochure on her lap. The house blinks back at her. Bright white-shuttered eyes. A happy, perfect place for happy, perfect people. She feels like throwing up.

"This is lovely," she says, the words coming slowly from her brain to her lips, as if through a broken transmitter. "Maybe the loveliest thing anyone's ever done for me without asking. But you know I can't possibly do this."

"Do what?" Gray does not look altogether alarmed. It's clear he was expecting a bit of resistance. He might be impulsive, but he's no idiot.

"Be 'a family.' With you. In this perfect house."

"But why not? Isn't that sort of what we're already doing?"

Maya shakes her head. "No, it's not. I'm an old friend you've kindly taken in while I sort my life out. And we've slept together a few times, which was maybe a mistake or maybe not. I'm still not sure—"

"Eleven times, exactly—not that I'm counting. But I don't think you can call eleven times a mistake."

"Eleven times we had sex, or eleven times I slept with you in your bed?"

Gray looks caught out. "Okay, eleven times slept and eight times sex. You are a stickler for the truth, aren't you?"

Maya laughs, then fights the urge to touch his face. She doesn't want to be patronizing. "Adam, I can't tell you how grateful I am for everything you've done for me and the twins. But you can't just ambush me like this. I'm tired of being ambushed. I want to be the one who decides my life, don't you see?"

Gray is silent. He licks his fingers and rubs his eyelids. When he opens his eyes they are red and weary. "I wish I didn't see," he says, "but I do."

CHAPTER 24

Nick

Slowly, slowly, Nick pedals up the mountain. The earth is red, cracked and burnt clay, the terrain is rough, more of a gesture toward a road more than an actual thoroughfare. The bike is moving so gradually it would almost make more sense to get off and walk. But not quite. (Nick has a speedometer and has done the math.) He works the dented, dirt-caked mountain bike over small boulders and in and out of ruts, its fat tires gripping the path then spinning out as the hill gets steeper. It is noon. High noon. A cowboy time of day. The Tanzanian sun blazes down on his back, soaking his jersey with sweat and dust as if he's been dipped in hot, gritty tea.

He hears the bus before he sees it. A braying diesel acceleration as the driver rips through gears to get up to speed. He swerves to the side fast and presses himself and the bike up against the rock face, as he's learned to do to avoid being flicked off the road like a bug. The bus doesn't slow—they never do—but rattles past at high speed, spewing dust and fumes, an audible trail of Bob Marley blaring from the loudspeaker over the windshield. Like all local buses, it's crammed to bursting with families, children, baskets of food and caged chickens, steamer trunks strapped precariously to the roof—a careening miracle on mud-crusted tires.

"*Mzungu! Mzungu!*" the children holler out the window—the Swahili word for "white man." Nick waves back with a big stupid grin, and the children scream in crazed delight. On the back of the bus is a hand-painted sign for Manchester City Football Club. Nick continues waving until the children's shrieking faces have flown around the mountain and out of sight. He gets back on the bike.

After six weeks on the road, he is tired. More tired than he's ever been. And yet there is elation in his exhaustion. He understands why those Buddhist monks walk for days, exhausting themselves in epic pilgrimages to sacred places. He never understood it before, but now he does. His hands are callused from gripping the handlebars. There is numbness in his wrists—nerve damage from white-knuckling it over bumpy roads. His body bears the marks of his journey. He is toasted dark on his neck, arms and calves, and paper white from collar to knees. A farmer's tan. His whole body hurts in a way that pleases him.

He rides alone all day, and when he reaches camp, he immediately pitches his tent alongside the other riders. He is friendly with a few but as a rule doesn't talk much. Keeps his story to himself. A big dinner from the canteen truck follows—huge, gluppy pots of pasta or stew sloshed into mess kits, perfect for riders burning hundreds of thousands of calories between them—usually complemented by a warm beer purchased from an enterprising local village kid, then to bed. Nick is sleeping well for the first time in months. Flat-out death sleep, nothing between him and the dirt but a thin, synthetic layer. It is so hot at night he sleeps naked on top of his sleeping bag, sweat vaporizing into the flimsy tent walls. He drinks gallons of water a day. Floods. Sucking up whole freshwater lakes. He dreams of home as he does this. Of the twins and their swimming lessons at the cottage. His mind, for the most part, is clear.

Up the mountain, then down again. He lets the momentum take him, standing high on his pedals to save his ass (also numb) from the impact of the road, breaking only for boulders or ruts in the path. This is Tanzania, a mountainous country of lush green forest, searing hot sun and raggedy kids running barefoot to school, their books strapped together with leather belts like in the olden days. Looking at these grinning children, he thinks of the things he will do with the twins: camping, picking blueberries, teaching them to drive, one at a time.

He hopes they will understand one day why he needed to take these weeks away—why the distance and the selfishness of it is actually his only hope to come back to them in one piece. He sees now, finally, what the problem was: fear. When the twins were born, he glimpsed something that terrified him. A love— there was no better word for it—that made him more vulnerable than he could bear. Maya poured her whole self into this love until she was consumed by it, the waters closing over her head. Nick resisted it until he was exhausted from the effort of refusing to surrender. Her smothering constancy became the counterbalance to his corrosive absence. The more she gave away, the more he withheld, until somehow they were both left with nothing. And everything. And now here he is. Not fixed, he now realizes, but finally coming to understand a fraction of himself. Not the old self or the new self—neither the mask nor the face—but the sliver-thin gap in between. This is the place where Nick has ended up.

At the bottom of the hill the terrain flattens out—a miles-long open stretch with no other riders in sight. He enjoys the flat ride, gearing down and spinning out his legs, letting the wind dry the sweat on his back and push him from behind. He practices going as fast as he can with minimal exertion, in an effort to cool himself down. It almost works. He drinks more water as he rides and, feeling that camp is near, squirts the last of it on his face to rinse away the dust. When he opens his eyes he sees the figure about one hundred feet in front of him. A Maasai warrior in the traditional red cloth robe, stacks of beaded necklaces and brace-lets, and a great ivory nose ring, raising his spear by the side of the road. Nick is surprised. Not to see the Maasai—they are com-mon in this part of the country, usually tending their goats—but to be summoned. The Maasai, particularly in rural areas, tend to be proud, composed and not particularly sociable with foreign-ers. But not this guy.

"*Mzungu*! Hel—lo!" he shouts at Nick as he pulls up on his bike. The man is dark-skinned with close-cropped hair, shaved almost to the skull. His face is friendly, though he wears no hint of a smile. When Nick dismounts, a staccato stream of English words fall from the man's lips. "Hello. Celine Dion. Barack Obama. Man City. Coca-Cola!" he says. If he means it as a joke it works. Nick laughs and the Maasai chuckles unsmilingly in shared recognition. It is as if the man has said, "You see? We are living in the same world." Nick thinks this might be all he wanted to say, but then the Maasai raises his long, elegant arm and holds out an object. It's a cellphone, a very old Nokia, battered and scratched, about the size of a jumbo Mars bar. Nick can see from the face that it's getting a signal, which is more than he can say for his state-of-the-art 5G model.

"Very nice," says Nick. He pulls out his own phone to show the Maasai.

The man nods, unimpressed. There is something else on his mind. He gestures with his head and points his spear into the long grass by the side of the road. Makes the universal sign for "Look over here. I have something to show you."

Nick looks around. Even though the road is long and flat and open, he doesn't see another rider on either quavering horizon. The Maasai is already striding barefoot into underbrush and motioning for him to follow. With a sigh, Nick sees he must go. It's not curiosity that propels him but a sense of fate. He drops his bike by the road and trails the Maasai down a path that looks animal-made. There are no huts or signs of human agriculture or civilization anywhere, and Nick has the strange feeling of being sucked back several millennia in time. He is considering turning back when the Maasai stops. He turns to Nick to make sure he has his full attention, then points with his spear.

Beneath a bush, there is a tail. Then a paw and a haunch. Nick squints, then staggers back in unmistakable recognition: a large male lion, having his mid-afternoon nap.

He scrambles back into the grass, stomach leaping up into his throat, choking him mid-jump. A powerful jolt of pure animal adrenaline shoots through his body like a lightning bolt. He's about to run when he notices the Maasai shaking his head, a would-you-look-at-the-crazy-foreigner expression on his face. Nick pauses and watches in receding horror as the Maasai pokes the big cat's ass with his spear. But the lion is still. Dead still. So dead still he is actually dead. Using his hands, the Maasai reaches down and heaves the lion over so Nick can see the football-sized hole in the beast's side. Maggots swirl over crusted blood. There is the hot, acrid smell of death. It's then that Nick notices the turkey vultures circling languorously overhead. Why hadn't he seen them earlier?

The Maasai flips the lion right side up again, and then turns to Nick and makes the motion of shooting a rifle at the beast. A poacher, Nick understands. He must have outrun his assassin and come here to die.

But why has the Maasai led him here to see this poor dead creature? Does he want to sell him his carcass as a trophy? Does he need help carrying the beast back to his village for food? Nick is confused, but this is clarified by what the Maasai does next: he takes his battered old cellphone, presses a few buttons and then hands it to Nick with an expectant look. He waves Nick back a few steps, then crouches down beside the dead cat and places his head on top of its mane. For a moment Nick wonders if he's performing some sort of tribal death ritual. A traditional animal funeral rite. But the warrior gestures toward the phone in Nick's hands, and it finally dawns on him that the man wants his picture taken. Nick sees it's been all set up—all he has to do is press the button, and so he does, three or four times, from a couple of different angles, until the Maasai seems happy. Safely snapped, the man stands up, takes back his phone and inspects the images, nodding to himself. Then he ducks his head in a gesture of thanks. And without a goodbye, the tribesman ambles off through the grass, leaving Nick alone with the lion.

He stares at the beast, breathing in the sweet, terrible smell of him. It's really not so bad, considering the oven-like heat; the rot must not yet have begun in earnest. Nick stares at the arch of his rib cage, his powerful haunches, and his heavy padded paws, each one the circumference of a baby's head, soft black pads like leather cushions. He has an urge to stroke the lion's nose, which is dry and grey and cracked like a drought-stricken mud plain. His lip is curled up at the side, revealing a long yellow fang, pointed and chipped at the end. Looking at the tooth, Nick decides that the lion was at the end of his prime, that he must have had a large pride and a distinguished life. It must have pained him yet also seemed somehow inevitable—his time had come. And instead of giving himself over to the poacher, he used his last dregs of energy to come here. To die a peaceful old man's death under a bush.

Nick crouches down and puts a hand on the lion's velvet flank. It's hot from the sun, but it's not a warmth that could be confused with mammalian blood rhythm. Instead of this, he feels the stillness. The absence of life. He crouches like that until his legs cramp. Then he gets back on his bike and carries on down the road.

CHAPTER 25

Maya

It is 7:00 a.m. and Maya is still curled beneath the duvet in Gray's spare room—the room she has insisted on sleeping in since she and the children moved in. When the twins creep in, as they always do, Maya pretends to be asleep. The creak of barnboard is followed by the soft thwack of small feet on bare floors, and for moment she can hear them speak as if they are alone. It's a little glimpse into their private twin-world and it thrills her every time. Isla speaks first.

"She's still asleep."

Foster, incredulously: "*Still?*"

Isla: "Yeth. I fink so. I'm waking her up."

Foster: "But what if she's grumpy?"

Isla: "Don't be a silly billy. She's only grumpy if we wake her up when it's dark. It's morningtime. Yesterday she was nice."

Foster: "Not as nice as Daddy."

Isla: "Of course she's just as nice. You just like Daddy better because he wrestles you. Mommies don't wrestle so much."

Foster (a tremble in his throat): "I do *not* like Daddy better. I just said he's nicer when we wake him up."

Isla: "But that's the same thing, dum-dum."

Foster: "Is not."

Maya screws her eyes shut and hopes the eel working its way down her throat will slither away before their bickering works itself up into a full-blown squabble and she has to intervene. She feels a poke on her hip through the cover.

"If we don't wake her up," Isla says, "she might sleep forever."

"Yes," says Foster, "but then we won't have to go to school."

Maya is puzzled by this newfound resentment of "school." Increasingly the twins want to be at home, where they can be alone together, whispering secrets in their private twinspeak. Since the split with Nick, she's noticed a change in their bond. While they still bicker like an old married couple, there is a new anxiety underneath it, an unwillingness to be parted even to go to the bathroom or have a separate play date. It is as if they think that by binding together, they can fill in the empty space left by the split.

"Stop poking her!" Foster's voice.

"I *wasn't*. I was just checking to see if she's awake."

"If she was awake, she'd have woken up by now."

Maya opens one eye theatrically, then growls deeply, like a mama bear stirring from her midwinter slumber. The children shriek with delight and jump back. Like sunglasses on a baby, it's a joke that never gets old. They pounce on her in turn, wriggling like puppies, begging for tickles and then screaming for mercy when they come. Once this ball of giggling, flailing hysteria has worn itself out, all three of them sprawl back on the pillows, panting for breath and sighing with the half-awake delirium that comes from early morning exertion.

"Mommy," Isla says as Maya listens to her daughter's heartbeat return to normal.

"Yes, sweetheart?"

"Can I ask you something?"

"Of course."

Isla composes herself. Raising her tiny, quivering chin, she pulls her pale curls out from under the collar of her nightgown. An oddly grown-up gesture that makes Maya's heart clench tight like a fist.

"When are we going to see Daddy again?"

The fat eel slithers back up into her throat, but she keeps a close-lipped smile plastered to her face.

"I told you, sweetie—Daddy's just gone on a little trip. He'll come back soon and you can have a nice long visit then."

Isla looks at Foster, then back at Maya. "But will we go and live at the old house once Daddy's back again?"

"Maybe," says Maya. "We're just trying to decide who's going to live where."

"When will it be decided?" Foster says this with his arms crossed officiously across his chest. Unlike Isla, who is inclined to probe the dark corners of things, Foster wants to determine where he stands and move on. Maya reaches over and musses his curls.

"Today. We'll decide everything today," she says. "Now, who wants pancakes?"

It's unsettling for Maya to be in the family courthouse as a client—a civilian in this soulless processing plant of human misery. The interior, she has often thought, resembles a discount airline lounge without the brightly dressed tourists, airplane noise or anticipation of sun. The people here are an invariably desperate-looking bunch. Everybody's life is hanging in the balance; everyone has the same lean, hunted look. These are people fighting over the two things humans are most willing to kill and die for: money and children.

Maya arrives half an hour early, as is her custom. She secures a private waiting room and makes sure to use the public washroom before the other side shows up—insurance against awkward pre-hearing run-ins. Only once she is secure in her territory, having removed her spring coat, reapplied her lipstick, smoothed her suit and procured a weak coffee from the vending machine, can she truly begin to gird herself for the battle ahead.

She is asking for half of all the family assets. She will not accept anything less, and she will not be tricked by creative accounting or offshore shenanigans. Given Nick's track record, she and Allison are alerting the judge to the possibility of both. She could have frozen his assets until the deal was done, but something made her stop just short of this. Maybe the new face Nick showed her was just a little bit real? The thought nags at her like a faint but persistent pain. Certainly his buggering off to Africa to find himself—a move she sees as an extended version of his selfish Saturday morning bike rides—is not a great sign. But she pushes the uncertainty from her mind and reads over the twenty-six-page statement of claim. Her proposal is that she keeps the house, which is paid off, and Nick takes everything else—a clean division of assets that will leave them both well taken care of. She also wants full custody of the twins and the minimum in child support. She knows Nick will disagree. *He always was all about the money*, she reminds herself. Girding.

Ahead of Maya in the court registration line is a young mother in a hooded sweatshirt who is hand-feeding Cheezies to a small boy in a stroller. He is a tall toddler—too big for a push-chair, really, and balking at the confinement. His mother tries desperately to calm him, but the approaching tantrum is inevitable, like storm clouds rolling over the hills. The boy, whose sweaty-looking ski jacket is covered sticky doughnut crumbs and sprinkles, arches his back into the stroller, then pitches himself forward until the whole apparatus shakes and threatens to tip. "Stay *still!*" says his mother, smacking the stroller handle with frustration. She touches her hair, which has been pulled into a tight but slightly crooked French braid, and looks around the room, possibly for her lawyer. Maya can see she is suddenly self-conscious—perhaps she feels guilty for shouting at the child she is fighting for.

Maya has a stack of work files to go through but finds she can't open them. Instead she stares around the place as if she hasn't been here a hundred times before. The blue vinyl bench seating, the worn industrial carpet, the windowless walls covered in corkboard stabbed with stern or threatening notices. "ARE YOU ENTITLED TO A MEDIATOR? FIND OUT NOW!" And "PLEASE BE ADVISED WE HAVE A ZERO-TOLERANCE POLICY ON STAFF ABUSE. MAXIMUM FINE: $2,500."

Maya reaches the front of the line and gives the clerk her name.

"Wakefield vs. Wakefield," the clerk says.

Maya nods, trying to effect a professional air, as though she's the lawyer on the case rather than the client.

The clerk shuffles her papers, a gnarled ballpoint pen clamped in her jaw. "Courtroom 24. 11:30."

She hands over a slip of paper that Maya doesn't bother to look at. Instead, she goes straight back to her private waiting room and is relieved to find Allison there, sitting primly with a large accordion file on her lap, scrolling through her email.

As Gray's favourite associate, Allison has been giving Maya's case extra-special treatment. Officially she knows nothing of the relationship between her client/colleague and her boss—they have never spoken of anything romantic at the office—but Maya realizes that people must be talking. Especially after the assault. A few of her colleagues said they were sorry, but most looked at her with wary eyes, as though she were the one who'd thrown the punch, not Nick.

Allison stands up and takes Maya's hand, half shaking and half squeezing it. "How *are* you?" she says, looking at Maya deeply and directly in a way that makes her want to cover her face in shame. Allison is twenty-six and wears her glossy brown hair in a long serpent-like side braid. Maya finds this somehow unsettling, though she can't put her finger on why.

"Fine," she says, a little more coolly than she intends. "Now, what do we need to go over before court?"

Allison takes out the statement of claim and reads it to Maya point by point. At this stage, Maya feels she could recite the document verbatim. When they finish, Allison leans back into the bench and scratches her neck thoughtfully, eyes still fixed on the open file.

"I don't think we're going to have a problem with the custody demands," she says. "It's just whether he wants to be fair about the money."

"Has his lawyer given you any indication of his position?" asks Maya, not for the first time.

Allison shakes her head bleakly. "No, it's really strange. In fact, I'm not even one hundred percent sure he has a lawyer. He didn't submit a statement of counter-claim to court in advance either, which is odd. I think you should brace yourself."

"Why?"

"Well, who knows what he's planning to spring on us."

An icy finger runs down Maya's spine. She blinks and shakes her head, as if to startle away a fly. *Focus*. "Let's hope he's just disorganized," she says. Though somehow, knowing Nick, she doubts it.

Two hours later, their case is announced over the PA and Maya and Allison enter the courtroom. They take their seats on the wooden benches at the front on the left side. The window-less room has a low-tiled ceiling and a carpet that matches the mood—a dull and soul-sucking beige. Several clerks and security guards mill about. On the other side of the room, sitting alone, eyes firmly fixed on his smartphone, is a middle-aged bald man in a navy suit. Maya recognizes him as a senior partner from a competing firm. A stone-cold killer famed for being the divorce lawyer of one of the country's most powerful media barons. This must be Nick's man. But where is Nick?

Maya switches off her phone and sits on her hands. Everyone

stands as the Honourable Mr. Justice Juan Hernandez enters, blinking around the courtroom through a pair of bifocals. He looks about sixty, short and portly. Maya has never been before him, but she has heard he is divorced himself. Never a good sign, since he may harbour lingering resentment. Allison looks up from her files and gives her client a pointed, if not terribly convincing, look that says, *It'll all be fine*. She grips the bench and feels the carpet sway beneath her.

The judge flips through the papers in front of him, then pushes them aside with undisguised impatience. He takes off his bifocals and looks at Nick's lawyer.

"I have read the statement from the claimant but have nothing from the respondent. Is your client planning to grace us with his presence today?"

"He's otherwise engaged," says the lawyer. "But he has read Ms. Wakefield's claim and drafted his response to be presented to the court by me."

The judge coughs, clearly annoyed. "So he was too busy to attend his own divorce hearing?"

The lawyer stands and buttons his suit jacket. In his right hand is a sheet of paper. "I think you'll understand his position once you read this. May I approach the bench?"

Judge Hernandez nods his assent and replaces his spectacles, shoving the frame back up his nose with a short sausage finger. The court is silent as he reads the proffered document. Finally, he turns the paper over and, finding nothing on the opposite side, sighs heavily. He takes a sip from the steaming mug on his desk and then directs his gaze at Maya.

"Mrs. Wakefield," he says, "I think you will be very surprised at the nature of your husband's response to your statement of claim. Are you happy for me to read it out before the court, or would you like a moment to look at it privately?"

Allison turns to Maya and whispers in her ear. "Do you want a minute?" she says.

Maya realizes she must look dazed. When she stands up to address the judge, her legs feel boneless and floppy. She keeps her hands on the bench in front of her for support. "I'm fine. Please go ahead." Somehow this seems better than reading it silently while the entire courtroom watches.

"All right, then," says the judge. He clears his throat in an almost theatrical way before reading out the note in a colourless monotone.

"'In response to my wife's statement of claim, I would like to grant Maya all our family assets both hard and soft, including all jointly owned real estate, art and furniture. Now that our marriage is over, I have no further use for them. With her permission, I will retain my portion of my commercial production business, my car and twenty-five thousand dollars cash so I can put down a deposit on and furnish a small apartment. I'm also happy to meet her demands for ongoing support. I would, however, ask to retain shared custody of our children, Isla and Foster. I am not proposing that they live with me half the time, but I would like to make myself available for regular childcare (in addition to their nanny, Velma) during the week when Maya is busy with work. Additionally, I would like to have them for sleepovers every other weekend and some holidays, once I have set up a new home.

"'I would also like to apologize to Maya, while she is still my wife, for my deceptive, erratic and at times confounding behaviour over the past year and longer. I am aware of my failings as a husband and father. I know that I have behaved badly, and for that I am now paying a heavy price. I want, more than anything I can think of, to ensure that things are as equitable as they can be between us. I may not be able to keep my family physically and emotionally intact, but at the very least I can keep them financially whole. I would ask the court—and Maya—to accept my wishes for a financial settlement in her favour without question. The time for fighting is over. Yours very sincerely, Nicholas Wakefield.'"

There is silence in the courtroom after the judge finishes. Maya stares straight ahead, her face weirdly numb, as if she's just seen the dentist.

"Mrs. Wakefield?" the judge is saying. "You do understand what this means? Your husband is giving you everything, without question. Do you have any response to this extraordinary request? Any response at all?"

Allison nudges Maya, her face barely concealing a grin. Maya recognizes the expression: it's the face of a divorce lawyer who's just watched her opponent give in without a fight.

Maya opens her mouth but finds she can't speak. The connection between her brain and her mouth has been severed.

Allison jumps in. "Your Honour, my client is in a state of shock. Do you mind if we allow her to absorb the news before responding?"

The judge shakes his head. "I'm afraid we're on a tight schedule here. Does your client have anything to say?"

Maya looks up and nods. "Yes," she says.

"Yes, *what*, Mrs. Wakefield?"

"Yes, I won't fight."

The judge doesn't smile. He takes out his gavel and thwacks the desk in front of him. "All right, then. The settlement will be drawn up according to Mr. Wakefield's stated request. Consider your divorce decree granted. All you need to do is sign the final papers. Court dismissed."

She finds him at the bar. Not quite slumped but hulking. Just another heartbroken middle-aged male hunched over a double Manhattan in a heavy-bottomed glass. He hasn't bothered to take off his trench coat and it rides up his broad back, straining and creased under the arms. Eventually he orders another with a swirl of his fingers. She looks at the bartender's concerned face and can see it's far from his first.

"Make that two," she says. Gray jumps at her voice.

By the time he swivels around to look at her, he's smiling. Even now, that beneficent, basset-hound grin. A smile that will forgive her anything.

"Are we celebrating your freedom?" he says as she takes her place on the stool next to him, suddenly aware of a new elasticity in her movements—the energy of the coiled spring unsprung.

"Of a sort," she says, popping the whole cherry in her mouth.

He laughs as she plucks the stem from her lips, perfectly knotted, and hands it to him as a gift. "Your old party trick."

"You can take the girl out of the kegger, but you can't . . . oh, never mind."

They sip their drinks in silence until Maya feels the caramel whisky burn the back of her throat.

"Think you'll keep the house?" she says finally.

Gray wipes his nose on a cocktail napkin and shoves it in his pocket. "Might as well," he says. "I can always rent it out."

"Real estate's never a bad investment in this town."

"You betcha."

He swivels his head toward her and she notices his jaw wobbling for a moment on his neck before coming to a quavery stop. The bobblehead-doll effect of day drinking. "You know, you may not want to hear this right now, but you really were *it* for me," he says. "You were the Big Thing. The prize. You probably don't want to believe that, but it's true."

Maya wrinkles her nose and shakes her head.

Gray smacks his hand down on the bar so hard it makes both their cocktails jump. She sees the smile clip off the bartender's face. He starts to walk over but sees her smiling and retreats.

"What's so wrong with that?" Gray says, a little more challengingly than she'd like.

"Nothing. It just makes me feel weird. Sort of *thingy*."

"*Thingy*?" His lids are heavy. He keeps having to remember to pull them open so he can see.

"What I mean is that it makes me feel a bit like a possession instead of a person. Anyway, it doesn't matter. I'm glad I found you here, because I wanted to say thanks for everything. You've been incredibly kind to me and the kids. We'll never forget that. No matter what."

"So you're moving out." He does not pose this as a question.

"I'm going to take a bit of time off. Take the twins to visit my parents' farm for a while."

"They're back from the Solomon Islands?"

"Yeah, but they ship out again to ride horses through the Andes next month. It was our only window of opportunity."

Gray snorts, nose half in his glass, as if he's trying to inhale the dregs. When he speaks there is a new flatness in his voice. "So you think I've been 'incredibly kind'? That's funny." His laugh is dead. "I've been a prick of the highest order."

Maya stares at the floor and waits for him to continue.

"I could've just let Nick stay with you—a 'changed man.' That's what he thought he was. Kept saying how different he felt about everything. How it was all new and good. But I couldn't let that happen." He shakes his head heavily. Maya has the distinct feeling he's speaking to an imaginary audience that may or may not include her. "Nope, I couldn't. And you know why?" He nods his head lazily in her direction.

"Why?"

"Because I was sick of him beating me. Better marks, better athlete, cooler career. Then he gets the girl too. It wasn't fucking fair. And just when I saw an opportunity to get in there and win something back, just when I could *taste* it, the fucker takes my plan—a plan that was designed to backfire on his jaded, cynical ass, by the way—and turns it into some kind of spiritual epiphany. He actually changes. He gets *better* at the very moment in the story when he should be getting *worse*. He should be bottoming out and getting his kneecaps broken in a ditch, and instead he goes out and claims the *fucking jackpot*." Gray's eyes are burning. His lips are wet and bitten.

"But how?" she says, not understanding. "Wasn't he just going to continue on with his life? With *our* life?"

"Don't you see?" Gray is exasperated now, determined to lay

it out for her. "He was supposed to lose everything because of his callousness, but instead I accidentally gave him the ultimate gift. I inadvertently showed him a way *to want what he already had.*"

There is silence as Maya absorbs what Gray has said. She keeps as still and small as she can.

"So this is all just about you and him?" she says as the narrative finally becomes clear in her head. "Some kind of exaggerated collegiate pissing match?"

Gray shakes his head. "Nah, I really was in love with you. I just . . . I guess I also had a point to prove."

"Which was what, exactly?"

He smiles at her again, but not in the old way. A new smile. He looks amused, like a parent chortling at the innocence of a child. "I wanted to win," he says. "Because really, what else is there?"

CHAPTER 26

Nick

The road is flat now. The Kalahari stretches west into Namibia and across the South African border, fanning out over the bottom of Botswana, a country of endless skies and angry-sounding plants: camel thorn, blackthorn, devil's claw and prickly pear. Nick is unprepared for this place. The beauty is almost brain-crushing, like a magnificent drug that is sometimes amplified, sometimes receding to the background, but always there at the fringes of his consciousness. He has heard people speak about the "energy of the desert" before and dismissed them as New Age fruitcakes—Burning Man acidheads or Joshua Tree stoners—but he gets it now. There is something in the sameness, the unnerving horizon, the sun's relentless glare that rises to a magical crescendo. *The landscape hums*—this is the only way he can describe it. The desert is like a vibration that becomes a sound, and the thrum of it fuels him in a way he cannot understand but is grateful for. He knows better than to question it. Each day he packs up his tent, throws it on the truck, and cycles fast and flat along the dead-straight roads across this country—past its undulating red dunes, spiny trees and ancient dried lakebeds where life used to be. The animals here are survival geniuses—jackals, springboks, snakes and spotted hyenas. They get their moisture from food, not water, and stare at the tour riders and their sloshing bottles with unvarnished contempt.

Nick's body has changed. He has lost so much weight, he barely recognizes himself in the dusty windows of the occasional passing bus. A week ago he took a selfie on his phone and it startled him: a dark, craggy stranger in a dusty bandana leaning his bike on a cactus tree. He does not take another.

He rides and he sleeps and he eats and then he rides some more.

This morning he takes it easy, spinning his legs out in high gear, his toe clips like gerbils dashing in their wheels. He stops at the lunch truck—a dusty canteen bus by the side of the road with folding tables swaying under the weight of enormous plastic coolers of water and fluorescent sports drinks. He drinks the orange stuff now because he's learned his body needs it. The sugars keep his glucose levels stable and the salt prevents his calves from cramping in the night. Nick has learned how his body works, because for the first time in his life, he's actually using it.

He nods hello to James the cook, a bearded vegan from Portland, Oregon, and sets about making himself six peanut butter sandwiches. He eats them fast and silently, staring out at the dunes, feeling the blistering wind, which he knows (but almost can't believe) is changing the shape of the landscape grain by grain by grain.

James the cook doesn't talk much, so Nick is surprised when he hops off the truck and saunters over to where he sits, on a campstool in the shade. "You've got a visitor," he says.

Nick raises his head, half a crust still hanging from his beard. "A what?"

"A visitor."

"Impossible."

"Apparently not. Just spoke to the boys at camp." He holds up a walkie-talkie.

Nick pulls out his phone. No bars. He'll have to sweet-talk one of the guides into letting him use the satellite phone to call Velma and check in with the kids again. He hasn't had decent reception for two weeks. Not since Tanzania. He's not even sure why he's still carrying his phone around. The illusion of connection. He gets up and wipes down his bike with a spare rag. Checks the chain and brake pads, squeezes the tires.

He gets back on the bike and he rides.

His body is a rocket with legs, impervious to strain or heat, an object in motion that will stay in motion, travelling in a straight line until something intercepts it. He is a man on a mission to nowhere. A still point in a fast-moving body.

It's fifty kilometres to camp, the longest leg of the day, but Nick does it faster than he did the previous thirty. The bike drives itself. It is as if he is being sucked forward by an enormous cartoon magnet—a blur of flesh on a desert straightaway.

All at once, camp materializes out of the sand, two buses rising like mammoths on the horizon. They quaver in the heat and threaten to disappear. Nick goes flat out, knees pumping, fleeing mirages and black magic. Sweat gathers under his arms and legs, drying in the wind before it can drip. He can make out the rest of camp now—the small tent city in the field behind the buses, the tarp for shade, the crew mechanic sitting at his post. It all looks the same, but it can't be.

He gets off his bike and walks. Staggers on a tumbleweed and catches his breath. He waves at the mechanic, who points behind the gear truck. Nick drops his bike where he stands and trips forward, choking on the hot wind in his throat. Then he pauses, a hand on each knee, and breathes deep.

Here she is. Sitting under the shade tarp on a folding chair, staring out at the red sand field, a paperback on her lap. A straw-blonde ponytail hanging down from a cotton sunhat. A T-shirt. That familiar galaxy of freckles.

It takes a long time for Nick to fully round the corner, to make his way to where she sits at the edge of the tarp, back up against a jury-rigged tent pole. The wind carries with it the familiar citrus smell of her skin, now mixed with clay dust and camphor. She turns, just a slight shift, and for a while neither of them moves or speaks. Eyes racing over each other. Faces wide open. She is the first to talk. Her voice lifting him up like a cool wave.

"The twins are with my parents," she says. "I had to see you. I hope you don't mind."

"No. Of course not. You came all this way?"

"I came to see you."

"All the way across the world?"

"Yes. You've changed."

"I have." It's not a question. This time he knows it's true.

"I'm not sure about the beard."

Nick lets himself exhale, and as he does Maya's face opens into joy—a smile that lifts them up into the desert vibration, the place where light and sound meet. He smiles back. They could go on like this forever.

Acknowledgements

STILL TK